THREE MEN... THE HOUSE SURROUNDED AND WERE DIRECTING GUNFIRE INSIDE

Return muzzle flashes were visible from windows on the first and second floors.

"Not good," Blancanales said from their position down the street.

"I don't get a warm, fuzzy feeling from this one," Schwarz agreed.

An older squad car blocked the road while providing cover for an officer with a shotgun, who crouched against the rear bumper. None of the armed men surrounding the house paid attention to him, a single deputy outgunned three to one by men with assault rifles.

"Gadgets, the gear," Lyons snapped.

The electronics wizard reached over the rear seat of the SUV and came up with an M-16 A4/M-203 for Lyons. He grabbed a second assault rifle for himself, a SIG 551, and a Belgium-made FN-FNC.

"Go around the sheriff and his deputy," Lyons said.

"What are you planning?" Schwarz asked.

Lyons grinned wickedly. "Going to give our friends up there a new target."

DON PENDLETON'S

STONY

AMERICA'S ULTRA-COVERT INTELLIGENCE AGENCY

MAN®

COUNTER FORCE

A GOLD EAGLE BOOK FROM

W●RLDWIDE®

TORONTO • NEW YORK • LONDON
AMSTERDAM • PARIS • SYDNEY • HAMBURG
STOCKHOLM • ATHENS • TOKYO • MILAN
MADRID • WARSAW • BUDAPEST • AUCKLAND

Recycling programs
for this product may
not exist in your area.

First edition June 2013

ISBN-13: 978-0-373-80439-9

COUNTER FORCE

Special thanks and acknowledgment to
Matt Kozar for his contribution to this work.

Printed in U.S.A.

COUNTER FORCE

CHAPTER ONE

Camp Shannon, Iraq

Captain Colin Pringle wiped a rag across the sweat on his neck and sucked in a breath as his sunburned skin rebelled at the motion.

We brothers weren't supposed to burn, he thought.

He'd been raised in the heart of Georgia, true, but they had humidity there and a lot of it. Not like the dry heat here. No amount of training, not even the intense Officer Candidate School course at Base Quantico, could've prepared him for this kind of arid heat. Ignoring pain *had* been part of that OCS training, though, and he let the moment pass by returning to his vigil on the preparations. He stood on the observation platform they'd attached to the massive warehouse that was their base of operations. Below him men were performing maintenance on vehicles and packing portable generators onto trucks. The place buzzed with the excitement and energy that could only come from fighting men who were going home. At last they would finally be rid of this piss hole of a country.

The war in Iraq was over and Pringle, for one, was damned glad about it. He yearned to see his wife, Kimberly, and he had yet to meet in the flesh their sweet little baby girl. He could still see the images of Kim holding that little treasured bundle at the hospital, kicking and active and sassy.

"Just like her mama," he'd told Kim over the LCD monitor.

He'd asked for a pass home from the Area of Operation but the fighting had been particularly intense during that time, and with the entire U.S. military working to un-ass this AO, the Marines couldn't spare him. Fine. He'd met his service obligations and pretty soon he'd be out of the uniform entirely. Then what—take a job in a stuffy office somewhere? Kim had her own ideas, but Pringle hadn't yet found the guts to tell her he was considering reenlistment. Aw, what the hell did it matter anyway? There would be plenty of time to discuss it when he got home.

"Sir?"

Pringle turned to the company first sergeant, Victor Brock. He'd been a hell of a mentor when Pringle first arrived at Camp Shannon more than ten months ago to take charge of Bravo Company after their first Commanding Officer bought the farm while leading a raid against Syrian smugglers. Brock had proved to be a tough son of a bitch with no time for nonsense. Simultaneously he acted like a Marine around the clock: motivated and talented in keeping his troops the same way. It was a tough job, but Camp Shannon had served as the single greatest deterrent in preventing arms and ordnance from reaching Iraqi dissidents and al Qaeda terrorists.

Brock stepped closer but didn't salute, and Pringle felt an inner glow. The war may have been over but Brock, a Marine through and through, wasn't about to give any potential snipers a chance to take out a CO. That would be a big notch on their belt, killing a Marine officer, not to mention what it would do to the morale of a company that had already lost its last CO to the murderous haji.

"What's up, Top?" Pringle asked.

Brock glanced at a crumpled sheet of paper in his left hand. He kept his right hand free, always free, in case he had to draw the Beretta 92 he wore in a nylon military holster on his hip. "Everything's accounted for in inventory save for water. We're running low."

"Anyone nearby who could loan us a buffalo? Don't need the water, just something to put it in."

Brock shook his head. "Already thought of that, sir. Closest unit is the 1-Two-7 on convoy twenty klicks north of here. The Transport Control Officer says he has an empty buffalo we could take, but the commander doesn't want to stop or divert. He's worried about an ambush."

"Aren't we all?" Pringle sighed, considering the issue. "Is the 1-Two-7 still in contact range?"

"Yes, sir."

"Get a radio tech up here and I'll talk to the CO personally. Maybe I can convince him to let us send a platoon to retrieve the thing."

"That's NCO-thinking, sir," Brock replied with a nod.

Pringle grinned. "I'll take that as a compliment, First Sergeant. Carry on."

"Sir."

The communications specialist, sweating profusely and breathing somewhat hard, reported less than three minutes later. Brock had obviously told the young man to double time his ass up to the CO. Pringle checked the Marine's nametag: G. Margolis. He looked to be about nineteen or twenty at most. Pringle vaguely recalled his reporting for duty six months earlier, but couldn't remember seeing anything extraordinary on his proficiency reports. Just a steady, performing Marine like all of them in Bravo Company—Pringle couldn't and wouldn't complain about good Marines.

"Specialist Margolis, did Top brief you yet?"

"Yes, sir.

"Good. Connect me with the CO of the 1-Two-7."

Margolis held out the receiver to the satellite radio pack strapped to his back. "Already on the horn, sir."

Pringle took the receiver with a nod. "This is Captain Pringle. Who am I speaking to?"

"Captain, this is the 1-Two-7, Major Douglas Compton commanding."

"Sir, thank you for taking time to speak with me."

"Of course, Captain. What can I do for you?"

"Sir, our orders are to abandon this camp and make for Exit Point Tango."

"Understood," Compton replied. "That's where we're headed now."

"We're about ready to go but we seem to be short on water. Um, check that. We *have* plenty of water, just no way to transport it. All the carriers we had for water had to be used for fuel."

"That's what I understand, Captain. I already spoke to your top and advised him I can't stop."

"I understand, sir. But the thought occurred to me that I could send a squad from my HQ platoon to retrieve the buffalo if you'd permit it."

A long pause ensued and Pringle was about to repeat his suggestion, concerned maybe Compton didn't hear him, when the 1-Two-7 commander's voice came back on the line. "I just spoke with my adjutant, Captain. That's putting your men at great risk. Are you sure you want to do that?"

Pringle tried not to take Compton's reply as a personal affront. They all had the same goals, after all: get every Marine home alive and in one piece. "I stand to put many more men at risk if I set off for a rendezvous nearly sixty kilometers away without sufficient water, sir."

"That's a good point," Compton replied. "And my adjutant and I agree that's your company and your call to make. Very well, Captain. Tell you what I'll do. You get those boys going and I'll dawdle, give them time to catch up. We'll have the buffalo ready for transfer when they arrive."

"Thank you, sir."

"*Semper fi*, Captain."

"*Semper fi*, sir. Out here."

Pringle smiled as he returned the receiver to the communications technician. "Specialist Margolis, go find First Sergeant Brock and ask him to report to me. Do it ASAP, Marine."

"Yes, sir!"

What Colin Pringle didn't know at that moment was that his squad would never make it to the 1-Two-7. They would be intercepted by the same terrorist force that surrounded Camp Shannon less than twenty-four hours later and cut off all communications.

A terrorist force on a mission to overrun Rifle Company Bravo's perimeter and kill 138 U.S. Marines.

Hancock, Montana

THE JANGLE OF THE PHONE on the bedside table startled Sheriff Gabriel Boswich out of a deep sleep.

Boswich cursed, rubbed his eyes and then glanced at the digital numbers of the clock through the blur as he fumbled for the receiver. "It's only 3:00 a.m. This had *better* be important."

Through the familiar static and crackle that told Boswich the call was being piped directly through the radio of one of his squad cars, the sheriff could make out what sounded like shattering glass and automatic weapons fire.

"Sheriff?"

Even through the panic, Boswich recognized Norman Harrison's voice. He'd hired his newest deputy less than six months earlier, an eager-eyed and fresh-faced recent graduate from the state law academy who'd decided he couldn't cut it with the "Staties" and opted to return to Hancock. And why the hell not? The kid had lived in Bear County his entire life and, given his high marks at the academy, he was prime material for the small-town life of Hancock. Even as county seat, the town wasn't that big and the people were friendly.

"What the hell is going on, Norm?"

"I got trouble, Sheriff!"

"Calm down, son."

"Calm down? Holy fuc—"

A fresh barrage of breaking glass and shooting assaulted Boswich's ears, this time interspersed with the *blam-blam* of shotgun blasts, most likely coming from the cruiser's Remington 870. Harrison came on once more but he was shouting so loud that Boswich couldn't understand a word. He ordered the kid to stay where he was and hung up.

Boswich leaped out of bed and cursed as he stubbed his toe while making his way to the closet. He'd tried not to wake his wife but that didn't make much difference, he knew. A ringing phone in the middle of the night had become much more commonplace than it had once been, and three-quarters of the time Suzanna just muttered for him to be careful, and then she'd roll over and go back to sleep.

This time she could sense something had gone very wrong—something about that woman's intuition—because she sat up and began speaking to him. "What's going on?"

"Some kind of trouble, nothing to worry about, I think. Go back to sleep, babe."

"You never could lie worth a damn," she told him. "I could hear the nothing-to-worry about through the phone, Gabe."

Boswich didn't say anything else as he eased his sock over his throbbing toe. He donned his uniform pants, shirt and vest before stepping into his boots. He slung his gun belt over his shoulder, stopped to scoop his badge and wallet off the nightstand and then headed for the safe in his office to retrieve the Colt AR-15 semiautomatic rifle. Five minutes later he floored the accelerator of his marked police unit, a Jeep Grand Cherokee. There were a few perks to the job.

Boswich turned on the GPS tracking system and got the location of Harrison's unit. He picked up his radio and was ready to call dispatch when he changed his mind. He dropped the radio on the seat and whipped his cell into play. Fifteen seconds later he heard Charles Pulley's voice come on the line. Chas, as they called him, had been Boswich's faithful and sole deputy for the past six years. With the increased population, Boswich had brought on Harrison to help offset the patrols and give them some of the extra manpower they needed. They were still desperately short on deputies but the county commission had been tight-fisted. He'd practically had to bribe the old codgers, three men and one woman, to even part with the cash for a new cruiser to replace the 1997 clunker he'd been driving.

"Whatever you do, don't alert county yet," Boswich ordered Pulley. "Norm didn't call them—he called me direct. He probably had a good reason."

"Where's he at?" Pulley said, obviously awake now.

Boswich gave him the directions and hung up.

Five minutes passed and he rounded the corner onto Trapline Road, gunning the engine when he spotted the flashing lights on Harrison's cruiser. He slowed a bit when he got within a quarter mile. The houses on the road were few and far between, most of them practically shacks—many positioned far off the road—on tracts that ranged between forty and a hundred acres.

Harrison's squad car happened to be parked in front of one of the houses close to the road, a place that had been the object of recent buzz in town. According to what Boswich had heard, the place had been put on the market after old widow Magarey had finally kicked off. She and her old man had never had kids and there weren't any other relatives that could be found, at least not by Boswich's meager resources. The place sold just a few weeks after it went up for sale to some sort of Arab fellow, a Pakistani or something like that.

Near as anyone from town had been able to tell, the guy was a quiet type, young and clean-shaven with glasses, and pretty much kept to himself. He'd apparently told the Realtor he was attending the tech school upstate. Boswich had heard through the grapevine that the young man had cleaned the place up and he didn't bother anybody, so Boswich figured to leave him in peace unless trouble reared its ugly head.

When he came within less than fifty yards, the house went up. Flames rocketed toward the black sky, the embers popping and dancing like fireflies. Heat from the red-orange tower of fire gushing from the propane tank was intense enough for Boswich to feel through the windshield of his vehicle.

The sheriff stopped a safe distance off and burst from the vehicle with his AR-15 loaded and ready. It only took him a few seconds to find the bullet-riddled body of Nor-

man Harrison slumped over the console of his squad car.
Part his face was missing and his car looked like it had
gone through a war zone.

Boswich could hardly believe the sight. What the hell
had happened here? And who was responsible for this?
Had the young Arab kid done this? Was he some kind of
terrorist or had it just been an accident? None of it made
sense. And now that a cop was dead, there would be a
state investigator coming in, maybe even the goddamned
FBI. Great…that's all Boswich needed. Some punk suit
from the state or Feds nosing around his crime scene.
Well, he wouldn't have it. One of his men was dead and
he was going to find out who was behind it.

And the son of a bitch would pay!

CHAPTER TWO

Stony Man Farm, Virginia

Silence reigned within the War Room as the five men of Phoenix Force tried to digest what Barbara Price had just told them.

Price had put them on alert when the first intelligence brief arrived from the White House following a meeting between the President and Harold Brognola.

"You can imagine the pure chaos happening at the Pentagon right now," Price continued.

"Indeed," replied David McCarter. As the leader of Phoenix Force, McCarter could appreciate what most of the Marine commanders were feeling right at that moment. "It's not every day you lose contact with an entire bloody company."

Price nodded. "We do have some preliminary data on that note. The current political environment is such that the Iraqi government is refusing to permit U.S. aircraft to enter their airspace. We could've forced the issue but the President wasn't prepared to do that given the current depletion of forces in the area."

"I'm almost sure I know the answer, but what about NATO?" Rafael Encizo asked.

Born in Cuba and naturalized as a U.S. citizen, Encizo remained one of the three original Phoenix Force veterans alongside McCarter and Gary Manning. He carried a reputation for being tough and resourceful, and specialized in underwater and maritime warfare. He also had the distinction of being the most skilled knife-fighter of the group, a fact made more evident by the numerous scars on his body.

"NATO can't interfere," Price said. "This isn't a NATO outfit. U.S. Marines are autonomous, and due to the nature of their operations they typically aren't ever attached to any NATO force. Not to mention they have no more fly-zone rights than the American military. No, we're on our own with this one."

Calvin James, a black American raised in Chicago and the team medic, stroked at his thin mustache with a thoughtful glance at the table. "Could we use our dedicated satellite?"

Price smiled. "Already in position and we're getting data back. From what we can tell, the unit is still within Camp Shannon. But in the terrain surrounding them we've identified hundreds of separate heat signatures profiling both vehicular and personnel assets. Our enemies, whoever they are, effectively have the camp surrounded."

"And because of the no-fly zone, we can't provide air support," remarked Thomas Jackson Hawkins.

A former member of Delta Force and the youngest of the team, Hawkins had stepped in after the retirement of McCarter's predecessor, the late and venerable Yakov Katzenelenbogen. His team often called him Hawk or just T.J. and often teased him mercilessly about his Texan roots. Hawkins had been somewhat of a hothead when first coming on board, but he'd matured as both a man and warrior through the years. His teammates touted him as an invaluable ally, steady and reliable even under the worst circumstances.

"We're also concerned that some of the vehicles may include SAMs," Price said. "There's presently a pretty dense storm moving through that area, so we can't get a good granular fix yet. But we'll have more intelligence on the ground once you're airborne."

"When do we leave?" Manning asked.

Gary Manning had been working with the Royal Canadian Mounted Police as a terrorism specialist when Stony Man recruited him. Even then he'd possessed an uncanny, almost encyclopedic knowledge of terrorist groups. He'd also undergone rigorous training with Germany's GSG-9 antiterrorist unit. He served as Phoenix Force's primary demolitions specialist.

"Within the hour," Price said. "Grimaldi's on his way back from Montana, where he dropped Able Team. He'll put down at Dulles, fuel up and you're out of here. Any questions?"

"Just one," McCarter replied. He scratched his neck and said, "Do we know anything about this enemy force? Are they terrorists or Iraqi nationals? Military? Maybe police militia?"

"I wish we could answer that question, David. Unfortunately, we can only make an educated guess. Camp Shannon was put in place primarily to act as a security checkpoint for the Syrian-Iraq border. Weapons smuggling along that border was big business, both before and during the war. According to the intelligence brief there were two nonmilitary personnel on site, as well.

"There's a complete dossier on the first man that's been uploaded to the onboard systems of the jet. You can study that en route. In short, he's an Iraqi scientist who developed a perimeter detection system that worked quite effectively during the war. Naturally, we don't want him falling into enemy hands. The second man is a CIA agent by the name of Paul Hobb. That's about all we know of him, since the CIA's not being overly forthcoming with his information. We have the President leaning on them now for their cooperation, but who knows when they'll finally give us something useful."

Hawkins frowned. "I don't mean to sound like some big baby, but we're not exactly equipped to go up against a hundred or more armed terrorists who've had time to dig in. Do we have any specific mission objectives?"

"We're going to have to leave the details to your own tactical devices," Price said. "We're not there and we can't do anything more than provide you with as much intelligence as possible. As I said when I opened the briefing, this is one of those missions unlike any we've ever sent you on before."

"I don't know about all that, luv," McCarter said with a shrug. "Intelligence is scarce, conditions are anything but ideal and all the numbers are against us. Sounds like business as usual!"

"You indicated we'll have help from the Jordanians," Encizo interjected. "What's that all about?"

"They claim to have an intelligence asset in Camp Shannon with information vital to their internal security. They've agreed to help us on the off chance we can get him out alive, and they've assured us we'll have all their resources at our disposal. Apparently they've built an underground that's become quite adept at getting in and out of Iraq. That's your ticket. Once you're there, do the needful and try to get everybody out of that camp alive. Including yourselves, and I can't stress that enough."

"We hear and obey," James said.

"Good luck, Phoenix Force," Price said. "And God-speed."

"NICE WEATHER HERE!" Hermann "Gadgets" Schwarz said. "If this were January instead of July, we'd have to be dressed in mukluks."

A cool morning breeze swept down the main street of Hancock as the three men of Able Team exited their rented SUV. Rosario "Politician" Blancanales had parked in front of the sheriff's office—not difficult to find thanks to the GPS system on board their vehicle. The drive from Bear Run County Airport had taken only about ten minutes.

Carl "Ironman" Lyons, a tall blond warrior and Able Team's leader, glanced around him and then directed his voice toward his teammates as they made for the front door. "I don't think we'd have to wear Eskimo garb to look out of place here, gents."

The other two men couldn't argue the point with him. They were attired in suits and ties, determined to play the part of FBI agents attached to the Department of Homeland Security. It was an old cover, to be sure, but one they had found useful in situations like this. Sheriff Gabe Boswich had reported the death of one of his officers and the explosion of a house owned by a man of Arab descent. That had triggered enough interest for the DHS to send a forensics team to the site and simultaneously notify the Department of Justice.

Brognola still had an official relationship with the DOJ and when the report came across his desk he'd considered it too important. After checking it out, the Stony Man chief had activated Able Team with orders to investigate and act on whatever they found.

Lyons pushed through the door and a hidden buzzer alerted the occupants of the station to their entry. A cute woman in civilian dress sat behind a tall desk past a small reception area that sported a couple of seats. She typed on a computer keyboard, her nails clacking furiously against the keys, and looked at the trio as they filed in.

Without stopping she said, "May I help you, gentlemen?"

Lyons reached to the inner pocket of his coat and withdrew the mock credentials. Price preferred to term them as mocked rather than forged since they were actually legitimate FBI credentials that had been produced for Able Team's cover. Half the time when dealing with members of law enforcement, it usually became evident in short order that the three urban commandos were a bit more than the average FBI professional.

"Agent Irons, Homeland Security," Lyons recited as Blancanales and Schwarz followed suit. "We're here to see Sheriff Boswich."

The woman stopped typing and tried for something that couldn't quite be defined as a smile—more like a forcing of the corners of her mouth. "Of course. You're expected. Please wait here."

The woman disappeared into a back room and Able Team took in their surroundings by pure training reflex. Not a large space, more deep than wide, and furnished with plain desks and chairs. Three doorways left to right were visible off the back wall of the main area and labeled Holding, Sheriff's Office and Restrooms respectively. The woman came out a moment later with a tall, lanky man wearing a uniform, light vest and tactical gun belt in tow.

The man stepped through the swinging waist-high door next to the high desk and extended his hand. "I'm Sheriff Boswich. Welcome to Hancock."

They shook hands in turn and then Boswich gestured for them to follow. They went through the doorway for the restrooms but continued down the hall past doors for male and female. The hall emerged onto a breakroom with a table, coffeepot, refrigerator and vending machine.

"Afraid my office is a bit small, so I hope this is okay."

"It'll be fine," Blancanales replied in as congenial a tone as possible.

Boswich offered coffee as Able Team took seats at the table. It smelled freshly brewed so Blancanales and Schwarz accepted. Lyons refrained, never having been much for the stuff. Instead, he thumbed some coins into the vending machine for a bottled mineral water and returned to his seat.

"I hope you guys can understand I'm a little resentful you've come here," Boswich began. "I just want you to know that up front. I like to cut the bullshit and speak the truth. It's nothing personal."

"This is your territory, Sheriff," Blancanales said. In most cases, his teammates preferred to let Blancanales take the lead in conversations like this. He'd earned his nickname for his gregarious manner and infectious charm. "We're not here to step on your toes."

Boswich squinted over a sip from a ceramic mug that had his name over an emblem of the Bear Run County sheriff's badge. "That right?"

"That's right," Lyons said. "We're here to help."

"Okay. How?"

Blancanales wrested back the conversation. "First, let's assume that this student you claim is of Arab ethnicity is in fact missing."

"Let me stop you right there, boys," Boswich said. "I can assure you that he is of Arab descent. His name's Hamza Asir. He's twenty-one years of age and a sophomore at Montana Regional Science Institute in Great Falls. He's there on some kind of fancy scholarship from what I could get out of the real-estate agent combined

with school records. Apparently he's from Pakistan.
Those points coupled with the circumstances surrounding the homicide of my deputy make him my number-
one suspect. Not a person of interest, a suspect. Get it?"

"Fine, so he's a verified Pakistani." Blancanales put
an edge to his voice. "We're not interested in his ethnicity—we're interested in his background."

"What do you mean?"

"I mean, where did he live before coming here? How
long has he resided in Montana or even been in the United
States, for that matter? Does he have any known associates? Is he religious? Does he attend a mosque? How
does a Pakistani student end up with a scholarship for a
school in Montana of all places? Where did he attend high
school? Where else has he lived? What was he studying
at this institute?"

"Okay, okay," Boswich said, raising his hand. "You
made your point."

Lyons said, "Look, Sheriff, I can understand you wanting a piece of whoever killed your deputy. I was a cop
once. I get it. But if this guy *is* a terrorist, then you can
bet he has friends. And if he's run to ground with them,
it could mean he'll be back."

"What makes you think so?"

Lyons's smile lacked warmth. "Fanatics typically like
to do something spectacular. More spectacular than, say,
killing a deputy sheriff. A real terrorist isn't going to
bring down a lot of potential heat on him just for one
cop."

"Sheriff, has the FBI forensics lab gotten back to you
yet on what caused the explosion?" Schwarz asked.

Boswich shook his head. "Not yet. Do you think that's
important?"

"It could be," Schwarz said. "I'm somewhat of an explosives expert and you can often tell a lot from those kinds of remnants. It might give us a clue as to who supplied them if we know what they are."

"I don't have any influence on those boys up there in Helena. Maybe we'd have more luck expediting things if one of you talked to them."

"We can do that," Lyons said. "Meantime, we'd like to check out—"

He never got to finish as the young woman, who they had learned was Paula Bacon, entered the kitchen.

"Sheriff, Chas just called in. More trouble."

"Chas is my other deputy," he explained to Able Team before saying, "What's going on?"

"Some kind of trouble on the Northbrook Road," Bacon replied.

Boswich nodded and climbed out of his chair. "Sorry to cut this short, boys, but duty calls."

"We'd like to tag along, if you don't mind," Lyons said.

"Why? I don't think this has anything to do—"

"Uh, Ms. Bacon here just said there was 'more' trouble," Blancanales urged. "I don't think she would have put it quite that way if whatever's happening now isn't related."

Bacon's expression remained unreadable but Boswich apparently decided to acquiesce because he didn't put up any more arguments. "You can ride with me."

"We have our own vehicle and equipment," Blancanales said. "We'll follow behind you, if you don't mind."

"Fine."

The three men made their way out of the office and were just getting belted in when Boswich emerged from a side road with his lights and sirens going. He turned the corner, nearly putting his Jeep Cherokee on two wheels, and tore down the main street with a squeal of tires churning dust and gravel. Blancanales expertly backed out of the spot and laid in a pursuit course. They didn't have a clue where Northbrook Road was but they couldn't afford to get lost. Blancanales had plenty of experience in high-speed road action so this wouldn't give them much trouble.

They raced behind Boswich's car for a time and Lyons finally said, "Have to admit, this guy's a bit impressive."

"A little on the hot-tempered side," Blancanales remarked.

"Well, you got to admit that it's probably chaffing his ass right now that he's got *federales*—" Schwarz made quotation signs "—horning in on his investigation. I think he'd just prefer to handle this himself."

"Doesn't matter what he prefers," Lyons said. "He's not trained for this and we are. If there's trouble, real trouble here like I'm beginning to think there is, he's going to need us."

They rounded another turn and straight ahead they could see something going down. Three men, all clean-shaven and wearing desert-style camouflage fatigues, had a house surrounded and were exchanging gunfire with whoever was inside. In fact, there were several occupants because muzzle-flashes were visible from windows on both the first and second floors.

"Not good," Blancanales said.

"I don't get a warm, fuzzy feeling from this one," Schwarz added.

An older squad car, this one a sedan, had taken a position in the road so as to block it while also providing the maximum cover for the deputy. An officer was crouched behind his cruiser with a shotgun in hand, back pressed to the rear bumper. None of the armed men surrounding the house seemed to be paying attention to him, but that was possibly because he didn't pose much of a threat, a single deputy outgunned three-to-one by men with assault rifles.

"Gadgets, pass out the gear," Lyons ordered.

The electronics wizard reached over the rear seat of the SUV into the hatchway and came up with an M-16 A4/M-203, which he passed to Lyons. He retrieved a second assault rifle for himself, a SIG-551 A-1. Chambered for the 5.56 mm NATO round, this little baby could put out 700 rounds per minute and boasted a muzzle velocity exceeding 850 meters per second. The last weapon he produced was a Belgium-made FN-FNC, a growing favorite of the Stony Man teams for its versatility and reliability.

"Go around the sheriff and his deputy," Lyons said.

"What are you planning?" Schwarz asked.

Lyons tendered him with a wicked grin. "To give our friends up there a new target."

CHAPTER THREE

Blancanales shouted for them to hang on and then veered off the road and into the ditch. He rode it as far as he could, his knuckles white as he fought the steering wheel, and when the opportune moment hit he swerved onto the asphalt. Now past the police vehicles, he jammed the brakes and jerked the wheel to put the rental into a power slide. He came to a halt in perfect position and the Able Team warriors went EVA.

The enemy combatants were Americans, or at least non-Arabs. They turned toward the Able Team arrival with surprise, but Lyons and his teammates were hardly about to let up now. The men stopped trading shots with the occupants, but bullets from the house punched through one adversary's body, driving him back as he danced like a puppet. Red splotches erupted in his belly and chest and he finally went down at the edge of the road.

All three Able Team warriors realized simultaneously that their enemies weren't standing outside. Something made it clear—although none of them would be able to later describe exactly what that something had been— the *real* enemies were inside the house.

Lyons responded by turning the muzzle of the M-203 in the direction of the window where the shots had come from and tightened the stock to his shoulder. He sighted in on the target, judged the distance at twenty meters and squeezed the trigger. The 40 mm grenade launcher recoiled with the force of a 12-gauge shotgun but it did the trick. The HE grenade blew as soon as it penetrated the window, and yellow flame mixed with dark smoke and debris erupted outward. It left a charred, gaping hole in its wake.

Able Team charged the house while the shooters inside were still reeling from the confusion at their arrival. Lyons shouted at the remaining pair outside to throw down their arms and surrender, although he didn't plan to stick around to see if they complied. Boswich and his deputy would just have to handle that situation. The bigger threat still seemed to be from those inside the house. Blancanales reached the door first and put his foot to it with the full power of his stocky frame behind the kick. The door gave and Able Team rushed through the doorway. They fanned out as they assessed the interior, pointing their weapons in the directions it seemed most likely they'd find trouble.

Schwarz caught the first hint of a light on metal in his peripheral vision. He whirled and triggered his SIG-551 A-1 from the hip. The reports were loud in the confines but Schwarz didn't even flinch. A volley of 5.56 mm rounds found their mark: the chest of a dark-skinned man with wiry brown hair and a beard. The impact drove him backward and flipped him over the arm of a heavy chair.

Two more men rounded the second-floor landing but didn't realize their mistake until it was too late to matter. They'd bunched themselves in the narrow stairwell in their haste to escape. Lyons and Blancanales took full advantage of the blunder. The pair opened up simultaneously, cutting a swathe of destruction across the path of the terrorists. The two men twitched under the onslaught and then tumbled in unison down the steps, one right behind the other. Only one corpse made it to the bottom of the stairs. The other one got hung up midway.

The gunfire died out and Able Team waited a minute, listening for any sounds of movement. Their ears were pricked for the slightest creak or groan of floorboards. The house was older and the warriors were confident if other occupants were moving they could hear it. After a time, they swept the rest of the house but found no more trouble so they made their way outside.

On the front lawn they found the camouflaged survivors on their knees, hands on their heads while Boswich and his deputy held them at gunpoint. Lyons could tell from the scowl on Boswich's face that the sheriff wasn't happy Able Team had interfered. Fortunately the guy had enough good sense not to bring it up in front of the prisoners. They'd catch hell for it, yeah, but Carl Lyons didn't really give a damn about that. They had a job to do, and they'd do it whether Boswich liked it or not.

Blancanales asked one of the men, "What's your name, son?"

"I ain't your son, *pops*."

Lyons's face screwed up in anger. "Watch your mouth, punk!"

"You look like military types," Schwarz said. "You militia or something?"

"Something," the other man said. This one had a calmer demeanor and looked a bit older. He wore his hair high-and-tight, just as his partner, and he wore his uniform just a bit too well.

"I don't think this is amateur hour here," Blancanales told his teammates. "In fact, I'm guessing these gentlemen are veterans. U.S. Marines, perhaps?"

Neither of them spoke or moved a muscle.

"They've asked for lawyers," Boswich said. "Going

to have to take them in. Obviously they're not going to say anything. And even if they did, you couldn't use it in court."

"Doesn't matter," Lyons replied as he reached into his pocket and removed his cell phone. He snapped each of their photos with the built-in camera. "I'm sure our people will be able to identify them using facial recognition, and especially if they've served in the military."

"You can't do that," the older man said.

Schwarz chuckled. "Well, actually, he just did."

"YOU GUESSED RIGHT, Pol," Barbara Price announced to Able Team. "They're both ex-Marines."

They were gathered around the main seating area of their Spartan accommodations at the Brown Bear Resort, a lodge catering to the city slickers who came to hunt. It was off season so they practically had the place to themselves, save for weekend fishermen. The laptop computer that boasted a secure satellite uplink to Stony Man Farm sat on a coffee table in front of them, but the space was too cramped for Price to be able to see them all, so Lyons took center stage.

"Doesn't really come as much of a surprise, Barb," Schwarz replied. "It was pretty obvious from the start that they had some sort of military training."

"The older of the two is Sergeant Donny Kapczek, a veteran of Afghanistan and Iraq, three consecutive tours. He's twenty-six years old and currently serving in the inactive reserves. The younger man is Kevin Weissmuller, a private with one tour who was released after nearly losing an arm. Both men are decorated and served honorably. No history of criminal records for either of them, either during or after service."

"Maybe they just never got caught," Lyons muttered.

"I don't think it's that at all," Blancanales said. He scratched his chin. "Neither of those boys struck me as idiots. Sure, the younger was mouthy but he certainly wasn't any type of leader material. The older one, this Sergeant Kapczek...I pegged him as the senior guy right away."

"And let's not forget what Boswich told us after they were taken into custody," Schwarz said. "Neither of them resisted when they were placed under arrest. That means they didn't have any criminal intent."

"Either way, we can't have just anybody running around with guns and blowing holes in people without authorization," Lyons rebutted. "Innocent people always get hurt in those circumstances. I'm all for home defense just as long as the right people get shot."

"The eye-opener is yet to come," Price said. "Both of these men served in the same unit together. Their last unit, in fact. They were attached to Rifle Company Bravo, part of the 123rd Marine Battalion."

"Um, Barb, isn't that...?" Blancanales began.

"Yes." Her tone became solemn. "That's the company at Camp Shannon in Iraq. Phoenix Force's mission, to be more precise."

"Phoenix Force's mission." Lyons scratched his chin. "Would someone like to catch me up?"

"I heard the 4-1-1 from Jack just before he dropped us off. He left in a big hurry because he had to get back and pick up Phoenix Force," Blancanales explained. He rose and came around the back of the love seat on which Lyons sat so he could see Price. "You think our assignments are connected?"

"You know what they say about coincidence in our line of work," Price replied.

"Let's back up a step," Lyons said. "Run it down for us from the beginning."

Price explained the details, starting with the communications block of Rifle Company Bravo to Phoenix Force's mission objectives.

Schwarz let out a low whistle. "Sounds like David and crew have a tall order."

"You can say that again," Lyons said.

"Sounds like—"

"*Not*," Blancanales said as he made a chopping motion with his hand.

"What it really sounds like is, we need to go question these two Marines at length," Lyons said.

"Don't know how easy that's going to be," Blancanales said. "This Sheriff Boswich is a decent enough sort, but the guy definitely likes to play things close to the vest. He's especially not going to just let us get our run at those two before he does, and that won't happen now that they've asked for lawyers."

"Actually, your mission now officially supersedes the murder of Deputy Harrison," Price replied. "As much as I hate to pull the rug out from under local law enforcement, this is an issue of national security. With these missions now being verifiably connected there's a good chance Kapczek and Weissmuller possess information that may assist Phoenix Force."

Lyons sighed. "Even if they do, we still don't have any way of putting that together with why they were engaged in an encore of the fight at the OK Corral. The four terrorists we took out inside that house have yet to be identified. There's not much left *to* identify of one of them."

"You didn't find anything inside the house that would be helpful?"

Lyons shrugged. "No time to search, Barb. I swear it

was like Boswich had the forensics and haz-mat teams on speed dial or something."

"It definitely sounds like you're right about him trying to rein things in."

"Well, we're just going to have to find some way to get around that," Blancanales said. "Our mission takes priority, as you've said. And I'm more concerned about the lives of more than a hundred service personnel than I am about the rights of two vigilantes."

"Agreed," Schwarz said. "For all we know, they could've just been looking for some payback and somehow connected those guys we took down with this Hamza Asir."

Lyons grunted with a nod and then returned his attention to Price. "Speaking of Asir, you got the information I sent you?"

Price nodded. "Yes. That was good thinking sending it ahead of time. Bear managed to run down everything he could find on Asir, and my analysis revealed some very interesting data on Mr. Asir."

"That's our Bear," Schwarz joked, referring to the Farm's computer expert.

Price cleared her throat as she referred to something out of view, probably her notes. "Asir was born in Pakistan but as a baby came to the United States as a refugee. His parents were apparently killed during a civil demonstration."

"That would give him no loyalty to the Pakistani government," Lyons said.

"On the contrary," Price countered. "This Hamza Asir has every reason to hate us. First, the demonstration took place in front of an American Embassy. Second, Asir was forcefully removed from the country and sent here against the will of his family. Apparently, when someone came here from Pakistan and tried to leave with him, they were arrested and deported, and Asir was returned to the orphanage."

"Isn't that just grand," Lyons said.

"So he could definitely have terrorist ties," Blancanales said. "Is that what you're saying?"

Price smiled. "That's part of what you need to figure out."

"Give us some time to talk to the two Marine prisoners," Lyons said. "Maybe we can coax some information out of them with the promise of a reprieve if they cooperate."

"Whatever will get you answers, Stony Man will back your play."

"Thanks, Barb. We'll be in touch. Out here."

Lyons closed the laptop, leaned back and rubbed his eyes as he let out a long groan. "It just gets better all the time."

"Actually, we could have an opportunity here," Schwarz said.

Blancanales feigned surprise. "Do tell."

Schwarz sat forward with an intent expression. "Well, let's just suppose that Asir is a terrorist and those four at the house were his buddies. You got something going down in Iraq and then two Marines formerly of the same unit in trouble decide to go pick a fight with Asir's friends. The big question I have is, how did they know?"

"Know what?" Lyons asked.

"How did they know where to look and who to look for? I mean, it's not like these terrorists went and took out an ad in the paper. Kapczek and Weissmuller had to have found something to tie these guys to trouble with their unit. That means they knew about it beforehand, maybe even before it came through official channels."

"He makes an awfully good point, Ironman," Blancanales said.

"I often make a good point."

Lyons said, "Well, we could sit here and hypothesize all day but that doesn't give us anything to act on. Let's go have us a chat with our two Marines."

HAMZA ASIR CROUCHED in the distance and observed the activities around what had been the house of his brothers and allies.

Now they were dead and the Americans were once more to blame for tearing him from the only people he cared about. Was it any wonder that he wanted them dead? These Westerners were ignorant and pathetic. Couldn't they just leave him and his friends alone? That sheriff had meddled in his affairs practically from the beginning. Asir knew about all the talk there had been regarding him by the people in the town; he knew the lies they spread about him. It wasn't really that much of a surprise to him, and he couldn't really say that he blamed them. An utter paranoia had spread throughout this country regarding any Muslim or Arab, even those born right here in their own country.

Good.

Asir *wanted* them to be afraid. He planned payback for the deaths of his comrades. The difficulty would be knowing where to start. He could only assume that the two surviving military types had been taken into custody. It would probably be some time before they released them so Asir couldn't wait—he would have to go to them.

The jihadist stepped away from the line of trees where he'd observed the police working the house and returned to his motorbike, which was parked out of sight. Under other circumstances a plan like the one he'd formulated would've been deemed crazy by his superiors, but in this case he'd elected to set aside any thought of punishment by them. This wasn't part of their plan but it had to be done. Blood had been drawn and blood was required to appease Asir's sense of justice, if not the will of his masters.

Asir worked the kick-starter twice and the engine revved to life. He turned in the narrow space between two massive trees and took off at an easy pace until he got to the next paved road. He watched both sides of the road but didn't see any observers. It would be dark soon and Asir would make his move then. He'd watched the office of the Bear Run County sheriff plenty since arriving in the small town and he knew their comings and goings well. They would most likely move their prisoners from the jail to the county holding facility tonight.

Yes, tonight would be perfect. Hamza Asir would make his move tonight.

"I DON'T KNOW HOW many times I have to explain this, Sheriff," Rosario Blancanales said. "This case is a matter of national security and that gives us precedence."

Able Team stood in Boswich's cramped office. The sheriff looked haggard, probably from not sleeping well since the loss of Harrison. Blancanales could feel for the guy but he also had to consider the fact their own men were at risk. Phoenix Force had no idea what awaited them in Iraq, and chances were good Kapczek and Weissmuller could shed some light on the situation.

"And I don't know how many times I have to explain this to *you*," Boswich replied. "But those turkeys are material witnesses to the homicide of a peace officer. That supersedes any jurisdiction of the FBI or Homeland Security. We're talking about the right of the state now, boys. Don't tell me the law, because I can quote most of it to you chapter and verse."

"Sheriff, we don't want problems here," Lyons finally said after initially letting Blancanales take the lead on the thought they could capture more flies with honey. "But if you refuse to let us speak to these men, we'll have to place you in custody."

Boswich's face reddened now and he stood slowly, placing his big hands on the desk for effect. "The only individual with the authority to arrest me in this county is the coroner, friend."

"I beg to differ," Schwarz said. "Under the Patriot Act, any U.S. citizen interfering with federal officers investigating a case of domestic terrorism is guilty of obstructing national security. Under those circumstances, we can obtain an order from the White House to place you in custody."

Boswich's face remained blank.

Schwarz looked at the gaping expressions of Lyons and Blancanales, shrugged and added, "Just saying."

"All right, we're done playing tiddlywinks," Lyons said, an edge in his voice. "You want to transfer those two guys in there to the county lockup, fine. We'll just wait to talk to them there."

"Nobody can talk to them," Boswich said. "Did you forget they've lawyered up?"

"The plain fact of the matter is that we're dealing with a terrorist threat," Lyons replied. "Now, I can understand you wanting justice for your man, and you want to make sure you hold up all of their legal rights so you don't lose your case in court. But understand we believe the men they were fighting to be terrorists. We also believe Hamza Asir is one of them."

"And let's not forget that those were fully automatic

weapons carried by that bunch," Blancanales added. "Not something they would've picked up at the local hunt shop."

Lyons looked around the office and then said, "Not to mention it doesn't much look like you're prepared to fight an army of Muslim fanatics."

Boswich let out a snort. "And you are?"

"Yeah."

Something in Lyons's eyes or perhaps his tone gave Boswich pause. Silence fell on the four men and Boswich, while clearly defiant at first, looked as if he might waver. Lyons knew the guy was no genius but he was far from an idiot. Boswich could see what was going on, that nothing was as it appeared. This wasn't just a bunch of good ol' boys involved in some tavern brawl near closing time—probably the most trouble Boswich had seen in his long career. These were veterans of the USMC shooting it out with Arabs toting assault rifles.

Boswich finally let out a sigh and rubbed his eyes. He was torn between doing his duty exactly as he thought he should do it, and getting to the bottom of who killed Harrison. "I still think you guys are barking up the wrong tree. This just looks like a case of vigilantism gone wrong."

"It doesn't really matter what it looks like," Lyons said. "Listen, Boswich, I've been where you are now."

"That right?"

"Yeah, that's right. I've been torn between following procedure because it was the law and following my gut because I thought it was right. And because I went with door number two, I ended up working with the sharpest tools in the shed. We've done a lot of good over the years, and we don't want to see innocent people get hurt. So you have to decide if you go with the letter of the law or the spirit of it, and you have to decide now."

After a long time Boswich said, "Fine, Irons, fine. We'll do it your way."

"You won't regret it," Schwarz said with a grin.

"I already do," the sheriff replied.

CHAPTER FOUR

Camp Shannon, Iraq

"Anything?" Captain Colin Pringle asked.

First Sergeant Brock turned from the radio and shook his head. "No, sir. We can't seem to reach anybody, even by satellite phone. It's like the entire Corps went black."

"Not likely, Top. Options?"

"Well, being that the squad we sent for the water buffalo hasn't returned and we were able to confirm with the 1-Two-7 they never arrived, I'd have to say chances are good they've been intercepted."

Pringle frowned. "But by who?"

"I don't know, sir. I can only guess."

"Then guess."

"Al Qaeda," answered a voice.

The two leaders whirled to see a somewhat rotund man with dark skin peering at them with dark eyes. He had smooth, brown skin and pudgy cheeks. His physical traits implied he'd never taken very good care of his body, but they knew his mind hadn't suffered. Abu Sudafi had designed the perimeter security system the Marines had used practically since establishing Camp Shannon five years earlier. The system utilized a sealed unit buried in the desert with an antenna that extended no more than six inches above ground. Connected to a satellite relay that returned signals to a dish at their base camp, the units were planted in a very specific formation. They could detect not only infrared signatures and changes in air pressure, but they also detected changes in seismic waves.

Anything larger than a desert hare and PSIDS—Perimeter Scanning and Intrusion Detection System— would immediately pick it up and alert the monitoring teams. The system had confounded the enemy, comprised mostly of dissident Shiites and al Qaeda operatives with remnants of the Hussein regime forced to flee the country. Sudafi's machines could even pinpoint targets of opportunity that could be taken out by planes or STS guided missiles, if called for.

"It's generally not considered good practice to eavesdrop, Mr. Sudafi." Brock did nothing to hide the disdain in his tone.

Pringle knew the two men hated each other. The commander couldn't really say he liked Sudafi, either, but the man had become a necessary evil. The relationship was symbiotic, and even if it hadn't been, orders were orders. Not that there was much love lost on the other side of the fence. Sudafi had turned on his own country in the hope of spending out his retirement in the United States. He'd entered into a negotiation with defense contractors who, for whatever reason, had decided to trust the guy. They'd convinced the U.S. government to grant the guy full legal residence in America with no questions asked. In return, Sudafi had built PSIDS and sold out his countrymen for his own betterment.

It didn't come down to a matter of patriotism or an ideology for democracy in Iraq. The guy just plain looked out for number one, and his shifty attitude had given most of the men in Rifle Company Bravo a reason to avoid him at all costs. He wasn't to be trusted and he'd found no acceptance among the enlisted men, which left him to confine his social activities to the officers and senior noncoms.

"I wasn't eavesdropping." Sudafi managed to smile but it didn't quite fit. "I came to advise you that the reason we no longer have communications is because they're being jammed."

"That's impossible," Pringle replied. "You can't jam satellite communications."

"You can if you interfere with the satellite dish intended to receive those signals."

"What're you getting at, man?" Brock demanded. "Quit talking in riddles and come out with it!"

Sudafi sighed and shook his head as if scolding a naughty child. "I'm talking about sabotage, Mr. Brock."

"You address me as 'First Sergeant,' Sudafi. Understand?"

"That's enough, men," Pringle interjected. "We don't have time for personal differences right now. Mr. Sudafi, explain what you mean by sabotage."

"There's visible damage to the satellite dish that not only provides your long-range communications but also data from the PSIDS interface."

"What kind of damage and how extensive?" Pringle asked. "And more importantly, can it be repaired?"

"I believe I can repair it if we have the appropriate materials. Most of this has already been packed, however, in anticipation of our evacuation. So we'll have to find the right containers and unpack them."

Pringle nodded. "Get on it. You can have three of my people from First Platoon to assist."

"I don't think I'll require—"

"That wasn't a suggestion, Mr. Sudafi," Pringle said.

"I'm the commanding officer of this unit and you do things my way. Understood?"

Sudafi looked as if he might rebut Pringle's directness but then apparently decided against it by nodding and beating a hasty retreat.

"I can't stand that douche bag," Brock muttered.

"Me neither, Top, but we don't have time to worry about him right now. He's not even close to being cut from the same cloth as a real Marine but he'll do his job or I'll shoot him myself."

"Permission to speak freely, sir?"

"Granted."

"I think in light of the fact we've had equipment sabotage and have no idea what's happened to our personnel from the squad we sent for the water buffalo, we should double roving patrols on the perimeter."

"Do it. I also want you to come up with a plan for cataloging all ammunition and squad-based weapons available to us, as well as any munitions or demo in reserves. Issue plus-fifty to all units assigned to roving guard. Also get me your recommendations for a scouting detail of four men, preferably from Hartman's platoon."

Brock replied with a salute, not reserved to doing so since they were indoors. "Yes, sir. The latter I can do right quick."

Pringle looked toward the darkening sky. "Good, because I get a gut feeling we're running out of time."

CAPTAIN COLIN PRINGLE didn't know how prophetic his words would be until just after sundown when the first strike came in the form of 102 mm mortar fire.

The squat building just to the east of the Technical Operations Center that housed the latrine and boiler became the first victim of the mortars. They arrived in tandem, first three then two, taking out the insulated metal roof and causing enough contained internal pressure to shatter the heavy plastic and frames that served as windows. Two Marines who happened to be inside relieving themselves were killed in the first wave.

"Holy fu—!" Brock began as he whirled and grabbed Pringle. He dragged his CO under the heavy metal table just in time. The next mortar grazed the roof of the TOC and blew out the southeast corner. Jagged shards of metal and wood whistled through the air but didn't come close enough to pose a threat. In any case, the loud report from the explosion and choking dust made it seem as if they'd come close to buying the farm.

Over the aftermath Pringle said, "Thanks, Top. You just saved our asses."

"All in day's work, sir."

"What I wouldn't give for a C-RAM right about now."

"We got something better, sir. Marines."

Brock took a moment to flash his superior a wicked grin before scrambling to his feet and running out the door of the TOC, now affixed only by a bottom hinge. He sprinted across the open space between the TOC and central barracks area. Even as he arrived his men were already hustling, geared up and heading toward their assigned posts. Squad leaders and platoon sergeants were shouting orders in a coordinated effort as Rifle Company Bravo took up a defensive posture on the perimeter.

Fortunately, Brock was experienced enough that he'd taken Pringle's order one step further and ordered members of Second Platoon to unpack all of the M-252 mortars put in crates by the weapons platoon. Led by Gunnery Sergeant Stuart Covey, the weapons platoon of Rifle Company Bravo had won numerous citations for their excellent marksmanship. Even as Brock watched

Covey command his men to get to work, the first sergeant beamed with pride.

Yeah, they were the best of the best.

The men in the first and second rifle platoons were taking up perimeter defense with their small arms as Covey's men prepped their equipment. The enemy seemed to be focusing their fire on key areas of the camp, although they had stopped the assault for reasons Brock could only guess. The enemy could've been planning a charge but Brock deemed that a suicidal move, at best. No commander worth his weight would order men to charge a well-defended perimeter in the dark unless he was insane.

"First Sergeant!"

Brock turned to see Lieutenant Hartman, Third Platoon's commanding officer, approach at a flat run. Brock opened his mouth to acknowledge him when Hartman's body came apart in a blast of heat and smoke. His left arm struck Brock in the chest full-force and combined with the blast it knocked the noncom off his feet. His ears rang and Brock shook his head to try to clear it. Before he knew what had happened, Brock felt strong hands on either arm and then sensed the steady rhythm of two of his Marines as they dragged him to cover behind a five-ton truck.

"You all right, Top?" one Marine asked.

Brock couldn't really recognize the guy through the patina of dust coating his eyes and face, not to mention the distraction of his ringing ears, but he nodded and mumbled, "Ship shape, Marines. Get to your posts…" He coughed. "I'll be all right."

"You sure, First Sergeant?" the second Marine asked.

"Fine, damn it! Now follow orders."

He couldn't have been sure but Brock thought he heard both men say *"Semper fi"* in unison before they left him.

The shock still had Brock out of it a bit and he never realized the mortar explosion he heard a few seconds later killed one of the Marines and wounded the other. It would only prove the beginning of a long and costly battle.

THE LAST THING Muam Khoury had expected would be for the Americans to have mortars of their own.

His man inside the compound had assured them that they would be unable to defend against a mortar attack because most of their combat had been, or would be, packed away. Their initial attack should've wiped out most of their munitions but instead the Americans were launching mortars of their own, and they were doing it with some accuracy. The first of the 81 mm shells fell short of their targets but his enemy was good and they adjusted in no time.

Khoury smiled. Excellent—at least he would be going against worthy opponents and not men ready to curl up and die when faced with adversity. Those were the types he'd been fighting up to this point. The war in Iraq had been anything but a challenge. He'd accepted his assignment from his masters in al Qaeda with excitement at first. He was to recruit and organize any insurgents that resisted the puppet democracy. He was to then train them and do whatever he could to disrupt operations against the Iraqi military.

He'd been successful the past few years in particular, probably because the majority of the fighting had ended and American forces were withdrawing in droves now. Most recently, they had abandoned a number of key positions and never even bothered to protect their retreat. But with the war winding down in Iraq, Khoury found himself wanting to return to his home in Afghanistan and lead his men there. Perhaps one day he could but for now he would have to bide his time and accomplish the mission at hand.

It would prove much more of a challenge if his enemy were worthy of the task and this one definitely seemed as much. Their latest volley of return mortar fire took out two of his emplacements and forced Khoury to order a retreat. Khoury instructed one of his squads—what remained of a former Iraqi military detachment that had joined forces with his group—to maintain interlocking fields of fire while the remaining weapons crews withdrew.

They had hit most though not all of the targets they intended on this round. They would continue to harass the Americans, launching regular attacks to destroy their equipment and supplies and wear them down. As long as they couldn't get communications out to their units, and Khoury had assurances from his spy as such, Khoury's hundred-man army could hold out here almost indefinitely. Of course, it wouldn't be a wise tactic to attempt to do that since the U.S. government would eventually risk violating the no-fly zone to rain hell from the skies on his men. By that time, however, it would be too late. Already the hills were providing an invaluable entrenchment point. Once completed, it would be very difficult to destroy them short of dropping a nuclear device. They wouldn't risk killing their own men.

That was the biggest trouble with the Americans, and the reason they had won absolutely nothing in Iraq. Lawlessness continued to abound in the cities and in the high-action areas. Well…they were fighting a battle they already lost. Unlike most of his Muslim brothers, however, Khoury did not view the West as filled with stupid people; rich and spoiled sinners abounded in America, perhaps, but they weren't uneducated. They knew they'd made a critical error in Iraq and many of their soldiers had been killed needlessly.

That thought didn't really bring any pleasure to Khoury. He sought no delight in the deaths of fighting men, real fighting men. He only wanted his countrymen to be free to practice their worship of Allah in their own way, without interference from outsiders. He felt the only way to secure those rights was the total destruction of any who sought to undermine the liberties of Islam. It was no more for a man or government body to determine this than it was for them to determine who should have children and who should not.

Khoury intended to make sure that never happened again.

The commander entered the base camp tent and found three of his field commanders bent over a map, arguing tactics among themselves. He almost became angry at them, disgusted by their endless bickering, but finally he shook his head and smiled. Whatever disagreements they had meant nothing—he was their commander and ultimately made all tactical decisions. They would obey as they had always obeyed him, or suffer the consequences: death by firing squad.

"My brothers," Khoury finally said as he poured a cup of coffee from the pot on the propane cookstove. "Why are you troubling yourselves with such details?"

"Sir, I've lost six men tonight," said Colonel Shabbat, commander of the weapons squad.

"I know," Khoury replied with a straight face. "I was there, too."

The meaning behind Khoury's reply seemed lost on Shabbat. "I will not continue to sacrifice my men while this American force has the ability to fight back."

"What would you have them do?" Khoury replied with

a laugh. "Stand up in full view and let you simply shoot them down?"

The other commanders laughed at Shabbat's expense, and Khoury could tell from the reddening in the colonel's face that he'd made his point. He didn't bother to remind Shabbat that the men he spoke of actually belonged to the jihad, neither did he feel it necessary to make the point that those men, like Shabbat, fought and died at Khoury's expense. He didn't like Shabbat—never had. The man was arrogant, and not much of a leader or tactician for that matter. But because Shabbat was the brother-in-law to al Qaeda's third imam he commanded special privileges that Khoury couldn't ignore.

Khoury didn't have to bow to Shabbat's every whim, however, and in this case he decided to defuse the topic simply by changing it. He turned to one of the other commanders. "How many of your men were injured, brother?"

"None, sir. They are all well and taking rest."

He nodded and told all three, "Make sure every man is fed. They will need to be fortified for the next assault. I want to begin the attack just before dawn. We'll have to reposition the mortars and double the infantry to provide covering fire for the mortar teams." Khoury tossed Shabbat a cold look and added, "That should prevent you from losing any more of your men."

CAPTAIN PRINGLE SAT in the reinforced bunker behind the factory building that had been converted into barracks years before and listened to the report from the leader of First Platoon, Lieutenant Ryan Dittmer. Dittmer had been a first-class officer throughout his tour, well liked by his men and a strong tactician. Because of this, Pringle had considered giving him control of Third Platoon with

Hartman KIA. Only problem was Dittmer didn't know squat about leading a weapons platoon and with nearly an entire squad being wiped out in the attack, they couldn't afford to lose any more weapons specialists or officers.

"Next best thing would be get some of *your* men trained on the M-252s," Pringle told the platoon leader.

"My Marines are ready and willing, sir. How many you need?"

"We lost four in this attack," Pringle replied. "And sure as shit the enemy's already planning their next attack."

"Agreed."

Pringle sighed and scratched his neck, now beginning to itch as the sunburn healed. "Give me a little time to think about it and I'll get back to you. Meanwhile, we go the usual. Keep up patrols, weapons cleaned, chow and rest in rotations."

"Yes, sir."

Dittmer hadn't been out of the makeshift headquarters half a minute when Brock came in.

"You okay, Top?"

"I got a little shaken, sir, but I'll pull through. Might have some hearing loss but doesn't much matter. I'm getting old anyway."

"Don't say that, Top!"

Pringle's reaction threw Brock for a loop. The guy was definitely stressing, and little doubt experiencing a bit of shell shock himself. The enemy had hammered them for nearly an hour, trading 60 and 102 mm mortar fire with machine-gun emplacements.

"Sorry, sir."

Pringle shook it off. "No time for apologies, Victor. We got bigger problems. I'm just touchy about any talk of you checking out on me. We've already lost good men today."

"Understood, sir. Won't happen again."

Pringle nodded. "Where do we stand?"

"Eight dead, six wounded. That's not counting our missing pickup squad."

"What the fuck is going on?" the CO muttered. "We're supposed to be getting out of here and instead we've had our communications knocked out and it feels like we're up against an entire division out there. How could this have happened?"

"I wish I knew, sir." Brock fired up a cigarette, a habit he'd finally managed to quit before assignment to Iraq. "But since we have no idea what numbers we're up against, it's possible we might not walk away from this one."

"I won't accept that," Pringle said. "Whatever happens, we're going to get our men out of this in one piece. You hear me, Top?"

"Loud and clear, sir."

"Now let's talk about a plan to turn this thing around."

CHAPTER FIVE

Hancock, Montana

"It's time to go," Sheriff Boswich said. "Let's move it."

Kapczek and Weissmuller looked up from behind the bars of the holding cell. They had circles under their eyes but they were no worse for the wear following interrogation by the three Feds. Boswich had a hard time believing Irons's men had any luck extracting information from these two simpletons, but he claimed to have learned quite a bit. He'd also promised to share it as soon as he could verify whatever Kapczek and Weissmuller had told him.

"Where're you taking us, sir?" Weissmuller asked.

Boswich couldn't repress a smile. It seemed almost too hard to believe this fresh-faced kid had actually spent nearly a year in a place like Iraq. He looked like he should be attending some prep school, not sitting in lockup for attempted murder. Frankly, Boswich felt sorry for the guy—both of them, really, although he knew Kapczek should have had the good sense not to try to influence his junior and former subordinate.

"County lockup. You're being held there temporarily until we can determine the final charges."

"What're we looking at?" Kapczek asked in a hoarse voice.

"At minimum, you're up for weapons charges. Posses-

sion of automatic rifles without a permit's illegal, even in
Montana. We don't like to deprive nobody of their gun
rights up here, but you still got to obey federal law. You
boys should've known better."

Boswich gestured for Kapczek to turn and slip his
hands through the bean slot where he cuffed him; he repeated the process for Weissmuller before actually opening the door. The sheriff stopped them in the hall of
the detention area—he'd had the place remodeled a few
years ago—to attach shackle clamps to their opposing
legs. Once in the transport, he'd chain the shackles together. That done, Boswich transferred them out to the
foyer where the three FBI agents were huddled and con-
ferring in low tones.

"Soon as these two are on their way," Boswich told
Irons, "I want to talk to you. So don't go anywhere."

"We're staying put, believe me," Blancanales replied.
"But you're not going with them?"

Boswich frowned. "Only one deputy now. Somebody
has to stay behind to police this town."

The trio nodded in understanding as Boswich es-
corted his prisoners out to the vehicle waiting in front.
He would've preferred to have a sally port but the current
office structure didn't support it, and there hadn't been
enough room on the side street for the county commis-
sioners to build one without revamping half the block
and issuing a new zoning ordinance. That had forced
Boswich to take any prisoners right out the front door,
something he didn't like to do. Of course, most of the
people in Hancock were peace-loving, law-abiding folk
who wouldn't have tried to bust a prisoner free, even a
family member. There'd never been anything like the
trouble they'd encountered the past few days, or the vio-
lence for that matter.

Chas Pulley waited in the sheriff's Jeep, the only vehicle they had big enough to transport two prisoners, not to mention it had the facilities needed to secure the ankle shackles. Pulley climbed out from behind the wheel long enough to assist getting Kapczek and Weissmuller into the backseat. A minute later Boswich had them shackled in and made a "get-going" gesture to Pulley. The black deputy smiled and took the wheel.

That smile would be the last thing Boswich remembered about his deputy. As Pulley backed out of the parking spot and put the vehicle in gear, glass exploded from the driver's window and a buzz of autofire blew his skull wide open.

"IF WHAT KAPCZEK TOLD US is true," Carl Lyons was telling his companions, "we sure as hell better—"

The sound of automatic weapons fire coming from the street cut him short.

The trio drew their pistols in near synchronized movements and headed for the front door. They emerged quickly but cautiously on the sidewalk and found Boswich moving in a crouch as his vehicle eased down the street very slowly. They couldn't see the shattered glass from that vantage point, but the screaming men in the back and the gray-red smears on the front passenger window painted the picture clearly enough for the Able Team warriors.

Boswich managed to gain access to the vehicle through the passenger door and a moment later he got it stopped.

Able Team had already gone into action, splitting up and moving up and away from the concentration of autofire coming from the roof of a building across the street. They couldn't see much of their attacker but they observed the muzzle-flashes. Pandemonium had already erupted on the street with women screaming and children bawling—what few men were present were doing what they could to get the former to safety.

Lyons went to check on Boswich and the prisoners while Blancanales and Schwarz split up and sprinted across the roadway. Lyons nodded as he observed their actions, realizing if they could make the opposing sidewalk without getting their asses shot off, chances were good the shooter wouldn't be able to take them at that steep angle. Not unless he had help from a mirror gunner, an unlikely scenario since this side comprised mostly single-story units. Blancanales and Schwarz made it, although no thanks to the efforts of the shooter.

"What the hell—?" Boswich said.

"Ambush!" Lyons replied.

"Asir?"

Lyons's jaw muscles flexed as he nodded. "Good bet."

It didn't really matter who was shooting at them as much as it mattered they get out of the line of fire. They also had to consider that if it were Hamza Asir behind this, he had probably killed Pulley first to neutralize the vehicle. That meant his real targets were Kapczek and Weissmuller. All of this Lyons considered in the moment before he instructed Boswich to get the pair out of the vehicle as fast as possible while he laid down covering fire.

Lyons swung around the Jeep until he found a good position of fire and leveled his Colt Anaconda. The big .44 Magnum revolver boomed in the afternoon air as Lyons squeezed off three rounds. The first two hit the parapet where the shooter had perched but the third managed to clip the forestock of the rifle. Black plastic shattered and pieces flew in all directions, the impact churning dust off the parapet. While Lyons knew he hadn't hit the shooter, his marksmanship had disabled the key threat.

Two more rounds came from the shooter's position a moment later, but they fell short of Lyons's position, obviously banged off hastily as the shooter tried to cover his retreat. Lyons turned to check on Boswich and the prisoners, heard Boswich say something about Weissmuller getting winged but that the two former Marines were alive, and then tore after his teammates.

BLANCANALES AND SCHWARZ reached the opposite side of the street and immediately skirted the building. They weren't familiar enough with the layout to know how the sniper had made his way to the roof, whether by rear stairs, a fire escape or some sort of attic access inside. However he'd gotten up there, he couldn't remain forever and he would eventually have to descend to make his escape.

It would be better to remain on the perimeter and wait for the gunman to appear than to attempt to seek him out. They advanced up the narrow sidewalk of the street running parallel to the building, pistols held at the ready. They slowed as they approached a side door and an old man happened to emerge just as they got close. He looked surprised at first, dropping his sack and raising his hands, but Blancanales shook his head and waved the guy on even as Schwarz bent to retrieve the sack and hand it to its owner.

"Please get out of here," Blancanales said.

The codger gave the pair a strange look but he complied with added haste, moving across the street as fast his doddering pace could take him.

The Able Team pair moved on, turning once at the sound of movement behind them as Lyons approached.

"Any sign of him?" he asked.

Blancanales shook his head but Schwarz couldn't help being his usual wiseass self as he replied, "Only one old geezer with a mischievous glint in his eyes who I doubt's our man."

"There!" Blancanales pointed down the sidewalk.

From behind the building emerged a lone figure, short and attired in black from head to toe. He had something in his hand, probably a weapon, but the sun had nearly set and the shadows obscured most everything on this side of the building. Even positive identification would make it practically impossible. It didn't change the name of the game, however. Able Team gave chase.

Lyons was far and away in the best shape of the three, possessing a physique of hard sinew and muscle. He'd never seen any real fat and had always maintained his physical conditioning through a regimen of swimming, biking, running and calisthenics that would've put most Navy SEALs to shame. His two comrades weren't quite as diligent, although years of combat and reflexes, combined with physical workouts to maintain endurance, had kept them in good fighting condition. Blancanales had always sported a slight paunch but it never seemed to interfere with his abilities.

The shooter rounded the corner of a building the next block up but Lyons had gained considerably on their quarry. He reached the corner and shuffled to a stop, Anaconda held high and ready. He counted to three, caught a deep breath and then stepped around the corner with pistol extended. He heard the roar of the motorcycle a moment too late to draw a bead and had to leap aside to avoid being run down. The bike erupted onto the street and turned south. It rocketed from Able Team's position with the high buzz of its engine and squealing, smoking tires.

Blancanales and Schwarz slowed and tried to catch their breath.

Lyons climbed to his feet and raised his pistol, but he changed his mind after seeing how much distance the motorcyclist had made. He holstered the Colt Anaconda and then inspected the rips in the knees of his pants, tattered from throwing himself to the ground—as was the skin beneath the fresh tears. "Damn it!"

Blancanales watched the steadily retreating bike. His eyes narrowed and he said, "I'm guessing that was Hamza Asir."

"That's just what I was thinking," Schwarz said. He looked at Lyons. "You okay, Ironman?"

"Yeah," Lyons grumbled, taking a moment to watch the motorcyclist escape. "But whoever that was won't be when I catch up to him."

"A MILITIA FORCE?" Sheriff Boswich said. "You have *got* to be kidding."

"Not kidding," Carl Lyons replied. "And because there are now automatic weapons involved and our people have confirmed that Asir may have ties to terrorists, this is automatically a federal case."

"Meaning?"

"It means we're taking over," Blancanales said.

"And we'll expect your full cooperation," Lyons added.

Boswich slammed his fist on his desk. "I knew this'd turn into a damn turf war eventually."

"It's not about turf—it's about common sense," Lyons said.

"I'd think you'd be happy for some assistance at this

point, Sheriff," Blancanales remarked. "The fact that you've now lost two deputies to these bastards should be enough to convince you it's folly to take this on yourself."

"He's right," Schwarz said. "Look, Sheriff, even you have to admit you almost bought the farm out there today, too. If we hadn't been around, who knows what might've happened?"

Boswich leaned back and shook his head. "You boys just don't get it, do you? This is my county and it's my job to police it. The people here expect me to keep them safe. That's why I was elected."

"Well then, you can best do that by starting to cooperate with us," Lyons countered.

Boswich rubbed his eyes and sighed.

Lyons said, "Look, we can empathize with your situation, trust me. But you have no idea what kind of shit you've stepped in. First, we have Kapczek who's flat out admitted he's the head of the Patriots' Charge. Did you have any idea whatsoever that a county militia had been formed and training for months?"

"Of course not," Boswich replied, waving in the direction of the holding area. "You already know that. They told you they've kept their activities secret."

"Then it also stands to reason you didn't know anything about Hamza Asir's ties to al Qaeda. We can't tell you everything, such as exactly who we are and our particular specialties. But the fact is you've got a war brewing right here on American turf and that's why we're taking over. We don't want any more dead cops and we sure as hell don't want innocent civilians getting pasted."

"We need to tackle this problem before it becomes any more of a train wreck than it already is," Blancanales added. "We're not superheroes but we're experts at taking down groups like this and keeping them down. Our solutions are radical but effective, and when the government doesn't feel it has any other choice it calls on us to take care of business."

"So what are you guys supposed to be, some kind of Delta Force or something?" Boswich asked. "I could believe it because it was obvious you knew how to handle yourselves out there today."

Schwarz smiled. "We have that effect on people."

"Well, I owe you my life and there ain't no denying that," Boswich said. "We'll do it your way from here out. But I expect to stay involved with this."

Lyons said, "If you're in, you're all in. And that means from here out I say jump you ask how high—no questions, no arguments. Clear?"

Boswich looked like he wanted to make a hostile reply but he finally nodded.

"Good." Lyons checked his teammates, who both nodded at him, then said, "Okay, here's the short version. Less than twelve hours ago a U.S. Marine unit in Iraq, a rifle company to be more precise, fell out of communications. They were part of a battalion involved in evacuating."

"The last unit, in fact," Blancanales interjected.

"Kapczek and Weissmuller served together with this unit," Lyons said. "And not coincidentally they went out and touched base with a whole bunch of others who served with that same unit."

"How did they found out about Asir?"

"According to Kapczek, Weissmuller was taking courses from the same school Asir attended. He apparently observed some odd behavior and, being naturally suspicious of any Muslim type, he started tailing the guy. Lo and behold, he finds out Asir's hooked up with others of his kind and I don't just mean choirboys at the local mosque."

"Mosques don't have any choirboys, Ironman," Schwarz joked.

"Shush," Blancanales muttered.

Lyons shook his head with a deep sigh. "When Weissmuller told Kapczek what he knew, they started digging for more information. They even had one guy who had some pretty significant IT skills and managed to start digging into Asir's background. I guess it became obvious pretty quick that little Hamza Asir wasn't everything he claimed to be, and that made them even more suspicious."

"That's when they blew it and took matters into their own hands," Blancanales said. "When Asir and his cohorts realized the Patriots' Charge had gotten their scent, they grew paranoid."

"Your first deputy killed, Harrison," Lyons said. "It was just his poor luck he stumbled onto them and they cut him down, worried that maybe the cops were working with Kapczek and friends."

"So where're the rest of the members of this Patriots' Charge?" Boswich asked.

It was Schwarz who answered. "We tried to get that out of them but they wouldn't cough it up."

"So they're still running around out there. Do we know how many?"

Lyons shook his head. "Kapczek won't give it up. He sees it as ratting out on his brother Marines and that wall is strong and silent. As you know."

Stony Man had dug into Boswich's background, as well, and discovered he'd served in the Marines. Able

Team had already agreed to disclose what they'd learned about the militia and al Qaeda agents operating in the area but the action on the street had stolen the opportunity.

"So what exactly did Weissmuller say he got on Asir?" Boswich asked.

Blancanales said, "Mostly just emails in Arabic. But included in it was a layout of the military facility where this unit is currently stationed in Iraq. The details were too good to be guesswork, even better than what Weissmuller said he remembered. He knew that information could only have come from someone inside the camp, most likely a spy. And with that Marine unit now completely incommunicado, we can only assume the worst."

Lyons said, "The other part we haven't told you is that some of our own men, our friends, are on their way right now. We have no idea what they could be stepping into, and if there's any chance we can find intelligence and pass it along, it would help. With each minute, we're falling further behind the eight ball. Kapczek won't give up his people but he's assured us of one thing. The Patriots' Charge won't stop until every last one of these terrorists is dead."

"Is that such a bad thing?" Boswich asked.

"What do you think?"

"We've already lost two fine law-enforcement officers over this," Schwarz said. "It's obvious that either side believes in acceptable casualties. We need to shut this down at the source and we need to do it fast. We don't mind killing terrorists but we don't want to have to keep looking over our shoulders for American veterans. Only problem is, we don't know this territory like you do."

Sheriff Gabe Boswich's expression looked grave now. "I understand."

"We could use your help," Lyons said. "Any ideas where either side might hole up?"

"Nope." Boswich replied. "But I'm pretty sure I know where to start looking."

CHAPTER SIX

Zizya area, Jordan

A stiff, hot wind greeted Phoenix Force as they deplaned at Queen Alia International Airport twenty miles south of Amman.

Stony Man had arranged to get the jet down in one of the cargo hubs without attracting any attention, really— no surprise considering the GID, Jordan's secret foreign intelligence service, maintained arm's-length alliances with the Central Intelligence Agency. In fact, it was a CIA cover Phoenix Force had been given by Stony Man to solicit the GID's cooperation in getting them over the border.

McCarter knew from years working with Britain's SAS that if any group could do it, the Jordanians could. Their reputation preceded them for recruiting and train-ing some of the toughest intelligence assets in the world, and frankly McCarter was bloody glad to have them on his side. It also didn't surprise any of his teammates when they were greeted by a muscular man with a beard and long brown hair.

The guy extended his hand. "Mr. Brown. You may call me Nawaf."

"Pleasure," McCarter replied. He introduced the rest of Phoenix Force by their respective aliases.

Nawaf nodded and gestured to a waiting van. When

they'd loaded their gear and climbed aboard, Nawaf got behind the wheel with McCarter on shotgun and left the airport. He turned onto an access road that took them in a direction opposite the highway.

"We're not going into Amman?"

Nawaf shook his head. "Your faces would attract too much attention. Our mission may already have been compromised. We can't afford any more exposure, you understand."

"What makes you think the mission's been compromised?" Encizo asked.

The man studied Encizo through the rearview mirror only a moment before returning his eyes to the road. It had grown steadily brighter since they'd landed—fast sunrises were not uncommon in this part of the world—which apparently had Nawaf increasingly nervous. The man's eyes never seemed to focus on one point more than a second, and yet he took in everything with a moment's glance.

"With the communications disruption to Camp Shannon and our not having heard from either our agent or his ally."

"You're talking about the CIA guy we have inside?" McCarter asked.

"Yes. Mr. Hobb."

"You know his name?" Hawkins inquired with evident surprise.

This brought a smile from Nawaf. "This shocks you but it should not. There have always been some relationships between your agents and those within my country. I know Mr. Hobb, as well. We have dossiers on practically every agent who has ever operated in our or any other nation in which we have an interest. It's how you say...symbiotic."

"They're supposed to use cover names," McCarter said.

"It wouldn't matter if they did, my American friend."

McCarter didn't bother to advise the guy he actually hailed from Great Britain. While he'd lost much of his Cockney accent over the years serving with Phoenix Force, any trained agent would've pinned it almost immediately. Not that it really mattered, since the Jordanians would never be able to pull his dossier. Such information didn't exist—anywhere.

Which was probably something Nawaf had already figured out. He said, "Our agent, code name Jeddah, had been working with Mr. Hobb. They had been working with each other in secret because Mr. Hobb believed that there was a potential spy inside Camp Shannon."

"Did he communicate to your man the possible identity of this spy?" Manning asked.

"I do not think so," Nawaf said with a shrug. "At least, he couldn't be sure. He did tell Jeddah he was very suspicious of the man named Abu Sudafi."

McCarter cracked the window as he lit a cigarette. "I don't know that I'd buy that, mate."

"Me, either," Encizo agreed. "Sudafi stands to lose entirely too much playing turncoat against the U.S. His detection system has allowed him to write his own ticket."

"Maybe it is not his own ticket he wished to write, as you put it."

McCarter glanced full-on at their associate. "Meaning?"

"I don't think you really need me to answer that question, my friend. Abu Sudafi was willing to betray his own for an exalted position and good life in America. Do you think it's so unbelievable he might be willing to trade that for other luxuries? Perhaps they threatened his life."

"Um, exactly *who* is it we're talking about?" Manning asked.

"This operation against your Marines could only have been the work of those with inside knowledge of the area."

"Agreed," McCarter said.

"What the insurgents and other subversives inside of Iraq do not have is the military resources to mount such an operation on their own. This means they had to have outside support. Our operatives inside these factions believe this support is coming from al Qaeda, and we're inclined to believe their assumptions are correct."

Manning tapped McCarter on the shoulder and whispered, "It makes sense."

McCarter nodded. Of course it made sense—not only because it was coming from the Jordanians but also because they knew the U.S. military's mission in Iraq to strip the disenfranchised of the country's citizens of access to internal resources had been effective. For any of the insurgents or terror groups still operating in Iraq to be effective, they needed external allies. Worse, they needed money and lots of it. Only al Qaeda had that kind of loot and only al Qaeda could arrange to get the necessary resources *into* Iraq.

"So what's your plan to help us?" McCarter asked.

"I think it's premature to speak of this," Nawaf replied.

"I think it's not. You can spill the details now or turn this thing around and take us back to the airfield."

The Jordanian eyeballed McCarter and obviously realized the warrior was dead serious. There were already too many unknown variables going into this mission and he wasn't about to leap before he looked, especially when it had to do with the security of his team and the lives of more than one hundred U.S. Marines.

Nawaf finally nodded as he put his eyes on the road again. "Long ago, when the war first started, we knew that our borders would be a point of concern and especially with Syria to the north. We decided it was in our best interest to establish an underground into the country. We figured we would need it, whether my government officially declared their support for the invasion of Iraq or not. As it turns out, we were right. We did not realize at the time, however, what sort of an asset it would become."

"Well, I for one can vouch for all of us when I say we appreciate your foresight," Encizo remarked.

Nawaf took the compliment in stride. "Make no mistake, our decision to do so has provided us with much good intelligence on the situation. While we wouldn't declare any official hostilities against Iraq without the full support of NATO, and unless we were attacked, we are not entirely without an understanding of the dangers they pose."

"You got danger all around you most of the time, partner," Hawkins said.

"This much is true, American. We are surrounded on all sides by enemies. Unlike the United States, we do not have the luxury of great distance. Terror is an ever-present danger and it has always been as much in Jordan."

"Regarding this underground…" McCarter said in an effort to get back on track.

"Yes. In this instance, it is the literal truth. As I said, we began building the underground shortly after the war started. The deserts and wilderness along our borders is vast. The Iraqis did not have the resources to monitor all of it. We started digging a tunnel, one that took many years to complete."

"Holy shit," Calvin James muttered. "You're talking a real underground route."

"Yes," Nawaf replied. "The tunnel is nearly eight kilometers in length, and wide enough in most parts to permit a vehicle five times the size of this."

"Okay, so you've built a tunnel," McCarter said. "What about once we're on the other side?"

"We have commandeered two vehicles at your disposal. They are older utilities, Jeeps, I believe, but they are solid and weapons-mount capable." He gave McCarter another one of his sideways glances. "You've brought weapons, I take it?"

"We did. Mostly small arms and ordnance, though, and nothing larger than an M-60 insofar as crew weapons go."

"I believe we can help you with this," Nawaf replied. "We have a considerable armory. I will see if Colonel Ravid will be willing to part with some of his heavier pieces for a time."

"You going in with us?"

Nawaf nodded. "I must! Jeddah is my friend but also my responsibility. We're as interested in getting him out of whatever situation he may be in as you are of helping your Marines."

"You'll get our full cooperation, then," McCarter replied. "As long as you can guarantee we'll get yours."

"You shall have it, American. My word of honor."

IT NEARED MIDDAY by the time Phoenix Force and its escort reached the rendezvous point.

The camp had been nestled in a outcropping of rocky hills and crags, this section being less than a kilometer from the Jordan-Iraq border. It provided the perfect cover for Jordanian military forces who had dug in steadily over the course of the war, a time the Jordanians had obviously used to their advantage while their Iraqi neighbors had their attentions focused elsewhere.

McCarter had to admit the base nestled within the natural terrain impressed him. They had a number of missile defense systems, complete for both surface-to-air and surface-to-surface contacts set up at decent intervals.

"Of course, there are no guarantees the Iraqis don't have a similar setup," Nawafi admitted.

"Even if they did, it looks like you've used the war to your advantage all the same," Manning observed as he studied the heavy field artillery that seemed to have been made practically a part of the bedrock.

Ensconced within these crags and short cliffs was nothing less than a military base, easily three times the size of Camp Shannon according to their intelligence. With the Iraqi forces in complete disarray, and the terrorist sympathizers too fractured and ill-equipped to be of any use against a military force of this magnitude, none of the men in Phoenix Force had any doubt believing the Jordanians could stave off anything short of a nuclear strike.

Of course, that was likely by design.

The structures that served to provide mess, supply, field and bunk facilities were constructed from special material that looked almost like adobe but was clearly fabricated. The material was coarse and painted to blend into the surroundings. However, when Nawaf showed them inside one of the buildings they found it comparably cool. They'd obviously been designed especially for the extreme and oftentimes unpredictable weather of the barren, desert wilderness. Dust storms weren't uncommon at this time of year, although McCarter knew they weren't far from monsoon seasons—he hoped they could beat those in their mission. Anything less would make them half blind, and that was no time to have to fight an enemy.

Nawaf led them across the squat structure past desks occupied by military support staff. While the Jordanians had their paperwork and administrative duties, just as any military force, all of the personnel at those desks were fit and carried the aura of men well trained in combat. This bode well for their allies as far as it concerned McCarter and his team—they wouldn't be saddle-bagged with any wimps, whoever got assigned to escort them over the border. McCarter hoped it would be Nawaf since he'd already established a rapport with the guy and genuinely liked him. He knew, however, that wouldn't ultimately be his call.

Nawaf ushered them into a very large office with two desks that sat perpendicular to one another. Behind the larger of the desks was a man in Jordanian combat fatigues with subdued rank insignia that belied his importance, although McCarter couldn't be sure *how* important. There was no mistaking, however, the black beret with a gold metal insignia on its crest, or the numerous other subdued patches above the breast pockets that indicated he'd engaged in paratrooper training.

The man himself was short and muscular with broad shoulders. His upper body tapered in a V-shape to his waistline, which was encircled by a military web belt and a holstered pistol. He had coal-black hair and eyebrows, deep brown eyes that seemed perpetually intent, and a neatly trimmed mustache as dark as his brows. His skin had been bronzed by the sun and enhanced by his Arabic lineage.

"Gentlemen, be pleased to meet Colonel Yousef Ravid," Nawaf said.

McCarter gave the man a salute and then extended his

hand, and Ravid looked none too surprised at McCarter's formal acknowledgment.

Undoubtedly, Ravid knew most, if not all of the details of their mission and that Phoenix Force was not a military unit. In the strictest sense, they were supposed to be part of a CIA special covert team, but one soldier knew other soldiers and Ravid returned the salute smartly before taking McCarter's hand in a firm but warm grip. Ravid then acknowledged each of the other men with a nod as Nawaf introduced them by their cover names, getting all of them right to everyone's surprise.

"Colonel Ravid has been briefed on your mission objectives and promised his full cooperation," Nawaf said.

"Mr. Brown," Ravid said in accented but discernible English, "we are at your disposal, sir. We understand you have an American military unit trapped behind enemy lines. I can understand your wish to get them out quickly. I would want the same if it were my men there."

"Thanks for that, Colonel," McCarter said.

Ravid nodded before continuing. "However, you can understand our reticence to utilize this passage to get you over the border. This is a highly secret operation and I am under orders to keep it that way. Every time we use it we increase the risk of its discovery by Iraqi forces."

"You'll pardon my presumption, sir, but there are greater threats to you being exposed than Iraqis," McCarter said. He glanced at Nawaf and then back to Ravid. "In fact, we're not sure of the present status of this unit. Our electronic surveillance is being blocked at the source, bringing a halt to transmissions that were continuous until forty-eight hours ago. What we can tell you is they've been out of contact too bloody long and the Iraq government is threatening harsh sanctions if we send in air support."

Ravid nodded and McCarter thought he could actually hear a sigh from the military man. "It always comes to politics. I understand this. You can be assured we will do everything we can to assist you, the bond of one soldier to another."

"I appreciate your cooperation, sir," McCarter replied. "Now if you'll show us to our transportation, we'd like to be moving out before the natives get too restless."

Ravid seemed to hesitate. "Um, nightfall would be better, tactically speaking—"

"Sorry, but we just don't have that kind of luxury," Encizo cut in. "We need to get to that unit as soon as possible. I hope you can understand the sense of urgency."

"Of course, of course." Ravid turned to Nawaf. "The transportation you requested is waiting. Two light-armored utility vehicles and we have equipped each of them with a .50-caliber machine gun."

"Thank you, sir," Nawaf said with a slight bow.

The men of Phoenix Force noticed Nawaf's almost show of obeisance but none commented on it. Such courtesies weren't unheard of among the higher ranking military personnel and their security counterparts in the Jordanian Intelligence Service. Yet it seemed odd and McCarter filed it for future reference, although he had no idea why the hell he had.

Once outside the building, Nawaf led the men to the entrance of the cavern with a steep downward slope. It could handle something the size of a tank but Nawaf instead took a walkway along one side that sported a thick plastic railing attached at the base of long metal grates wide enough to permit passage single file. The gloom seemed to close around them as they descended, the only illumination from portable lanterns hung along the walkway side of the cavern walls. None of Phoenix

Force could tell how far they'd traveled but it had to have been at least a kilometer or so before things leveled out. They emerged into a staging area. Against the far wall they spotted makes varying from Jeeps to military-grade Humvees.

Beyond that point Phoenix Force could see a massive tunnel stretch into darkness, almost as if it ran forever. The Jordanians had indeed been busy throughout the Iraq war.

"Quite impressive," James remarked.

Nawaf nodded and waved toward the black expanse beyond them. "It's nothing short of a marvel of engineering. Desert terrain like this is unforgiving. There were many cave-ins, many things that impeded their progress to be sure. But we persevered and the tenacity of my countrymen eventually won out."

"How long has this been in operation?" Manning asked.

"Two years." Nawaf got a faraway look. "It took us more than six years to complete this tunnel. It sees less traffic now than it did when completed, but of course that was at the height of the war. It has not been used much and at one point they had talked of dismantling it. Or at least burying a part of it beneath rubble, but my government refused to see the work go to waste so we've managed to keep it open."

"Must take quite a bit of cash to keep up something like this," McCarter said.

"The maintenance is surprisingly simple," Nawaf countered, scratching his beard. "But we have spent too much time here. I know you are anxious to depart…as am I."

Nawaf waved them toward the vehicles in the staging

area and Phoenix Force headed in that direction. It was time to venture into hostile territory.

Into the heart of the enemy stronghold.

IT SEEMED it took forever to navigate the dark tunnel, only the headlights of the two vehicles providing illumination.

Nawaf drove the lead Humvee while one of Colonel Ravid's special forces commandos—Nawaf had introduced him as Sergeant Dakuwami—manned the wheel of the second. McCarter rode shotgun in the lead vehicle accompanied by James, and Hawkins manned the mounted .50-caliber machine gun with a butterfly trigger. They had decided to let the Jeep with the machine gun take point in the event they encountered any choppers, as Nawaf had hinted Iraqi regulars were beefing up combat air patrols along the border.

In the second Jeep, they had also mounted a crew weapon but this was a Heckler & Koch 23E. The Jordanians had managed to acquire a significantly large stock of them. It chambered 5.56 NATO ammunition and could fire burst or full-auto utilizing the same shared feed action as its predecessor, the HK-21E. This tough, versatile bastard could spit eight hundred rounds per minute at 900 meters per second. Rafael Encizo planned to make full use of it if the opportunity arose. Manning had taken shotgun position alongside Dakuwami.

Because the second vehicle was light a man, Phoenix Force had stowed most of its gear in that one—but not before fully rigging themselves out to the last man. Each of the battle-hardened veterans wore a side arm, carried an M-16 A-4 assault rifle, with James and Manning packing detachable M-203 grenade launchers, as well. All were harnessed with suspenders dangling with various implements handy for imminent hostilities. As the designated rifle marksman of the team, Manning also had a special operations electro-optical scope attached to his rifle that he could switch interchangeably with the modified PSG-1 sniper rifle packed in the gear.

"I assume there's some reason you're going this slow," McCarter said.

"We've had minor cave-ins before. I do not wish for our trip to end so soon as it has begun."

"Guess I should bloody well shut it and let you concentrate on the road, then."

"It is appreciated, this."

McCarter didn't hear anything in Nawaf's tone outside of good-natured ribbing. He had to admit the more time he spent around the Jordanian the more he liked him. Not that his government probably hadn't made a careful selection when agreeing to this little alliance. But then, Nawaf had as much of a stake in it as Phoenix Force, and they were going to have to cooperate with each other if they were to each achieve their own objectives.

As if he'd planned the timing, Nawaf killed the lights and McCarter could see the brightening ahead. They were close to the alternate entrance. He could only wonder how the Jordanian military had managed to keep this thing under wraps that long. Hiding such a tunnel wouldn't be easy, not even with the most advanced camouflage techniques. How would they have prevented heat signatures from registering, for example, or keep a plane or chopper from not noticing such a gaping opening from the air?

It wasn't until they'd ascended the tunnel that McCarter got his answer. It opened onto the mouth of what appeared to be a cave, a natural formation dug into the living rock. Beyond it they had streamed some sort of netting, several layers he saw in fact when they stopped and Dakuwami assisted Nawaf with pulling it back. McCarter thought it strange that they didn't have anyone guarding the mouth end of the exit and he said so as Nawaf climbed behind the wheel and they proceeded.

"Just because you didn't see them doesn't mean they aren't there, American. Ha!"

This caused McCarter to look back but he still didn't see anything. They didn't stop to replace the camouflage netting, however, and McCarter knew that somewhere the guards were concealed and would emerge only after they had passed beyond view. It was really a masterful setup and McCarter could only shake his head in utter amazement.

The Phoenix Force leader was still pondering it more than ten minutes later when the first of their troubles appeared. Along the horizon—a vast irregular outline now brilliant beneath the scorching noonday sun—the gleam of light on metal caught McCarter's eye. When they had emerged from the mouth of the tunnel he'd noticed Nawaf and Dakuwami had been required to navigate some rather precarious canyon trails and switchbacks. Like the other side of the tunnel in Jordanian territory, a craggy outline of rocky hills helped mask their entry point.

Now they were in the open and speeding across the massive, slippery desert with nothing but miles of barren land in every direction and as far as the eye could see. They were most likely now visible to any surveillance the Iraqis had in place, a fact that appeared quite evident in view of the square metal shapes glimmering ahead and raising a considerable cloud of dust in their wake.

"What is it?" Hawkins called over the rushing wind.

McCarter raised binoculars to his eyes, careful not to touch them too close as the Jeep's path jarred and bounced them along the rugged terrain. A wee bit more focus and…armor!

"Bloody hell," David McCarter muttered.

CHAPTER SEVEN

Of all the resistance they'd expected, Phoenix Force hadn't considered their enemies might possess armor. What bugged McCarter more than that fact, however, was when Manning's voice came over the radio a moment later. He'd obviously viewed the convoy through the powerful scope of his sniper rifle.

"You want good news or bad news first?"

"Roll the dice," McCarter snapped.

"Okay, good news it's only one tank. Other three vehicles are wheeled and unarmored."

"Hear that?" McCarter said to his teammates in back. "*Only* one tank, per the eternal optimist."

"Bad news is," Manning's voice continued, "the tank's an M-1 A-1."

McCarter frowned. "An Abrams? You think they're on our side?"

"Not likely, boss. It's sporting colors along the side and a designation that definitely isn't American."

"Iraqi army, most likely," Nawaf said.

"That doesn't track," Hawkins said, shouting to be heard above the wind. "They don't travel alone. Tanks are always deployed in units."

"Forward recon unit?" James offered.

"No," Nawaf said. "Your friend is correct. If there is only one, then it is either a remnant or the tank is stolen property."

"Well, they aren't friendly whatever the hell else they might be," McCarter said. "Let's go around."

The unmistakable boom of the tank gun resounded through the clear desert air, and Nawaf slammed on the brakes and turned the nose away from the enemy. The shell exploded wide and short of their position, but it didn't lessen the tension as the men waited for the shell to hit. They had wanted to avoid hostilities but it now seemed evident their unknown attackers weren't going to let them off so easy.

"Turn this thing around and get us the hell out of here!" McCarter ordered Nawaf.

The Jordanian shook his head. "We must go toward them."

"You're suggesting we attack?"

"Yes."

"Are you out of your bloody mind or what?"

"If they are one tank, as you say," Nawaf said, "then they are either terrorists, guerrillas or pirates. In any event, they may know something of what's happened to your people at Camp Shannon. We must seize this opportunity to gain information."

"Look, Nawaf, our job's to go directly to Camp Shannon. We aren't to pass Go and we aren't to collect our bloody two hundred dollars. So that's what we're going to do."

"I'm sorry but we need more intelligence if either of our missions are to succeed, American."

Nawaf spun the wheel hard and signaled for Dakuwami to follow as he gunned the engine and headed in a mad rush toward their enemies. McCarter resisted the temptation to pull his pistol and shoot the Jordanian in the side of the head. He'd have to deal with him later, but for now they were committed to a course of action that on

any other scale would've been nothing short of suicide.
Two machine guns in unprotected wheeled vehicles and
some grenade launchers were hardly capable of slugging
it out with an M-1 A-1 Abrams tank.

Even in the hands of the inexperienced, the M-256
A-1—a 120 mm smooth-bore cannon of the A1 and A2
variants—boasted no prejudices. The heavy main gun
could fire an assortment of projectiles and in this case it
appeared its operators had chosen high-explosive antitank
shells. A .50-caliber M-2HB and twin 7.62 mm M-240
machine guns, the latter pair typically fire-controlled by
computers, rounded out the standard arsenal for the tank.

"We don't stand a snowball's chance in hell," Hawkins
reminded them as he made live the .50-caliber by actu-
ating the charging handle.

"You think?" James quipped as he primed his M-203
with a 40 mm smoker.

McCarter bit back any replies to the sentiments despite the fact he agreed with them. He hadn't expected
Nawaf to countermand his orders, but there wasn't much
he could do about it. After all, they were here only due to
the generosity of the Jordanians and Nawaf didn't work
for him. He took his orders from somebody else and that
was just the way it was going to be, irrespective of what
the Phoenix Force leader thought. That didn't mean he
wouldn't take the guy to task for putting their lives and
mission at risk. But then on the other hand the guy might
just be crazy enough to pull off such a crazy stunt like at-
tacking superior forces expecting them to run. McCarter
gave Nawaf high marks for originality.

McCarter checked the action on his M-16 and then
squinted into the distance even as another boom thun-
dered through the desert air. This shell was closer but
still off by some distance and it made McCarter wonder.

As if reading the Briton's mind, James said, "Our friends in the tank are either overanxious or a group of college pranksters who decided to jack a tank."

"Yeah, those guns target using computers," McCarter replied. "It's almost as if they were firing on manual or something. But whatever the case it's apparent we're not dealing with pros. Maybe we got half a bloody chance to make something of this. It's possible, Nawaf, your instincts were spot on."

Nawaf didn't acknowledge, favoring the rough terrain ahead with his full attention. Among the sand and dirt of the desert was also brush just high enough to get caught in fan blades, as well as divots in the sand with rocks sharp enough to tear their tires to shreds. Then there were the very dangerous sandstorms that could come up suddenly and flip them right onto their side. No, the Jordanian was right not to participate in such banter.

Over the radio, Manning's voice called, "Stay sharp. Several of those vehicles from the convoy are coming straight for us."

"But they're not sending the tank?" James asked more to himself than anyone in particular.

"They might figure they stand a better chance against us with wheeled vehicles. Tanks can maneuver but not as well as these Humvees," Hawkins pointed out.

"Who needs a Humvee when you've got a 120 mm cannon," James pointed out.

"Touché."

They weren't left with any time to banter as their enemies closed in. If the men of Phoenix Force, veterans with a combined seventy-plus years of experience, knew anything they knew how to take the offensive and this they did.

McCarter led the charge. He stood on his seat, braced

his knees against the door and opened up full-auto on the driver of the closest enemy vehicle. An older European job, the foreign-made SUV had been dismantled to the level of a dune buggy and mounted with weapons that gave it the appearance of something out of *Mad Max*. Two men occupied the front seat and a third stood in the back behind a mounted light machine gun.

While most men would've considered the machine gun the biggest threat, McCarter knew differently—a machine gun was dangerous, yeah, but it was much less effective on a vehicle that couldn't go anywhere. The rounds from McCarter's assault rifle left spiderweb patterns on the windshield and continued into the driver's chest and head. McCarter was rewarded with a bloody spray as the vehicle swerved out of control, hit one of those many ruts and smashed to a stop with its front tires punctured. The impact threw the machine gunner clear even as steam began to belch from the radiator.

Nawaf steered clear of the utility vehicle and McCarter thought at first he planned to circle so Hawkins could take out the survivors with the machine gun. Instead, Nawaf continued pressing his wildly dangerous approach on the tank.

"What the hell are you doing?" McCarter demanded.

"I have a theory about that tank."

"You're going to get us all killed, bugger!"

"Just wait," was all Nawaf replied.

As they swung onto the left side of the Abrams, the main gun boomed another report.

McCarter glanced to the rear to see their comrades in the Humvee weren't far behind. The angle of that gun was far too steep that it would be able to hit them. So if the Abrams occupants weren't attempting to destroy Phoenix Force, who the bloody hell were they shooting at? McCarter finally realized the answer just about the same time Nawaf answered the question.

"They're firing blind!" Nawaf said.

The two M-260 machine guns mounted to the tank were manned, however, one positioned toward the right rear and the other by the Tank Commander. Since these guns could be controlled by a target-and-fire computer, along with the main gun, McCarter surmised either the computer was incapacitated or the tank operators didn't know how to use it. Either way, that gave them the advantage and McCarter planned to use it. He keyed up the radio and communicated his suspicions to Manning, who agreed McCarter's assessment bore merit.

McCarter directed his next question to Nawaf. "You think you can get us into a position where we can take that thing intact?"

"I will do my best," the Jordanian replied.

And the best he did as he swung the nose of their vehicle wide, angling from the tank on its weak, left side. As the Humvee came around Hawkins realized he now had a perfect angle from which to take out the rear gunner. He steadied the barrel of the .50-caliber best as he could under the rugged terrain and depressed the butterfly trigger. The weapon delivered a steady, chugging report and with it a volley of heavy-caliber suppressing fire streamed across the tank, the rounds sparking as they were deflected by the homogenous armor.

"Damn American engineering," James snapped as he got his M-16 sighted on the gunner.

The small arms of the assault rifle would result in better accuracy than the .50-caliber mounted to the jouncing Humvee, although even as James sighted on the gunner he watched Encizo take out the man in the TC position with a steady barrage from the HK-21E. The rounds punched through the man and his body jerked before he slumped dead over his weapon. James triggered several 3-round bursts, missing on the first two attempts but scoring hits on the third. The gunner twitched as holes appeared in his chest accompanied by a gory spray. As the Humvee slid past, the Abrams did a sudden ninety-degree turn and began to move in the direction of the remaining pair of utility vehicles that had made up the bizarre convoy.

McCarter keyed the radio and ordered Manning's group to run interference while they set about the task of attempting to disable the tank. Nothing in their current arsenal would penetrate that armor but chances were better than good they could blow out the track. It wouldn't disable the vehicle beyond potential repair but it might damned well remove whatever hope remained among its surviving occupants. And they just might learn a damn thing or two from those inexperienced operators about what they potentially faced on the road ahead. Of course, McCarter realized they might just be dealing with some pirates or local dissidents who'd stolen the tank for little more than amusement. Either way, they wouldn't find out until they brought this battle to an end.

Unfortunately for McCarter and his teammates, the remaining two utility vehicles proved more of a nuisance than they'd hoped. The combatants aboard them were more experienced than the tank operators and they'd split apart, each on its own mission to engage the two Humvees in a grisly game of hit-and-get.

The newer of the vehicles, a restored Land Cruiser, proved to be suited to its element as the gunners aboard fired from points along the sides and the roof. While they didn't have any mounted crew-based weapons, they were sporting assault rifles—mostly AK-47s with a Chinese

Type 63 thrown into the mix—and firing on their enemies with a surprising ferocity not seen from the first group McCarter had disabled. Angry 7.62 mm whizzers, including some tracers, cut into the body of their Humvee or cut hot paths through the air around them.

One round came close enough to James he heard its passing. "*Sheeeeit*, it's getting serious now!"

"I think we got past serious a long time ago, pal!" Hawkins retorted during a lull in the firing.

"Gary, we could use a hand here," McCarter called into his radio.

"We're on our way!" Manning replied.

GARY MANNING clicked off the radio and gestured for Dakuwami to change course, one that would give them a better angle against their enemies.

Manning had to admit that this entire idea had been nothing short of crazy. Something McCarter had said keyed Manning into the fact that a frontal assault against a tank hadn't been *his* idea, which meant Nawaf had probably taken matters into his own hands. He didn't like it but he knew there wasn't much McCarter could do about it. Nawaf played by his own rules, and if they wanted his help McCarter would have to acquiesce to the Jordanian's whims.

Well, that wasn't his problem—let McCarter handle that end of it. His job was to get the heat off the other team and that was something he and Rafael Encizo could handle. It was simply a matter of doing what they were trained to do: kill bad guys. Dakuwami took instructions well, however, and in a moment they had the flanking position they needed. The occupants of the Land Cruiser were just opening up with a fresh salvo when Encizo triggered the HK-21E. The first 5.56 mm round punched through the back of the head of a gunner leaning out the side. Blood, bone and brains exploded under the impact.

Encizo swung the muzzle of the HK-21E in a sweeping motion, directing the fire stream from the top down rather than starting low and letting it ride up on its own. Round after round smashed into the windows and body of the Land Cruiser, several puncturing a rear tire. The vehicle fishtailed as the driver fought to keep control over the slick mixture of soft sand and loose gravel that made up the majority of the desert floor. This particular area also had some lime deposits that, when mixed with the other elements, created laterite and made conditions even more hazardous.

The driver was skilled enough to keep from ditching his vehicle entirely but it slowed the Land Cruiser considerably, which was all Manning needed. He brought his over-and-under into play, the M-203 primed with a 40 mm HE grenade. As they passed on the far left side of the Land Cruiser, Manning aimed low and squeezed the trigger. Smoke belched from the muzzle of the launcher and a moment later the big Canadian was rewarded with a dense explosion that blew off the fender and had enough intrusion force left to decimate the left side of the engine and shred another tire.

The Land Cruiser rolled to a halt as secondary flames broke free from the windshield shattered by the impact. As Dakuwami put the Humvee in a hard turn and brought it back for another pass, the trio glimpsed the effects of their handiwork. The three passengers still alive crawled from their wrecked vehicle while a fourth sprinted away, his clothes completely engulfed in fire. Encizo delivered a short burst of mercy fire and ended the life of the screaming torch. The survivors looked like they might hold their ground and fight, but as soon as they saw the

Humvee bearing down on them they ditched their weapons and threw up their arms.

Their fight had ended.

WITH MANNING AND ENCIZO making short work of the Land Cruiser that had pursued them, McCarter and his men could focus on the last vehicle. It was similar to the first European-made SUV they'd encountered, although this one wasn't quite as stripped down or tricked out. Still, the men inside saw the odds were quickly stacking up in favor of their enemies. The driver decided the best tactic was to shadow the Abrams and attempt to flush McCarter's team into the open. The tactic didn't work. Phoenix Force had played this game before, even written some of its rules. All this did was strengthen their resolve.

Nawaf opted to swing wide of the tank and come up on the rear end of the SUV. Even as they heard the explosion from Manning's handiwork, Hawkins began to tap out a message for their enemies in terms they could understand. The .50-caliber sung like music to the former Delta Force commando's ears as he held low and steady while keeping the butterfly trigger depressed. At a rate of almost 600 rounds per minute, Hawkins hammered the vehicle with heavy fire that began to take the SUV apart piece by piece. Glass shattered, metal crumpled and accessories disappeared under the onslaught.

The driver finally veered off the parallel course it had been running with the tank and Nawaf stayed on its tail, although one bad turn nearly tossed Hawkins out of the Humvee. Only James's quick hand on Hawkins's equipment harness saved his friend from going over the side. When Hawkins signaled steady, James turned his attention to the SUV. He brought the stock of the M-16 to his shoulder, sighted through the open back window and triggered a pair of 3-round bursts. The driver's headrest split apart before the driver's head, and then the vehicle swerved out of control and flipped onto its side. The passenger in the front seat was visibly crushed by the sudden topsy-turvy fate of the SUV.

A pair of gunners in back were smashed against each other, the one's body cushioning the other's from colliding full-force with the door on the side of the vehicle grinding to a halt against the unforgiving desert floor. They scrambled to get clear but Nawaf had already brought the Humvee to a halt. James heard something clink, looked in Nawaf's direction and shouted in protest just a moment too late. Nawaf tromped the accelerator as soon as he'd let go of the grenade and managed a safe distance before the SUV blew apart.

"Now we deal with the tank," he said.

"When this is through, chum, you and I need to have a little chat," McCarter told him.

CHAPTER EIGHT

It didn't take Phoenix Force more than a tense moment to disable the Abrams. Working in concert, the two teams hit the track in a vital point with their grenade launchers, which in turn neutralized its mobility. McCarter had been reticent about disabling the tank, figuring they might be able to get the computer working and give themselves an edge against whatever they might find at Camp Shannon. Only Hawkins's assurances that the tank probably carried spare parts to repair the track gave McCarter the confidence to move forward with the operation.

When they were through, Phoenix Force had a relatively intact tank at their disposal along with two prisoners, one of the three survivors having died a few minutes after he and his team surrendered to Manning and Encizo.

"Took a couple mortal hits during the skirmish," James reported to McCarter. "Just took some time to bleed out. Sorry I couldn't do more."

"Nothing you could do," McCarter told James. The Briton turned to the remaining two prisoners. "I know at least one of you blokes speaks English, so I won't bother asking if you don't bother pretending."

"And if you only speak Arabic," Nawaf added, "I will be happy to translate. But I think my friend's right, and you do speak English."

"So what's it going to be?" McCarter asked, trying

not to show his irritation at being interrupted. "You talk to me or we just kill you here and now, save ourselves all a lot of trouble."

"You won't kill us, Western dog," one man replied in a tone that dripped with disgust. "We are not afraid of you."

"You shouldn't be," McCarter said. "Since I don't torture and I'm not an overly patient man, worse I could do is blow your head off."

Hawkins cracked his knuckles and said, "Well, boss, if you really want to you can tie them up and let me sing to them. Half hour of songs back home and I guarantee you they'll be ready to talk."

"You think you are funny," the talkative prisoner said. "I think you are sad. A sad excuse for a fighter."

"Now you're just looking to get your ass beat," Hawkins said.

Before any of the Phoenix Force warriors could react, Nawaf pulled his pistol from shoulder leather, aimed and shot the smart-mouthed Iraqi fighter point-blank in the face. The back of the man's head exploded under the impact of the .45-caliber slug and his body jerked before falling to the side. Weapons came up in reaction from every Phoenix Force fighter save one.

Rafael Encizo stepped forward as Nawaf turned his gun on the second prisoner and clipped the man's hand with a karate chop to a nerve in the meaty part of the forearm where it met the elbow. Nawaf produced a shout of surprise mixed with pain and the pistol sprang from his grip. Encizo stepped inside and grabbed a handful of Nawaf's fatigue collar, his muscular arm shoving backward like a piston as he tripped Nawaf with a heel to the back of his calf. The Jordanian landed hard on his ass and glared at Encizo with a wild-eyed stare.

"That's the second time I've watched you kill helpless

men without provocation," Encizo said. "I see it again and I'll put a bullet between your eyes. You hear me, amigo?"

Nawaf was still too stunned to reply even as Encizo reached down and offered a hand. The Jordanian looked Encizo in the eye and noticed Dakuwami hadn't moved a muscle. Nobody was going to step in on his side this time around, and Nawaf could obviously sense that if he pushed his luck he would have more enemies than allies. He didn't take Encizo's hand, choosing to get to his feet on his own, but he made no hostile moves and he said nothing more.

"I'll take that to mean we have an understanding," Encizo said.

The Cuban bent to pick up Nawaf's pistol, turned and nodded at McCarter as he handed him the pistol before returning to his original post.

The Briton nodded in reply, glanced a moment at Nawaf and then gave his full attention to their remaining prisoner and one potential hope of finding out what the situation was at Camp Shannon. While McCarter felt the chances this guy knew anything about the situation were slim, he had to at least try to get the guy's cooperation and see what he did know.

"Any information you can supply us would be helpful," McCarter said. "If you choose to answer my questions, of course."

The guy looked nervously at Nawaf, who had stepped a distance from the group and lit a cigarette. The smoke curled around his face in the hot breeze, wafting away in thick tendrils, and the Jordanian had a faraway look in his eyes. For the moment, however, he appeared to be ignoring the group and their prisoner.

McCarter tried to smile reassuringly after looking in the direction of Nawaf. "Nobody's going to hurt you.

Even if you choose not to talk to us, you're going to be treated humanely."

"*That* man has killed my friends!" the prisoner barked. He spit into the dust and studied Nawaf with unmasked hatred. "Why should I trust any of you who have befriended a murderer?"

"He's not our friend," McCarter said. "He's an ally and you know as well as we do that allies are necessary in a place like this. Now, you can either agree to help us or you can just keep quiet. It's your choice and I promise protection either way. But we're not here to wage war against the Iraqi people. We're simply trying to help a company of United States Marines. We've lost contact with them. They were at Camp Shannon. Do you know anything about it?"

The Iraqi rebel looked at Nawaf one last time, and McCarter snapped his fingers. "Hey, chum, stop worrying about him and talk to me. Okay?"

"Yes, I know this place," the man replied. "And I know what is happening. They are surrounded by…how you…?" The prisoner switched to Arabic.

"What the hell did he just say?" James inquired.

"Al Qaeda in Iraq—AQI," Dakuwami translated.

"So the Farm was right," Manning said. "This does have something to do with backing by al Qaeda. In fact, it is al Qaeda."

"With some Syrian assistance thrown in, I'm sure," Hawkins added.

"You're a Sunni fighter, then?" Encizo asked. When the prisoner nodded, Encizo said, "That means he's probably part of the Sunni Awakenings. That would make a whole lot of sense, and probably his intelligence is pretty solid. I think we can believe him."

"Where'd you get the tank?" McCarter asked.

"Taken from an Iraqi unit that came to protect us," the Sunni fighter replied. "And yet we found out when they arrived with many tanks that they were not there to protect us at all, but they had gone over to the side of our enemies."

"So you're saying the AQI has set up some kind of operation against Camp Shannon?"

"I do not know who is this AQI," the rebel said. "But yes, this is what has happened to your Marines."

McCarter sighed deeply and exchanged glances with his comrades. There wasn't any question this was more than they'd expected to encounter on this original mission. The fact that al Qaeda was operating in Iraq came as no surprise to anyone who knew what the hell was going on in the country, but to think that they would have the resources and gumption to wage all-out war against an entire U.S. Marine rifle company seemed a bit over the top.

McCarter ordered Hawkins to conduct security and offer water and food to the prisoner while he pulled the others aside to conference. Nawaf and Dakuwami participated, as well, since McCarter saw no reason to exclude them, but it was apparently obvious to everyone in the group that Nawaf's heart wasn't really in it. McCarter did his best to make a peace offering by returning Nawaf's pistol to the Jordanian. A tense moment followed as the man checked the action but ultimately he holstered the pistol.

It almost seemed as if everyone let out a sigh of relief at the same moment.

McCarter would have to watch the guy from here out. For a moment he considered sending the two Jordanians back to their country with the prisoner in tow but he knew the chances of the guy's surviving the trip were negligible. They couldn't take the guy with them, and they couldn't really press on without Nawaf because he knew the territory much better than they did. There was a third option, and that was simply to strike out on their own and send the Jordanians back, but again they would have to bring the prisoner along. McCarter brightened at that thought, considering their prisoner probably knew this terrain well and certainly knew it much better than Dakuwami or Nawaf.

"What do you think?" McCarter tossed out the question for anybody to comment.

Manning was the first to speak up. "I think he's telling the truth."

"Ditto," Encizo said.

"Okay, so he's telling the truth," James said. "I still don't see how that's going to help us."

"It'll bloody well help us if he can give us some idea of what we're up against," McCarter pointed out. "Look, mates, if this guy knows enough to be able to tell us who it is that's cut off communications with Camp Shannon, then he probably knows more than that. We should be able to at least get a position of enemy forces, a number and maybe even what they have planned."

"What I don't understand is the logic behind AQI's move here," Manning said.

"Go on," McCarter replied.

Manning scratched his chin in thought. "Well, I'm pretty familiar with the majority of terrorist outfits and their methods of operation. The AQI has always been about destroying the Muslim Sunni population in this country."

Manning waved in their prisoner's direction. "We already know this much from our friend over there. So what purpose would they have in cutting off communications with a fully armed and equipped unit of U.S. fighting men? How does this achieve any of their religious or political aims? Seems to me that even if they had the backing and equipment that such a move would seem more like suicide."

"Maybe Nawaf's been right all along," Encizo said. "Maybe there's a chance Abu Sudafi sold out to the highest bidder and he's the one who turned them on to PSIDS technology."

"I don't know what good that would do them now that the war's basically over," James said.

"This war is not over, American," Nawaf said in barely more than a whisper. When all eyes turned toward him he continued. "This war will never be over, at least not for the people in my country. The conflicts here in the Middle East will go on forever. There won't be peace any time soon, no matter how much we might want to bring it. And while you may not agree with my methods I can tell you that it's those in groups like the Sunni Awakenings and the AQI that continue to make this region dangerous for my country. If I get the chance to eradicate them, I will."

"Not at the risk of United States Marines or our mission," McCarter said.

"I have a stake in this, too," Nawaf said.

"*We* have a stake in it, my friend," Dakuwami reminded him—reminding all of them really. "There is one man who possesses the answers to all of your questions."

"Jeddah," Encizo said.

Dakuwami and Nawaf simultaneously answered by way of curt nods.

"Okay, so we have to acknowledge something up front here," McCarter ventured. "You guys probably don't really trust us and we don't trust you. But we have to cooperate and if we continue the way we're going chances are good we'll step on each other's toes. So I have a proposal."

"I'm open to suggestions," Nawaf said as Dakuwami nodded his agreement.

"You guys take one of the Humvees, we'll take the other." He turned to Encizo and James. "You guys think you can make any of those wheeled units road worthy?"

"Maybe that first one you took out," James said as his eyes scanned the carnage around them. "Obviously neither of the other two are salvageable."

"Fine, check it out and let me know just as soon as you can tell whether the thing can be fixed."

"Even if we can change those tires, how do you propose to get it out of that ditch?" Manning asked, squinting against the ever-increasing brightness and heat of the desert sun.

McCarter smiled. "Well, we got us a tank now. Don't we?"

WITHIN THE HOUR, Hawkins had the tank track repaired with Dakuwami's assistance and they got the SUV-turned-dune-buggy out of the shallow ravine. Some blood remained in the cab but had since dried under the sun and flaked, most carried off by the increasing desert winds. During the recovery efforts, Nawaf kept his eyes toward the west. After a time he seemed to stop being interested, but McCarter didn't let off for a moment. He couldn't seem to get past Nawaf's cold-blooded murder of one of the Sunni Awakenings rebels, although on some level he understood it. The Jordanians were hard people living in a hard world comprised of enemies on every side. It wasn't any wonder they did things like what he'd just witnessed.

Men like Nawaf didn't consider that murder—to them it was often just part of the brutality of war. It was a lesson military leaders and soldiers of a cause had learned long ago, particularly during World War II when the Nazis exterminated so many Jews, ultimately defending their actions as "duty" at the trials in Nuremberg. Of course, to a man with McCarter's sensibilities—or those of any of the men of Phoenix Force—it was murder plain and simple.

"You okay?" Encizo asked, intruding on McCarter's thoughts.

The Briton broke from his reverie and looked into the dark eyes of a man who'd fought alongside him for many years. Too many damn years, it sometimes seemed. He looked to ensure Nawaf wasn't in earshot and then said, "Yeah, I'm okay. Just thinking about that little incident with the prisoner. Thanks for stepping in."

"I figured somebody had to," Encizo replied with a shrug. "I certainly couldn't let him waste the only intelligence we had. But you're welcome, for what it's worth."

"I should've been Johnny-on-the-spot about it frankly."

"You had no way of knowing he'd do something like that, David. None of us did."

"It just…" McCarter felt distanced now.

"What is it? Spit it out."

"I was just going to say that it throws off our rhythm." McCarter withdrew an OD-colored handkerchief and mopped his brow. "We're used to operating as a team and reading each other's moves. We have a rhythm and a wild man like Nawaf throws off that rhythm. It can be dangerous. Now we're going to have to watch our backs."

"We'll watch each other's backs," Encizo replied. "Just like we always do. And I can guarantee you this much.

If I see that guy make one wrong move I'll put a bullet in him quick as that."

"I hear you," McCarter said. "Just don't get too itchy on the trigger too soon."

"Agreed." Encizo clapped his friend on the shoulder. "Now what say we go over our plans. Vehicle's out of the ditch and repaired."

McCarter turned and the pair made their way back to the main group. They all formed on McCarter in the relative shade of the tank. The Briton jerked a thumb at the monstrosity and inquired of Hawkins its status.

"Thing's in pretty good shape. Computer's completely shot, though, including the FCS. Highly unlikely we'll be able to get the Future Combat System running again. I'm guessing some kind of internal damage."

"She's sound enough to move though?"

"Yeah, but I don't know what good it's going to do us. Damned thing will run but she won't run very far."

"Why not?" Encizo asked.

"She doesn't have any fuel reserves. Our Sunni prisoner...uh, whose name is Uthman, by the way, tells me they have fuel tanks back at the base camp but chances are good we don't want to go back there."

"Did he ever say why they attacked us to begin with?" James asked.

Hawkins shook his head. "Don't know that, partner. He just said he was following the orders of the leader. I guess that was the guy in the SUV Nawaf blew up."

"And unfortunately none of the guys in the tank survived after we disabled it," Manning added. They had tried to take the tank operators and gunners alive but when they were met with small arms fire they'd been forced to defend themselves and destroy their enemies.

"We're damn lucky any of them are alive," James said. "These Sunni fighters are almost as fanatical as the AQI."

"So we could take the tank along but probably be dead in the water by late afternoon," McCarter said.

Hawkins nodded.

"I say we bring it along anyway, mates. Never know how it might come in handy." He looked in the direction of Uthman, who for all intents and purposes sat morosely some distance from the group and munched at the dried fruit bar from an MRE they'd supplied. This was the guy's second and from the looks of him he could've used all the extra weight they could put on the poor bastard.

"Hey, Uthman!" McCarter called. The Iraqi looked at him and McCarter gestured toward the tank. "You know how to drive this thing?"

Uthman nodded.

"Good, you just volunteered to be our new tank pilot," Encizo added. "Unless you'd prefer we leave you here."

This produced a negative reaction and McCarter was satisfied they could trust the Sunni guerrilla not to try anything stupid. He decided since Hawkins seemed to be the resident expert on the armored vehicle that he could ride along as TC. The others would ride in the Humvee and SUV—one pair to each of them—with Dakuwami and Nawaf taking the other Humvee once they transferred their equipment. They didn't concern themselves with fuel for the SUV since the thing had nearly a full tank and there were two spare gas cans in the back that had somehow managed to survive the battle and subsequent crash.

Within a couple of minutes the odd-looking convoy was on its way, the Abrams having no trouble keeping up with the three wheeled units since it could travel at up to sixty miles per hour. According to Uthman they were less than four hours from Camp Shannon, assuming they didn't run into any trouble along the way.

"Somehow," McCarter had said in reply, "I'm not sure our luck's going to hold out that long."

CHAPTER NINE

Nobody would've believed what they were seeing unless they'd witnessed it firsthand.

This was something Jeddah could hardly believe and he *had* seen it with his own eyes. How could a ragtag outfit from the AQI, even with money from the deep pockets of al Qaeda and its allies, have managed to pull this off? Surely they hadn't done it solely on their own and nobody would be able to convince Jeddah otherwise. They had to be working with someone on the inside at Camp Shannon, or at least with connections to Rifle Company Bravo.

Could it really be that Abu Sudafi was behind all of this? Jeddah found that difficult to swallow—he considered Sudafi one of his few friends. The guy had stuck with him throughout his mission over the past two years. The withdrawal from Iraq hadn't gone quite as fast as the Americans promised, not that his superiors at the Jordanian Intelligence Service hadn't already known this would be the case. One didn't occupy a country this long and then just pack it up and ship out overnight. Even back when war had been less "efficient" during the 1970s and 1980s, the Soviet army's departure from Afghanistan had taken time.

The Iraqi dissidents and the war between the AQI and Sunni resistance had also made it more difficult for the Americans to conduct an organized retreat. Even now the

AQI had set up a solid foothold in the hills just outside Camp Shannon, and unless Jeddah intervened he knew they stood little chance of getting word out to their generals waiting at the rendezvous point—the same rendezvous point they thought nobody knew about.

Jeddah had been there when they ambushed the convoy sent for the water buffalo, but he'd not been able to interfere. Not only would that have compromised his mission but he would also have not stood a chance against a force with that kind of numerical superiority. Beside the fact he was one man, it also wasn't his job to dig the Americans out of a trap of their own making. If he could provide some sort of assistance without jeopardizing his own mission or risking his neck he would do so, but he didn't owe it to them. If an entire company of U.S. Marines couldn't take out some roughly inexperienced AQI terrorists trying to play soldier, Jeddah couldn't help but wonder if they even deserved to survive. Only fate could decide that, however, and if Jeddah wanted to get out of this with his own skin intact—not to mention bringing a prize like the PSIDS back to his country—he'd have to do something to help out.

Penetrating the external security of AQI camp hadn't been easy. They were well entrenched in their current positions with a considerable fire zone setup. Their fields of fire were strongly interlocked, and they had the perimeter guarded by roving patrols moving on random points of convergence. Their people were neither soft nor lazy. They were diligent fighters, this bunch. The main problem was that they didn't have much experience and what they had failed to do, while watching the front lines of the camp ahead of them, was to secure their rear areas effectively enough to prevent someone from doing exactly what Jeddah had managed to do.

Jeddah took the first of the two sentries he encountered with a knife to the kidney, severing the arteries supplying blood to that area as he clamped a hand over the man's mouth, dug in and twisted. The man lost consciousness in seconds now that his left flank had been turned to scrambled eggs, and only minutes elapsed before he suffered shock and died from blood loss. The second sentry turned out to be more alert and thus posed a stronger challenge when he came to investigate why the first hadn't reported in on schedule. Jeddah had seen the radio on the body of the first guy but he hadn't thought they might be running checks at regular intervals. Perhaps they weren't as stupid as he'd originally thought, although the man who came to investigate wasn't really expecting trouble, either. Jeddah neutralized him by cutting his throat.

So now the Jordanian war spy had to decide his next course of action. He couldn't very well fight this battle for the Americans—this was a battle they had to fight for themselves. He could give them some idea of the weaknesses of the camp, and this might—*might*—be enough for them to secure a victory. Somehow Jeddah thought they wouldn't be smart enough to take it. He also knew the chances of him getting back to Camp Shannon and reporting this hole in security before the AQI terrorists discovered the breach and plugged it up was slim.

He had to try, though, because if they managed to defeat the Marines here it would surely compromise any chance of his people taking control of the PSIDS. It would prove much easier to snatch the thing out from under their noses by handing them a victory, even if somewhat hollow, than it would be to risk having the entire system end up destroyed—or worse yet, fall into the hands of the al Qaeda scum. And there were the Sunni rebels to consider. This was their home turf and for the most part they were a ragtag group that had done their best to keep the AQI dogs at bay. But Jeddah knew they could no more allow this territory to fall under the control of the Sunni warlords than the despots leading the AQI.

The best bet would be to get back to the Americans, something that would compromise his cover.

After thoroughly hiding the bodies in brush and sand, Jeddah stole away from the AQI camp, blending into the night shadows like a ghost.

CAPTAIN PRINGLE and First Sergeant Brock couldn't believe their ears as they listened to Abu Sudafi explain the presence of the man next to him. The newcomer looked like an Iraqi native, a desert rat wrapped in rags for clothing and dirty from head to toe. The veins began to grow ever bigger in Brock's forehead as he listened to Sudafi's tale of having befriended the man some months ago. He'd been feeding information to the man all this time, and although Brock had been right in his mistrust of Sudafi he hadn't expected the Iraqi scientist to ally himself with a Jordanian spy. It seemed like an unlikely alliance, at best.

Pringle scratched at the two-day growth of beard on his face. "So let me get this straight. You're telling me that you've been combining your efforts with a member of the Jordanian Intelligence Service while collecting a paycheck from the government of the United States?"

Sudafi replied, "That would seem a bit presumptuous, Captain."

"That right?" Brock's face reddened. "Seems presumptuous, does it? I think the only one who's been presumptuous around here is you, Sudafi."

"All right, let's not get carried away," Pringle snapped.

"What we *don't* have time to do right now is squabble among ourselves."

"Sir, may I respectfully request a minute in private conference?" Brock asked in a surprisingly quiet voice.

Pringle considered the request and then nodded. The two left the makeshift TOC they'd established in an un-used part of the enlisted men's mess and stepped into an adjoining area packed with crates that were supposed to have been shipped out when the company evacuated the camp. Unfortunately, with the destruction of the better part of the S1 trailer that had served as the Tactical Op-erations Center up until the first mortar attack, space had been limited and they'd been relegated to remove what-ever intelligence and equipment that survived to part of the old warehouse-turned-barracks when the Marines had first converted Camp Shannon into a headquarters for border-monitoring operations.

"Permission to smoke?" Pringle nodded and the first sergeant fired up a Marlboro before saying, "Sir, I can't recommend you listen to anything either of these men have to say."

"On what grounds?"

"On the grounds they've been working with each other all this time without consulting you. Not to mention that this guy, who claims to be part of Jordanian intelligence, has actually been made privy to top-secret information regarding military technology."

"What are you recommending?"

Brock took a hard pull at the cigarette, visibly con-sidering his response before he said, "I think we ought to lock up both of them, sir, until we've assessed our options. Then once we're out of here we can turn them over to Military Intelligence and let them handle it. That would be going by the book."

"I agree with you, Top," Pringle replied. "But unfortunately we're not really in a 'by-the-book' situation at the moment. Are we?"

Brock huffed. "No, sir."

"And let's not forget we have an unknown number of enemy troops out there with superior firepower and the high ground. My first responsibility is to the safety of every man in this company. We've already lost more Marines than I can logically account for, and every man's mother will expect me to have an answer for that. And the thing that really grinds on my guts is I don't have any answers for them."

"But, sir—"

"I'm not finished, First Sergeant," Pringle said with a shake of his head. "Now, maybe Sudafi's broken every fucking rule in the book and if that's the case then yeah, I'll make sure he answers for it. But right now our situation is what it is, and if this Jordanian has any information he wants to give us to turn this thing around then I, for one, plan to at least listen to what the man has to say."

"And if this turns out to be a bust?"

"Then you can shoot the haji bastard personally. But that doesn't happen until the word's given, you hear me, Top?"

"I hear you." Brock took a last hit off his smoke and dashed it out underfoot before they returned to the makeshift TOC.

"Okay, we've agreed to hear you out, sir," Pringle told Jeddah. "Tell us what you know."

GUNNERY SERGEANT STUART COVEY led the first squad of his platoon through the dark, ankle-twisting terrain of the desert hills less than two klicks south of Camp Shannon. The mission had been a risky one when first presented

to him, but Covey—a veteran of three different wars—
wouldn't have backed out of this for all the cash equivalent of oil this dung hole could offer. He was an American
fighting man, a U.S. Marine and veteran of countless
battles. He'd never lost one of them and he didn't plan
to start now.

The captain had told them the information was coming from intelligence sources outside their circle of influence but that it was believed to be as reliable as they
could verify. They had found the telltale signs of where
this mysterious source had camouflaged the two bodies of the enemy sentries, and they'd been further told if
there weren't troops combing the area they had a good
chance of getting inside the camp. Covey could hardly
believe his ears when Captain Pringle had told them they
were going up against an unknown number of al Qaeda
in Iraq terrorists and that their mission was strictly to
gather intelligence.

"Under no circumstances are you to engage the enemy
in any fashion unless your only escape route's cut off,"
Pringle had ordered. "You're to observe and recon the
enemy encampment as best as you can and get back here
no later than 0200 hours. Specifically we'll need a rough
count on troop strength, and any information on the number and types of weapons and equipment. We're especially interested in any vehicle, particularly armor of any
kind."

Covey had indicated his understanding but was surprised when First Sergeant Brock had pulled him aside
after the briefing before he departed to prep his men.

"Listen to me and listen good, Stu," Brock had said. "I
want you to follow the captain's orders to the letter, make
no bones about that. But where this intelligence comes
from and what the asset's interests are in, or that of his

pal Sudafi, I don't give a shit. You don't take risks and you verify everything, and I mean every fucking thing. You hear me, Gunney?"

"I hear you, Top."

"And you bring your collective asses back here in one piece. I've already told Captain Pringle I don't agree with this but he's in a hard place right now, and after talking to him this is probably his best option to get all of us out of here alive. But don't you lie down and die like a dog, either. If it comes to it, you run or you stand and fight—you do that based on whatever option the enemy gives you."

Covey had nodded in complete understanding and within a half hour they were out of sight of the camp and circling on the rear flank of the enemy's hillside encampment. It turned out to be unprotected to some degree and Covey wondered as they crawled stealthily toward the first signs of life on the camp perimeter if maybe they didn't have a chance to launch some kind of assault against the place. After all, they had more than one hundred U.S. Marines at the camp, not to mention a good amount of ordnance just waiting for use.

Of course, Covey would've preferred a tank division as backup, but beggars couldn't be choosers. What Covey hoped to do was to get some way of establishing communications with the mass of men and equipment headquartered at Exit Point Tango. If they could get a signal, any kind of signal to the base there, General Weeks would send everything he could throw at them, the evacuation be damned. Covey wondered why they hadn't sent a flyby, as had a number of other NCOs, until their LT had reminded them of the no-fly zone instituted by the Iraqis.

"Fuck them," one of the corporals had said early on. "We've been over here bleeding and dying for their sorry asses the past decade. We should damn well be able to fly wherever the hell we want."

It was a sentiment echoed by every man in the platoon but it was utterly moot under the circumstances. Mostly, the war had ended in their minds and they just wanted to get out. If the Commander in Chief said fight, then they were Marines and they'd damned well do it; otherwise they saw no point in sticking around and pressing their luck. Covey knew the way to survive was to follow orders, in general, and he also got the agreement of every man in the squad before adding to the parameters of their mission. They would do everything the captain had told them but they would do one additional thing—find a way to communicate with their comrades at Exit Point Tango.

Their initial sweep of the southwest perimeter proved the most treacherous to negotiate, but it didn't reveal all that much in the way of intelligence. Covey ordered a pair of the men from his squad to do a brief reconnoiter of the next section to find a way inside the perimeter. Successful penetration wouldn't be worth a rat's ass if they ended up caught inside and all points of escape were cut off. In that instance, they'd have to fight their way out and his Marines were good but they weren't *that* good. No way in hell could they go up against a hundred-odd armed terrorist fighters, or at least their intelligence was convinced that's how many were encamped in those hills.

Covey had wondered—although he hadn't dared ask Brock—why, if they were relatively evenly matched, they didn't just launch a full-out assault against the terrorists. The answer seemed pretty obvious after Covey considered it. First, the enemy had been afforded the time to become entrenched in the high ground. Second, they were equipped with a significant amount of ordnance, whereas the unit inside Camp Shannon had been operating off minimal supplies in every area. Already they had lost a dozen or so to infection or shock due to an inadequate amount of penicillin, saline bags for fluid replacement and pain drugs.

Covey meant to ensure they didn't lose any more, orders be damned.

The recon team returned several minutes later and conferred with their platoon sergeant. Covey asked Lance Corporal Baker, "What's the layout? Any way inside?"

"Looks like a straight line, Gunney," Baker replied. "I think we can get in and out without being spotted. You going to send the full squad into the Area of Operation?"

Covey shook his head. "Are you kidding? We can't afford the time it would take to get out, not to mention leaving nobody for cover fire in the event we have to un-ass that AO." The gunnery sergeant turned to Private First Class Mike Wilson, who everybody called Taz. "What's your take?"

"I'm with Baker, sir," Wilson said. "I think we ought to go for it."

"Let's rally the others then and I'll give you the battle plan," Covey ordered.

Once they were reunited with the rest of the squad, the unit formed up on Covey. He used the blade of his Ka-Bar fighting knife to draw a line in the sand showing the ingress point along the perimeter and their current position. He then drew a circle off that main area of his impromptu map and said, "Okay, this is our rendezvous point, which is about 250 meters due east. Once we have the communications system, our exit squad will create a diversion and we'll get clear. Then we'll meet at the rendezvous point and get back to base. If there are any questions about what went down, I'll do the talking.

The rest of you will say you were simply following my orders. Is that clear?"

After every one of the men nodded, Covey said, "You understand if we do this and it doesn't pan out, I'll probably get court-martialed?"

"I remember reading somewhere that risks are the only things that make life worth living," Wilson replied.

"You can read?" Baker gibed.

"Okay, let's cut the bullshit and get this done."

And with that, the men of second squad made ready to save the lives of their entire unit.

That's if we don't get ourselves all killed in the process, Stuart Covey thought.

CHAPTER TEN

Hancock, Montana

Carl Lyons was hopping mad.

Somebody had tried to kill the prisoners in their charge, not to mention tossed shots at the local law enforcement and his teammates. The thing he couldn't quite place his finger on was why. Clearly this had something to do with the two former Marines, but for the life of him, Lyons couldn't understand what the terrorists operating here would stand to gain by murdering them. Their presence had already been discovered and before too long Able Team would uncover their operational headquarters. Whatever the explanation, all three of the urban commandos knew Kapczek and Weissmuller had the answers.

As they waited inside the jail for the federal transport team to arrive, Lyons took the time to grill the two prisoners. As usual, it was Kapczek who did all of the talking. Weissmuller only spoke when spoken to, and he didn't say much mostly because Lyons hated to listen to his long and drawn-out answers. Blancanales, an experienced reader of people if there had ever been one, looked for any indication that Kapczek wasn't being forthcoming, but he didn't spot any and during the infrequent breaks he told Lyons as much.

"I'm serious, Ironman, I don't think these guys know any more than they've already told us."

"Oh no? Well, let's just see about that." Lyons reentered the interrogation room and said, "My friends are convinced you've told me everything. I still think you're hiding something. So I'm going to ask you a pointed question now and you're going to answer it. Otherwise, I'll make it my personal mission in life to make sure you're locked up for good, Kapczek. You reading me?"

"Yeah," the Marine replied, muttering because he'd been sleep deprived.

"If you're such low guys on the totem pole, how come a group of al Qaeda terrorists risked exposure just to try to shut you up?"

"What are you talking about?"

"You know what I'm talking about!" Lyons said, slamming his fist on the metal table. "Now you listen to me, asshole. You've been jerking my chain ever since we saved your collective asses at that house. There's no reason for professional terrorists to risk exposing their cover to waste a couple of former veterans unless they were afraid you could tell us something of importance."

Kapczek stared at Lyons a long time before he finally shook his head. "I can't do it, Irons. I can't risk my brothers, and I figure that is something you have to understand. Would you risk spilling the beans on either of these two?"

When he'd gestured at Blancanales and Schwarz, Lyons had to stop to seriously consider the question. It wasn't something he'd been expecting, although he couldn't determine why it surprised him so much since he knew Kapczek had been hiding something. Now wasn't the time for second-guessing, however, since it appeared he had Kapczek on the ropes. He couldn't let up now, even if he'd wanted to—it was just too damn important.

"All right," Lyons said. "I know I wouldn't give these guys up for anything. And yeah, I understand loyalty. But the fact of the matter is, pal, that you're going to prison no matter what. You're already going to do time on a federal beef for illegal possession of automatic weapons. The only question that remains is how you do that time. I can tell you this much, and that is, what I say about you at the hearing will go a real long way with a magistrate. They might even see their way past letting you and junior here do a stint at Club Fed.

"But if you don't cooperate," Blancanales added, "you might just wind up at Guantanamo Bay."

"They wouldn't send Americans there."

"They would if you were believed to be colluding with terrorists," Schwarz interjected.

"We're not in collusion with Asir!" Weissmuller shot back.

"Shut up, Kev," Kapczek muttered.

"But do you hear what they're saying to us?"

"I said shut up."

"I don't care if I go to prison, man," Weissmuller insisted. "But there ain't no way in hell I'm going to let them send me up for committing terrorist acts. We were protecting our nation, Sarge. You need to tell these guys what's what and set the record straight. I ain't going to have my reputation—"

"Shut the fuck up!"

Lyons reached out and grabbed a fistful of Kapczek's shirt collar, keeping his voice low. "Why don't you just slow down, Kapczek. Stop being so hard on the guy. He's right."

Lyons released Kapczek and the Marine finally sat back and swiped at his face. He smacked his lips, rolling his tongue inside his mouth.

"You want something to drink?" Blancanales asked,

turning to leave the makeshift kitchen and adding, "Let me see if we can get these guys some water."

To Lyons's complete surprise, Kapczek opened his mouth and delivered a flood of words. "All right, I'll level with you. The fact is that we're part of a team of Marines, all of us having served at Camp Shannon one time or another. For years we've been putting this together. You see, we started doing a summer camping thing every year on the anniversary of Captain Shannon's death. Some of us served together during the tour, others had served before and they got our names from this website we all signed up to. It was kind of a tradition gig, at first—you know, like they used to do back when by signing a rock or carving their names into a big slab of wood with a Ka-Bar. Whatever.

"Anyway, we started this thing and it just kept going on. When we got out, a bunch of us hooked up and decided to do an annual retreat here in Hancock. Then one of the guys who happens to live here stumbled onto this group of hajis running this sort of Islamic religious group out of the technical school up north."

"The Regional Science Institute?" Schwarz asked.

Kapczek nodded. "Right. So our buddy, you see, he was going to the school, as well, and he started to see some things he thought were pretty suspicious. He tried to report them but the school people just pooh-poohed him. Then he tried to reach out to the cops in Great Falls, and they blew him off, too."

Lyons sighed, already able to see what was coming next. "So he decided to call up a few of you and let you know something was up. And you just couldn't resist coming up here and looking for trouble."

"We found more than trouble, Irons," Kapczek fired back. "We found a whole hell of a lot of bad shit going on. Did you know that a good number of these guys were taking chemical studies, showing particular interest in explosives and munitions? And guess what else they were looking into—nuclear materials. Yeah, that's right—you don't have to look so damn surprised."

"So why not bring that kind of information to the FBI?"

Kapczek delivered a laugh of derision. "You're kidding me, right? After our buddy had already been blown off by the school officials and the local cops, you think the FBI would've listened to him? Maybe you aren't as smart as I gave you credit for."

"He's smart enough," Schwarz said.

"So then what happened?" Lyons pressed.

"Well, we started to do some more digging and we all came up here for our annual shindig, just so as not to call attention to ourselves. By the time we got together, two or three of the guys had already been up here and were staying with Bobs."

"Who's that?"

"Well, his full name's Joe Bobinawski but we just call him Bobs, because the guy's head bobs like a chicken every time he runs. Nickname just stuck."

"Never mind the nickname malarkey," Lyons said. "So Bobinawski was the one who originally got onto Asir's scent and then you guys came up to join the party. That about sum it up?"

"Yeah," Kapczek said.

"And we weren't going to start any trouble with these guys until we found out about Camp Shannon and their plans here," Weissmuller offered. He jabbed Kapczek with his elbow. "Tell them about that, Kappy."

Kapczek eyed his friend with a sour look as Blancanales returned with two bottles of water. Kapczek waited until the warrior had set them down and then continued. "So in this most recent time that Bobs was tailing these guys, he follows them from Asir's house to this place out west of here, some place on the fringes of the county. Turns out they had a whole mockup of the camp set up out there in the middle of nowhere. It's mostly in miniature and all, but the place was replicated to practically every detail. I swear, they even had those Army men to show the placement of every Marine's station there, not to mention the vehicles and other equipment. The water supplies and barracks were specially marked, along with the TOC. When Bobs told us everything he saw, that's when we knew the camp was in some kind of trouble."

"Is that when you started your plan to ambush these guys?" Blancanales asked.

"But unfortunately you were too late," Lyons finished. "A couple of your guys went out to scout the place and never came back. And that's when you ended up at Asir's house and were trying to blow him and the rest of them to kingdom come."

Kapczek nodded as he opened the water with thanks of appreciation to Blancanales, who smiled at the Marine in return. The gregarious Able Team warrior had a definite way with people. Lyons was too slap-'em-up-side-the-head and Schwarz just didn't have the serious attention span to give most people more than cursory acknowledgment. But that was just Blancanales: he was the good cop to Lyons's bad cop, the soft touch to Lyons's more direct approach.

"So where are Bobs and the rest of your crew now?"

"Not sure," Kapczek said.

"Aw, and you were doing so well to this point."

"No, it's not that. I'm not shittin' you, sir. I'm just saying that I don't know where they might be at this particular time. They might already think we're dead and they'd be proceeding on target to destroy this camp."

"You don't think they'd try Asir's house again?" Schwarz inquired.

"I highly doubt it. I mean, the place was practically rubble by the time you guys got done with it. They wouldn't go back there."

"How many others are in this group of Asir's?" Lyons asked.

It was Weissmuller who replied, "We estimate it at ten, maybe more, but no more than twenty. We're pretty sure of that much."

"Including the ones we took out at the house?" Lyons asked.

"I'd say that's a safe bet."

"Where's this camp?"

Kapczek replied, "Bobs and his spotter disappeared before they could give us the exact location. We went to Asir's house because we figured they'd been captured. But now we know they aren't."

"Which means they could be either alive or dead," Blancanales pointed out. He looked at Lyons. "There's a good chance those guys are deceased. The rest of the group may go looking for payback, and they'll start with hitting this base camp first."

"Don't know what difference that's going to make," Kapczek said. "Even if our guys had decided to hit their little hidey-hole out there, I don't have the first clue where it's at. I'm not sure any of our other guys know, either."

"Six probably knows," Weissmuller said.

"Who?" Lyons asked.

"Brad Shtick," Kapczek explained. "We called him

Six because he was, like, obsessed with his abdomen. Dude was constantly working them things."

"You know, I'm starting to get a headache trying to keep track of all these guys," Schwarz complained.

"Let's just suppose for now that they know where this camp is at and they plan to launch an operation against it. Who would be the leader?"

"Six…I mean, Shtick. He was a corporal and my second."

"You were the leader?"

"After Bobs disappeared, yeah. He was actually a lieutenant until he got out on a medical. Guy has one leg, man. Lost the other and ended up with a prosthetic."

Weissmuller added, "Damnedest thing you ever saw. He still exercises and jogs and everything. Hell, you can't even tell he's got it most of the time."

"That is impressive," Blancanales said.

"Well if you were the non-com of this bunch and you don't know where this alleged camp is at, what makes you think Shtick would know?"

Kapczek said, "I'm making a best guess, okay? I don't know a damn thing, really, which is exactly what I've been trying to tell you clowns from the start."

"Hey! Watch the name-calling, chump," Schwarz said with an expression of righteous indignation.

"Go on, Sarge," Blancanales said.

"Sorry. All I meant is that Bobs and Six were kind of tight. I'm not sure why, but they were the first two in our group to serve at Shannon…um, '03–'04, I think. Anyway, I guess Six pulled the LT out of there when he got his leg blown off. Saved his life and all, although Six never got the medal for it. That really bit at him. But still, those two were tight as brothers after that, practically inseparable. I heard Six went to see Bobs as soon as he wrapped his tour. Lot of guys thought maybe they were Don't Tellers or something, but I never saw that. They just clicked, you know?"

Lyons nodded. "I know. So you think if we find Shtick that there's a good chance he can show us where this camp is?"

"Probably."

"Okay, sit tight." Lyons rose and gestured for his friends to follow.

They decided to powwow in Boswich's office. The sheriff had finally gone home for a few hours of shuteye. The fact he'd left the men of Able Team to watch over the prisoners pretty much cinched the assumption he now trusted them. Not that he had much of a choice since he now had two dead deputies on his hands and couldn't leave the town as the only law-enforcement officer. Lyons had managed to get Stony Man to pull strings with the state police, and help would be arriving before too long in the form of a couple of temporary deputies from the ranks of the Montana State Police reserves.

"Okay, so what do you think?" Lyons asked his friends.

"I think this whole thing stinks," Schwarz said.

"He's telling the truth," Blancanales said. "He has to be, Ironman. There's no way they could make up a story like that."

"Maybe they want to put us on a trail chasing ghosts," Lyons said.

"To what end?" Blancanales shook his head and ticked off the points on his fingers. "First, we know they were engaged in a gun battle with known terrorist affiliates. Second, we have plenty of information to suggest that Hamza Asir is a known al Qaeda operative, probably working for the AQI cell. Finally, the idea they would make up a story about Camp Shannon being set up in miniature in the middle of nowhere and there just so happens to be a bunch of Islamic radicals running around the area? No. If that's a tall tale then those guys should get some kind of award for being able to deal the biggest pile of bullshit this side of the Mississippi."

"Okay, I get your point," Lyons said. "So they're probably telling us the truth. But the fact still remains we have no idea where to start looking. Not to mention we could be up against some of our own kind out there. I don't know about you guys, but I'm not keen on the idea of shooting a bunch of veteran Marines just because they're looking to protect their home turf."

"Well, we do know the place is within the county and it's out west of here," Schwarz said.

"What's your point?"

"Why not get some air support up here and start looking for it? They obviously spent a lot of time at this place given they had time to build such a model of Camp Shannon to scale and in the detail Kapczek described. Surely they'll have needed generators and other equipment. Any camp of that size holding terrorists has got to be giving off some decent heat signatures. I have plenty of my equipment with me, and we could set that up."

Lyons nodded. "Sounds like a plan. Why don't you get on the horn to Bear Run County Airport and see if we can charter a flight."

Schwarz nodded and grabbed up the phone.

"Pol, why don't you keep an eye on our prisoners, see if they can tell us anything else of use?"

"Okay, what are you going to do?"

"I'm going to get on the phone to the Farm and give them an update. I'm also going to run these new names by Bear, see if he can tell us anything more about these former Marines turned hillbilly homeland security. I'd like to know what we're up against, at least from a psychological standpoint."

"I couldn't agree more," Blancanales said. "Like you, I'm not fond about maybe having to shoot it out with any American veterans."

"We'll do whatever we have to do," Lyons said. "But yeah, I completely agree it's not the most ideal situation."

"We're also forgetting something."

"What's that?"

"Not only are these America's favorite sons, they're also Marines," Blancanales said. "They'll be well equipped and you can be sure they know how to fight. Any serious resistance from them won't be an easy act to follow. I'm just as worried about keeping our own asses alive, as well as theirs."

CHAPTER ELEVEN

It was midday by the time Able Team got airborne.

Carl Lyons still didn't have much confidence in their plan, but he knew it was the only viable option available to them. He trusted Schwarz implicitly; the team's resident electronics wizard had enough smarts that it had earned him the "Gadgets" moniker.

Able Team had managed to acquire the use of a Bell 206L-4 headquartered at the airport for the Bear County EMS Search and Rescue teams, which included a pilot on twenty-four-hour standby. It took a bit of coaxing of the medical director, but eventually he gave in and approved the chopper for no more than two hours of their exclusive use. Of course, the ten-thousand-dollar honorarium promised by the United States government helped the EMS director to come around to Able Team's way of thinking.

They cruised over the rugged terrain, Schwarz manning his equipment with Blancanales offering an assist where needed. Lyons left the pair to focus on the scanning. He used the time to close his eyes and rest his weary bones. He'd learned the trick of getting sleep when and where he could. The Able Team leader had always been able to steal ten or twenty minutes, and that was enough to keep him going for long stretches of combat or intense activity. What he'd never learned to do was to stave off boredom.

"The more you try not to fall asleep, Ironman, the more difficult it gets to stay awake," Blancanales said into his ear to be heard over the noise of the chopper.

Lyons opened his eyes. "Well, the job can't all be fame and glory," he replied.

Schwarz grinned and turned his attention to the infrared screen and began to aah as his brow furrowed. He gave every indication he'd discovered something of importance but he didn't immediately say as much. Instead he donned the inboard headset, which gave him direct communication access to the pilot, and requested he alter course, make another pass over the area on the reverse vector. It took two passes before Schwarz was convinced he'd found what they were looking for.

"No question about it," he told his friends. "There is definitely some activity going on down there."

Lyons nodded and gestured toward their equipment bags. "Get us a more complete rundown on whatever you can using that thing. Pol, you and I can prep the weapons."

The pair turned to the equipment bag. Lyons's first draw was a Mossberg 935 automatic shotgun. In addition to its three-and-one-half-inch payload and rugged frame, the weapon boasted a fully rifled choke and weighed less than eight pounds. The synthetic stock supported a webbing shell holder loaded with twenty shells of Lyons's preferred load of No. 2 and double-0 buck. Following a quick check of the action, Lyons removed an M-16 A-4/M-203 combo with five 40 mm HE grenades. Lyons planned to take both into the zone for the sake of versatility, convinced if they found things as Kapczek had claimed they might, he'd be able to adjust to battleground changes with relative ease.

Blancanales went next, securing a Beretta AR 70/90.

The weapon first got its chops in the wars in Afghanistan and Iraq. It chambered 5.56 NATO ammunition and could fire more than 600 rounds per minute to an effective range of 500 meters. Blancanales had used it many times before and come to rely upon it. He checked the action with the efficiency of a combat veteran, then put the weapon on safety and turned his attention to preparing Schwarz's weapon, although he knew his friend would check it again all the same.

Blancanales didn't mind. He withdrew the SIG-551 A1 and unfolded the Swiss stock with a glimmer of admiration. The weapon sported a rotary diopter sighting system. A new addition to the SIG-Sauer line of law enforcement and military models, the weapon retailed at approximately two grand. Stony Man's armorer, John "Cowboy" Kissinger, had told them when first adding it to their arsenal, "Take care of these babies because they cost a-plenty."

Blancanales ensured the weapon was in safe mode before passing it to his friend, who accepted it with a short nod.

Lyons ordered the pilot to put down a good half klick from the dense set of infrared signatures Schwarz had marked and locked. When they'd touched down, Lyons said, "We should be in and out, so wait for us. You carry a gun?"

The pilot shook his head. "I'm on the reserve police force but mostly I work medical evac. Don't typically pack for those missions."

Lyons handed him a pistol with a nod. "I won't go into who we are or what we do, but chances are better than good we're going to run into some less than nice folks."

The pilot arched an eyebrow. "Would these folks be of the terrorist persuasion perhaps?"

"Perhaps," Lyons replied suspiciously. "Why do you ask?"

He shrugged with a knowing grin. "Small town."

"Just stay put and if anyone tries to take you or the chopper for a ride you put as many holes into them as you can." He handed him a spare magazine and added, "Meaning a lot. Understood?"

"Roger that."

Lyons returned to the rear compartment. Blancanales already had the satchels and other equipment waiting just outside the chopper. Schwarz had his equipment powered down, and a compact tracker hung from a lanyard around his neck while he performed a quick double-check of his SIG-551 A1.

Once they were boots on the ground, Able Team headed in the direction of the suspected hardsite with Schwarz on point. Blancanales brought up the rear and Lyons took middle position, but offset to avoid being sandwiched between them. They also kept about a twenty-yard spread to prevent any terrorist sentries from taking them down in a thick fire ambush. While the men of Able Team were specialized in urban warfare, no one could have accused them of being strangers to rugged terrain. They had fought in some of the most inhospitable places on the planet and were just as comfortable trekking through mountains and deserts as through the concrete jungles of any city, big or small.

They were also trained to spot trouble well before it hit them, and so the two terrorists who tried to surprise them ended up being the ones caught off guard.

The pair opened their ambush from behind a couple of thick-trunked ferns. The autofire buzzed just past Schwarz's head but the warrior had already spotted them, signaling his friends to fan out before going for his own cover. Where the ambushers had failed was to cover metal parts with nonreflective material, and the beams of sunlight off the metal of their rifles and equipment gave away their position.

Lyons swept to the left and brought the M-203 into action, sighting on a point between the terrorists before he triggered the grenade launcher. The HE shell wrecked the situation for the terrorist pair, the heat and blast of fragments nearly taking the leg off one of the prone shooters at the knee. The other was fortunate enough to avoid most of the concussive effects although he did wind up with shrapnel fragments in his left side.

Schwarz moved on cue and ended the agony of the terrorist who'd lost a leg by triggering a short burst that blew his head apart. The other terrorist rolled from cover, rose and tried to retreat, but Blancanales caught him in the spine with a single shot from the AR 70/90. The man's body continued in forward motion until his foot caught on an exposed tree root and he tumbled to the mossy floor of the increasingly dense woods.

Able Team remained under cover a time before forming on each other to continue their patrol.

"I guess that seals up any doubts we might have had," Blancanales said as they started out once more.

Lyons looked at his teammate with a glib expression. "You think?"

So FAR, nothing had gone as Hamza Asir had planned.

First had been the loss of valuable members of their team at the house he'd bought, a purchase that had nearly depleted the remaining funds al Qaeda had provided him. Then he'd failed at his one chance to eliminate the American Marines who could possibly exploit their operations here in Montana. Now the American operatives who were not, as nearly as Asir could tell, part of the FBI or Homeland Security, had somehow managed to locate their secret base of operations. And while this wasn't the last place from which Asir and his men could hold out, he knew they would be left with their only remaining option of retreat if security here at the camp were breached.

Asir didn't want to think about that now, even though he knew he *had* to consider it with the latest development. The location of their base had somehow been discovered, and according to their latest intelligence the Americans had broken through the outermost ambush point. The approaching force was of unknown size or capability but it was assumed they numbered between ten and twenty, and moreover they were heavily armed and well equipped.

"Burn everything," Asir had told one of his comrades as soon as that last information arrived. "And set the thermal explosives to trigger when the perimeter is breached. We shall implement a scorched-earth policy from this point on. Leave nothing that will alert them to our plans or our affiliation with the efforts of our brothers at Camp Shannon."

It didn't somehow seem like enough, but Asir knew they didn't have much choice, really. The Americans were coming and they wouldn't stop until they had reached their objective. Asir had to wonder at the accuracy of their numbers but he had no reason to doubt the reports. Even if they were exaggerated—Asir had only seen three Americans plus the sheriff in Hancock when attempting to kill the Marines who had murdered his friends—they would surely send a force of more than three men.

What those men didn't know but Asir was counting on was that the American vigilantes, a group of ex-Marines that considered themselves a militia, were gathering to plan their own raid against the camp. Asir could only hope that each would cross the path of the other and while they were battling it out, completely oblivious to the fact they were killing their own kind, Asir and his small band of remaining fighters could slip out quietly. From there, they would proceed toward their last refuge to the north, an urban keep of sorts in Great Falls. Asir had hoped not to have to resort to such a retreat, but they couldn't spare any more men at this point.

The operation in Iraq should be well under way by now, anyway, which meant that their efforts were now secondary. They had put it all together for Muam Khoury and his people, gathering what intelligence they could from the former Marines who had served at Camp Shannon all the way to providing the technical specifications needed to build their ultimate weapon. Within the next twelve hours, Asir and his men expected to hear of their success and then they would attempt to escape this cursed country.

He hoped their plan would be so crazy the Americans wouldn't become suspicious or worry about an escape attempt. While crossing the border into Canada would've seemed the safest way to go, their plan was much riskier and at the same time bizarre. They had open tickets to fly out of Great Falls to Denver. From there, they would make their way to Mexico City. Escape from Mexico to a neutral or Arab-friendly port would be much easier and less suspicious, particularly since the last place the Americans would think to look for them would be Central America. Canada was always the suspected haven for the smuggling of terrorists into and out of the United States.

Asir hoped it wouldn't have come to that, but with news of impending arrival of American commandos, special operatives from who knew what organization, he realized it was more likely now the only course of action left to him and his men. Yes, it was plainly inevitable.

"Is it done?" he asked ibn-Habad, his trusted friend and ally of more than ten years.

Ibn-Habad had worked alongside Asir during the operation, hardly ever leaving his side as their efforts stretched into the early hours of many a morning at the apartment near the university they both attended. While they worked tirelessly to develop the special weapon that Khoury would use against the Marines at Camp Shannon, they had made a point of staying away from each other at the school. Somehow one of the Americans had connected them in some other way, perhaps due to their religious affiliations with Islam.

The whole idea of acting out their roles as Muslims and American students had been to cast off suspicion. The Westerners had become so paranoid about racial profiling that it was less effective to "act" Americanized when it was apparently obvious they weren't. For a while, anyway, they had seemed able to carry out the facade. Who would have suspected one American Marine home from the war would be able to pick them out so easily and identify them for what they were?

Asir's connections had managed to clue him into the man who had been following them from the school, observing their activities and reporting them to the American police. Asir had wondered where this ex-Marine felt it his duty, like some self-appointed watchdog, to report them to the local and then state authorities when they had done nothing to him. The paranoia with which this former Marine had operated annoyed Asir and had almost pushed him to putting together an operation to eliminate him once and for all. Ultimately, he dismissed it as attracting too much attention. How the hell could they have suspected that the American dog would rally others to his cause, taking it upon himself to interfere with their operations?

"I directed the men to place the charges where we planned, and they are set to detonate within the next fifteen minutes."

"Excellent," Asir said with a nod.

Ibn-Habad added, "If we are to go, it should be now, Hamza. We don't want to be close when the explosives go up."

"What are you worried about?" Asir asked as he lifted a backpack onto his left shoulder and slung his AK-47 onto his right, in ready position for firing. "The Americans are coming with the expectation they will find us unprepared. Instead, it is they who will be unprepared."

"Yes, but we have a considerable distance to cover and we understand they have air support."

"The woods should cover our retreat nicely. And if we move by day it will go all that much more quickly. I am ready. We should be able to make it to the ridge overlooking the camp by the time the Americans arrive."

This brought a smile of satisfaction to ibn-Habad's lips. "Yes. I anticipate it will be quite a spectacle to behold."

"Let's go."

And with that, Hamza Asir and his men departed the mock Camp Shannon for the last time.

THINGS WEREN'T JUST quiet on Able Team's approach to ground zero—they were *too* quiet.

Rosario Blancanales had been a veteran of many battles in many inhospitable places, and as such he'd learned to mistrust coincidence. The sudden, almost deathly silence that greeted their ears as they neared the perimeter of the encampment seemed all at once expected and yet completely out of place. Blancanales couldn't quite put his finger on that queer sensation of duplicity, but he knew it wouldn't bode well for them if he didn't heed the internal alarm bells.

Blancanales made a faint noise to get the attention of his teammates and then indicated they should get low. Lyons and Schwarz went to their bellies. Following suit, Blancanales crawled in their direction and gestured for them to join him. It was risky, to be sure. One well-placed grenade or a savvy fire team and it would be curtains for Able Team and their mission.

Fortunately, Lady Luck smiled on them.

"What's up?" Lyons inquired.

"How close are we to the target site?" Blancanales asked Schwarz.

Schwarz checked the handheld device around his neck. "Maybe twenty yards."

Blancanales nodded and looked at Lyons. "I smell a trap."

"We already sprung the trap," Lyons countered, jerking his thumb in the direction of the ambush. "Back there. Remember?"

Blancanales shook his head. "No, I'm not talking about that. They could just as easily put a whole army out there to guard the perimeter. Instead they left only two sentries and they were pretty far out at that. I get the sense they *wanted* them to engage us that far out, buy them time to evacuate this location."

"Yeah, but evacuate to where?" Schwarz asked. "I mean, you don't really think—"

"Shh!" Lyons hissed.

The pair froze and looked at him, the Able Team leader now as rock still as a gargoyle on a Medieval church with a stony expression to match. The only thing that moved were the ice-blue eyes probing the foliage around them. The forestry had thickened considerably the closer they moved to their position. At first they couldn't make out anything but then it registered. Blancanales was utterly amazed at his friend's almost superhuman hearing. They were definitely the sounds of movement, the kind of sounds made by a small unit of men on an approach vector to the camp. The movements weren't really coming toward them, however, as much as it seemed like they were *around* them.

In a moment of horror and revelation, Blancanales understood the significance of that oddity. It was a risk they had taken in the hope it wouldn't actually materialize. Unfortunately the cards hadn't fallen in their favor. It appeared Kapczek's people had found the camp, as well, and Blancanales knew the odds had been long against such an eventuality. Somehow Hamza Asir had arranged events to fall out this way in the hope of destroying all of his enemies at once while he and his men made their escape.

Blancanales wrote one word into the dirt: "Marines."

His friends read it just a heartbeat before the first explosion resounded in their ears.

CHAPTER TWELVE

Brad Shtick understood war.

He also understood the enemy they faced, because he'd done battle against them every day for three years of his life. His friends and family had thought he was crazy to volunteer for a second tour in Afghanistan, but they'd flat out called him nuts when he returned for a third. What they didn't understand, could *never* understand, was Shtick's dedication to his friends and unit. It wasn't that Shtick had a death wish or some kind of survivor's guilt—they could save that bullshit for the hospital psychiatrist or the clergy. No, what kept Brad Shtick going was love for his country and the Corps.

So it hadn't been any stretch for Shtick to join his fellow Marines and friends to put down a guy like Asir. The man stood for everything Shtick stood against, and when it came to his attention that Asir was part of a band of Islamic extremists bent on spreading terror right here American soil, it didn't take any prompting for Shtick to rally to Bobs's call for help. That's how this had started, and with the likely death of Bobs and a couple more of their own now in custody, Shtick had taken charge of the unit with one purpose: destroy the enemy. Unfortunately, Shtick hadn't considered the consequences of his actions or those of his friends. He realized a moment too late the very dear costs all of them would suffer for their lack of foresight. There was an old rule among enlisted men in the Marine Corps that the job of the leader was to keep his men alive.

Shtick could taste a part of that failure when the man to his right cried out in surprise just a moment before his body blew apart under the concussion of a thermate-filled explosive. Showers of molten iron spread across the immediate area and a small patch landed on Shtick's forearm, the majority passing over his head as he hit the dirt in reflex action to the explosion. Three years as an Iraqi veteran saved his life, but the thermate filler knew nothing of that and it burned quickly into his flesh as it seared its way toward bone.

Shtick groaned through gritted teeth as he snatched a scoop of mud from the forest floor and slapped it onto the wound. The thermate burned with oxygen and the mud patch would smother the heat, but not before a significant amount of damage would be done to the muscle and bone. He had to get it out and do it now; otherwise he'd be effectively out of the action, something they couldn't afford if the shouts of turmoil and pain coming from somewhere ahead were any indication.

Shtick snatched a combat knife from his belt. He wrapped the sling of his rifle above his forearm and used his teeth to pull it taut, then got the tip of the knife under the mud patch and flipped it away. The intense burning started again and Shtick let out a cry of anguish as he wedged the blade past the blackened, charred flesh and pried under the metal. The tip of the knife became red-hot nearly instantly as the molten iron connected with it, but Shtick flipped it out and away from his position. Wherever it landed nearby it produced a burning, acrid smell and a hiss as it continued to do its nasty work.

Shtick pulled a canteen from his belt, doused his fore-arm with water and then returned the canteen before slapping a thick combat compress on the wound. He tied the dressing securely with the attached wrapping and cinched a knot directly over the padding. Shtick got to his feet and grabbed the cover of a thick tree trunk, watching as the rest of their team fanned out. He'd heard at least a half dozen distinct blasts, he thought, and if all the thermate filler had spread then any number of casualties might have ensued.

Asir and his cronies had set a trap for them, and Shtick had been stupid enough to walk his friends right into it. They'd trusted him to keep them alive and he'd failed. Their numbers had been reduced to nearly half between the deaths of two friends, coupled with the arrest of Kapczek and Weissmuller. If they lost the battle here, their fight would be over for good and Hamza Asir would go on spreading terror and succeed in whatever plans he had for Camp Shannon.

With new resolve, Shtick broke cover and skirted the line he'd traversed in the hope of breaching the perimeter of Asir's encampment by another route. The trees immediately ahead shimmered in the morning sunlight, and plumes of dirt began to rise around him as the report of a machine gun resounded in the distance. That didn't take Shtick by surprise since he'd expected they might attempt to stay to defend their position against intruders rather than abandon it. Their resources would be limited; this much Shtick and his comrades had assumed to be true.

What Shtick hadn't expected was to have someone grab his shoulder and yank him off balance. His back slammed onto the ground just a heartbeat before the area where he'd been standing came alive with the buzz of autofire. A good dozen heavy-caliber slugs chewed up the earth and Shtick realized whoever had grabbed him had saved his life. He turned his head—a foggy buzz lined the periphery of his vision as the impact had all but knocked the wind out of him—to find a pair of hard blue eyes staring into his.

The man had blond hair and a medium complexion, with facial features that looked like they'd been chiseled from stone. Near as Shtick could tell, the guy had a physique to match and there was no mistaking the intensity of an experienced combatant in that hardened visage. It was enough to cause Shtick's breath to catch in his throat and render him speechless.

"Who the hell are you?" Shtick finally stammered.

"The guy who just saved your ass," the man replied.

THE EXPLOSIONS hadn't taken the men of Able Team by surprise. The shouts of surprise—and in one case a scream of pain—were another thing entirely.

Somehow the disorganized band of vigilantes had managed to penetrate the immediate area without Able Team even knowing about it, and that disturbed Carl Lyons greatly. They must've been getting soft because he didn't realize they weren't alone until just a moment before he heard them, followed by the explosions. Before they could react, Lyons observed a figure in forest camouflage carrying a .223 assault rifle—a semiautomatic civilian version of the M-16—crash through the brush to his right and head straight for the machine gun fire being poured on their position.

Lyons had managed to yank the new arrival out of the line of fire before the unseen gunner connected. Not the best way to make introductions but they'd hardly expected this mission to be a cakewalk. There had always been a chance they would encounter friendlies in the strictest sense, but Able Team had hoped to put down Hamza Asir and his terrorist bedfellows before it came to such an encounter. This was something their little self-appointed militia had probably planned from the start, which implied Kapczek hadn't been entirely forthcoming in his statements. This didn't really come as much of a surprise to the Able Team leader, but it appeared the guy he'd just saved from destruction hadn't expected to find allies here.

"Do you have any idea the problems you guys have created?" Lyons demanded.

"Look, pal—"

Lyons shushed him with a swipe of his hand. "Not the time! Keep your head down and stay out of this. And give me your ammo."

"No way, man. No way will I let you leave me defenseless while you guys—"

"Um," Schwarz cut in, "could we perhaps work this out later?"

Lyons looked as if he had more to say but he clammed up, reminded they weren't out of the woods yet.

"What's your name, friend?" Blancanales said.

"Shtick, Bradley R., Sergeant, USMC retired."

"How many more of you out there, Shtick?" Lyons asked.

"Six others on the team, but we lost one in that initial blast."

"Any chance he's alive?"

Shtick shook his head with a grim expression.

"Okay, you got radio contact with the rest?"

"No, we didn't have time to get any radios."

Great, Lyons thought. Bunch of young Marine fire-pissers came out here to face off with experienced terrorists like a band of drunken hunters looking for a good time during deer season. This was why such activities were better left to the professionals, although Lyons knew these guys hadn't thought of it in those terms. While they were probably a fine bunch of Marines fighting against dense Iraqi dissidents and ill-equipped guerrillas in Iraq, they didn't know the first thing about fighting hardened al Qaeda terrorists.

"Options?" Lyons asked his teammates.

"I'm guessing our Marine friends tripped booby traps," Schwarz said. "Looks like a thermate mixture of explosives, probably part of the home-cooked ordnance in evidence at Asir's house."

Lyons nodded. "That was my thought."

"If they bothered to booby-trap the place, I'm guessing they've abandoned the camp," Blancanales said.

"A diversion to keep us at bay while they escape," Schwarz said.

"But escape to where?" Lyons asked. "Not to mention they've got us pinned down by that machine gun."

"I'll take care of that," Blancanales said.

Blancanales patted the scope mounted to his AR 70/90 before he climbed to his feet and ran in a hunched position, skirting the perimeter far enough outside so as not to trigger any additional booby traps the enemy might have set. Already, the remaining three men could feel the heat coming off the encampment, a tall flame visible just beyond a particularly dense copse of trees and brush. A thick, dark cloud of smoke had begun to waft through the trees and coat everything with a layer of thin ash, an indicator the fire had burned hot and fast.

"What the hell did they do?" Schwarz asked. "Start a forest fire?"

Lyons shook his head. "It's the mockup of Camp Shannon. They destroyed it. That's why the thermate."

Shtick looked puzzled. "No reason to be so gleeful about it...*friend*."

"You should be a little nicer," Schwarz deadpanned. "You're in enough trouble already without adding rudeness to the list of charges."

"For your information, Marine, I'm downright tickled about it," Lyons said. "Don't you see what it means? They wouldn't have bothered to take the time to destroy the thing if they thought we actually knew what they had going on here. We already know about what's happened in Camp Shannon and we have some of our men there right now to correct whatever may be wrong. But by Asir going to the extra effort to destroy everything here, that indicates he doesn't *know* that we know."

"Well, here's something else you may not know," Shtick said as a new barrage of autofire opened up. When it subsided he said, "You may not know that Asir and some of his chumps were doing a lot of work with chemical and biological elements."

"You mean, the thermate?" Schwarz asked.

"No, this was a lot more serious than that," Shtick replied. "I'm talking about nukes, man."

Lyons nodded. "Kapczek said something about that before."

"What about your lieutenant that found all this out?" Schwarz said. "Bobinawski's his name, I think I remember?"

Something went hard and simultaneously broken in Shtick's expression, and Lyons remembered what Kapczek had said about the bond he'd formed with Bobinawski. Despite what Kapczek had intimated, Lyons could understand the kind of bond between these men. He knew a similar bond with his two friends, and Lyons had never dared wonder what life would be like without his longtime friends and fellow warriors. The three had been through hell and back too many times to count.

"What do you think happened to him?" Lyons asked.

"I'm not sure I want to say," Shtick replied. "But I sense he's dead."

The machine gun opened up again but this time the reports were abruptly silenced. Somewhere amid the firing, much closer to their location and just milliseconds before, they heard a single shot. Another tense moment followed before the radio receiver earpieces worn by Schwarz and Lyons beeped and were followed by Blancanales's voice, his tone almost proud.

"Scratch one terrorist."

Lyons keyed his mike. "Good job. You got an opening?"

"Roger that."

"Good deal. Stand by and we'll converge on your location."

"Copy. Out here."

It took Able Team another forty-five minutes for the heat and flames to die enough that they could make a closer inspection. They used the time to attempt to find the remaining militia members, but had no luck.

Lyons had a hard time choking back his anger, but he knew to take it out on Shtick wouldn't do him any good. If they wanted the guy to cooperate with them, they'd have to bring him around to their way of thinking. Lyons wasn't sure why they would've scattered and run but he had a feeling they had either spotted Blancanales and, realizing he wasn't a part of the team, had broken off on a prearranged signal, or one of them had observed the interaction between Shtick and Able Team and they'd decided to split.

Once they were aboard the chopper and headed back

to the airport, Lyons said, "We aren't any closer to wrapping this up than we were before."

"It's pretty clear they think their mission has been accomplished," Blancanales pointed out. "Otherwise they wouldn't have abandoned the camp."

"So now you think they'll do what?" Schwarz asked. "Just run?"

"I don't know what else they could do."

"Maybe we should run what we know by the Farm," Blancanales said out of Shtick's earshot. "Bear could probably run it down a lot faster from his end than they could."

"He would only be doing what we are. Guessing," Lyons returned.

"Maybe so," Blancanales replied with a shrug. "But I feel a whole lot better about his guesses than I would most other people's facts."

"He's got you there," Schwarz noted.

They didn't speak more about it until they landed. They barely had their equipment off-loaded when the sheriff's cruiser, lights going full blast, squealed to a halt a safe distance from the chopper blades that were still winding down.

When Boswich climbed out from behind the wheel he didn't look happy. There was a grim set to his mouth and his eyes flashed with what looked to be renewed anger. As he stomped toward them Lyons couldn't help but produce a deep groan.

"Oh, boy," Schwarz said. "He looks none too happy."

"So what else is new?" Lyons replied.

"What in the blue blazes do you guys think you're doing?" Boswich's face had taken on a dangerous red hue, and a purple vein stood pronounced along the left side of his nose.

"Before you blow a gasket," Blancanales said, "you might want to let us explain."

"Explain what? Explain how you guys just took off and didn't give me the first clue about where you were headed or what you were up to? I got to learn secondhand after calling around half the county that you'd chartered a helicopter by apparently offering a bribe to the EMS director of the medical district in this county, and that you were seen flying over the western hills. Then I get a call from a ranger station about forty-five minutes later saying some hikers had reported not only a possible forest fire but also indicated they heard automatic weapons being fired. Just what the fuck is going on?"

"Well, this is Brad Shtick," Blancanales said, not missing one congenial beat. "And we ran into Mr. Shtick here while he and his Marine friends were attempting to assault a terrorist camp being run by Hamza Asir."

"It's true? There are terrorists running around this county?"

It was Lyons who replied, "Yeah. And apparently they've been running around here planning some sort of major operation against Marines fighting in Iraq. Right under your noses."

"Now look, Irons, I'm not saying—"

"I don't care what you're saying. What we're saying is that apparently this group of Marines felt it necessary to take the fight to the terrorists because when they reported the issue to the FBI and local law enforcement they got shot down. A report I would think would've been shared with your office. Am I right?"

"Well, I…"

"And have we mentioned yet that one got blown up during their little assault, the victim of a booby trap set by that maniac Asir?"

"And they also tortured and mutilated my lieutenant," Shtick said, his voice cracking and eyes welling with tears.

Lyons hadn't planned to mention that in front of Shtick, but now that the cat was out of the bag there wasn't any point in holding back. They'd found the incinerated remains of a body, left to burn with the camp, and among those charred remains they had pried a set of dog tags belonging to Bobinawski. The other Marine who had died in the initial assault, a private named Carlos Madera, Shtick had managed to positively identify.

Upon explaining this, Lyons added, "We still have four missing in action. We're hoping they don't make any further attempts against Asir. Shtick here has agreed to tell us where they've been operating their headquarters, so we'll start there. We're also going to have our people running down some possible exit points for Asir and his men."

"All right," Boswich finally said, obviously over his initial anger. "What can I do to help?"

"We need you to take custody of the sarge here," Lyons replied, gesturing at Shtick.

"For the time being he's not under arrest, since technically he hasn't broken any laws," Blancanales said. "Call it protective custody and get him somewhere safe."

Lyons looked the Marine in the eye and said, "And you need to stay there, Shtick. I'm telling you straight. Step out of line and I will recommend you go straight to jail. Got it?"

"Yes, sir."

"All right, boys," Lyons told his friends. "Let's get restocked and contact base. We have some Marines to find."

CHAPTER THIRTEEN

Iraq

Nawaf stood in the Humvee, which Dakuwami now drove, and raised his fist to signal the convoy to a halt. McCarter went EVA and approached Nawaf's shadowy form, illuminated only by the blanket of stars far above. They had been traveling for more than four hours, waiting in shelter for the hottest part of the day to pass and setting out at nightfall for the final leg of their trip. Now the time on McCarter's watch closed on the midnight hour.

"What's up?"

"Shh!" Nawaf said. He cocked his head and then said, "Listen…"

McCarter's first thought was to deliver a stinging retort but then he thought better of it. There was already enough bad blood between them and McCarter didn't want any more trouble for the moment. They could always deal with that part of it when the timing was better, but acting like two stiff-legged dogs right now just wasn't the answer. The Phoenix Force leader had more critical things to consider, and Nawaf's behavior up to this point suggested he felt the same way as McCarter about it. Perhaps the bloke had decided after all to put aside their differences for now.

McCarter also positioned an ear in the direction of Nawaf and after a moment he heard it. Small-arms fire!

It didn't mean a whole hell of a lot since they couldn't be exactly sure from which direction it originated and the very sound of gunfire in Iraq meant even less. But they had to be getting close to Camp Shannon according to their maps and the weapons reports could only reinforce the thought they were getting close.

"I hear it now," McCarter said, and turned back toward his Humvee. "Let's go."

"We should not rush into this!" Nawaf called after him.

McCarter froze in his tracks and turned. "Are we going to digress here, chum?"

Nawaf dismounted his own vehicle and approached McCarter, causing the Briton's muscles to tense. He knew the guy wouldn't likely try anything here in front of Phoenix Force, but it didn't mean he'd blindly trust the Jordanian, either. To the team's way of thinking this guy was a murderer, in effect, and they weren't just going to hand him the keys to the castle when it came to their mission. The U.S. Marines at Camp Shannon were McCarter's top priority, and he didn't intend to let anybody stand in his way.

"I can see the look in your eyes, even in the dark," Nawaf said. "You do not trust me."

"You have to admit you haven't given me or my men much of a reason."

"I cannot expect you to understand why I did what I did, but I can assure you that my killing that man was completely justified."

"In whose eyes?" McCarter challenged. "Yours?"

"I don't wish to quibble with you over these matters any longer. The facts are what I know them to be, and the matter is closed in my mind. I will only say that if one of your men puts his hands on me again I will not hold back."

"No offense, bloke, but neither will they. So why aren't we going to help whoever's out there?"

"Because we don't know that the shooting is between your Marines and the al Qaeda terrorists. It could be anybody fighting out here."

"This close to Camp Shannon?" McCarter inquired with a disbelieving tone.

"You have evidence to the contrary?"

"I don't need evidence, pal. And even if I had some, it wouldn't make a bugger's difference since coming all of this way would be pointless if we don't investigate. It could be guerrillas fighting, or even drunk Iraqi army shooting off rounds in the sky. But whatever it is, we're going to check it out, and you can come along or stay put. Either way, I don't give a shit."

McCarter whirled and returned to his Humvee, ordering Encizo to put the thing in gear and get going and gesturing for Hawkins—who'd taken up the TC position in the Abrams—to follow. The Humvee and tank moved on and McCarter noted Dakuwami and Nawaf apparently didn't mean to follow them. That was fine with him; he didn't have any more time to baby-sit the bloody chumps. He'd sort of taken a shine to Dakuwami, who was more military-minded than his intelligence counterpart, but he knew the guy would stick by his own countryman before entertaining the notions of a bunch of foreigners. Still, McCarter thought he caught something from Dakuwami, some moderate expression of disdain at having to stay behind and miss out on the action. Yeah, he was apparently a real soldier at heart.

They proceeded another ten minutes before Manning tapped McCarter and pointed in the direction of a group of hills. They could see some tracers passing between the hillside and the low ground, and when they called Encizo's attention to it, the Cuban turned in that direction and increased speed. The Abrams managed to keep pace with them, not a surprise since the tank was actually capable of speeds exceeding sixty miles per hour. Their biggest problem was, as Hawkins had already advised, a shortage of fuel.

McCarter had decided to risk it, convinced that if they could get the Abrams to Camp Shannon the Marines there might just have some mechanics who could fix it. If they didn't have much in the way of armor, if any armor at all, McCarter figured it couldn't hurt to at least bring some show of force. When they got close to the battlefield he could tell his hunch had paid off. The rounds were being fired from machine gun emplacements, invisible to the naked eye other than the tracer rounds that blazed sporadically down the hillsides.

They approached on the side that appeared to be neutral and eventually came upon a high fence that not only looked as if was electrified but was topped with three strands of barbed wire angling inward. A second, triangle-tiered cyclone fence of concertina wire lay another ten yards beyond that to form the DMZ perimeter-style fencing so common to military camps and bases, not to mention secured areas such as nuclear storage facilities and federal training areas.

McCarter turned to Hawkins and jabbed his finger at the hillside. "Get that one-twenty-mike-mike going, mate!"

"We can't target shit, boss!" Hawkins shouted.

"Don't need to hit nothing, just send a message that we're bringing home the big guns!"

Hawkins tossed a casual salute and then ducked into the Abrams.

McCarter turned to Manning. "Let's see if we can raise anybody on the radio. You got a frequency for today?"

Manning nodded and set the field radio they had brought to the frequency of the day. He then reached into a satchel and retrieved the pass codes. RC Bravo hadn't been able to communicate long-range but the intelligence from Stony Man suggested they would likely have shortwave radio abilities and that as long as they didn't run out of juice they would be monitoring the daily frequency. So far, the tracer rounds hadn't come even close to this rear of the camp and McCarter had to wonder at their security. The Marines at Camp Shannon wouldn't have purposely left their rear side unguarded.

McCarter found his thoughts to be prophetic when without warning they had a half dozen Marines approaching from the leeward side of the fence before Manning could even raise anybody on the radio. McCarter immediately raised both hands to signal he wasn't in a fighting posture and shouted an identifying phrase across the fence to be heard over the continuous exchange of autofire between the hillside emplacements and the forward perimeter of Camp Shannon.

"Who are you?" one of the Marines demanded.

McCarter couldn't see his rank but he figured the guy was probably a squad or platoon sergeant. "U.S. Special Operations Group! We were sent by your friends at the 8th and I!"

That caused every Marine to visibly hesitate, and McCarter knew he'd just authenticated without even giving the password of the day. Not that that would've mattered since Manning had finally reached somebody on the radio in time to tell them they had encountered one of the Marine roving patrols, telling them to order the group to stand down to keep from getting their heads blown off. Manning looked at McCarter in surprise when he heard him say it

"Quick thinking, David," Encizo said, picking up on the phrase.

The "8th and I" was absolutely Marine Corps slang, a reference to the Marine barracks in Washington, D.C., at the corner of 8th and I streets. Practically every Marine knew the significance of that term and anybody with less than the level of McCarter's experience wouldn't have thought to use the term in circumstances such as these. That proved, at least to this group of tired-looking combat troops, that McCarter was definitely a friendly.

The apparent leader of the group turned to his comm. spec a moment later, listened with an inclined head and then nodded. The guy looked at McCarter and he could see the man was grinning from ear to ear. "Just got the word…you check out! Move along the perimeter here and proceed about fifty yards. We'll let you in through the rear gate."

McCarter nodded with understanding but just as he took his seat in the Humvee, all three of them nearly had their eardrums shattered by the massive report from the M-256 A-2 gun on the Abrams. The first shell landed square in the middle of the hillside and sent up a heavy, roiling red-orange ball of explosive fury. The turret turned a mild ten degrees, keeping its angle of deployment, and the gun sounded again with similar results on the hill a heartbeat later.

To nobody's surprise, the firing from the hill completely ceased and the return fire from the camp followed a minute later, blanketing the entire area in an eerie silence that caused gooseflesh on McCarter's neck. They had at last arrived at their objective, but he couldn't help but wonder just exactly what the hell they had walked into.

"YOU'VE WALKED STRAIGHT into hell, Brown," Captain Colin Pringle told David McCarter. "But I don't mind saying you're a sight for sore eyes."

"Damned straight," First Sergeant Brock added. "You boys military?"

McCarter smiled. "Why do you ask?"

Brock shrugged. "Just want to know if we should be saluting you or other way around. Not that I'm hung up on rank, you see, but the captain here runs a tight outfit."

"Well if you must know, we're a paramilitary operations unit attached to one of those organizations you don't read anything about," McCarter said. "Meaning there's not a lot I can tell you. What I can tell you is our orders come from straight from the Man himself."

"'The man'?" Pringle inquired. "You mean, General—?"

It was Gary Manning who shook his head and said, "He means the President."

That got their attention, and while Captain Pringle might have looked a bit confused, they couldn't mistake the glint of something between satisfaction and hard knowledge in Brock's eyes. Of course there would be—an old warhorse like Brock would know that such units existed. Unlike Pringle, who had been trained to believe special operations happened utilizing only sanctioned military units, Brock could understand why certain missions required a covert unit instead of a solution like Navy SEALs, Delta Force or even a USAF Combat Controller team.

"Well, if you're under orders from the White House, then can I assume you've brought good news?" Pringle asked. "My people tell me you have a tank."

McCarter's lips quirked at the suggestion. "I don't know if I'd call the bloody thing a tank, Captain, but I suppose it'll do in a pinch."

"Now, what the hell is that supposed to mean…sir?" Brock added the honorific at the last moment, not sure whether military courtesies were necessary.

McCarter didn't do anything to dissuade him—he'd need cooperation and if these two thought he outranked them then at least they would follow orders with fewer questions. "It means the thing's more of a derelict than much else. We confiscated it from a group of Sunni fighters we encountered on our way here."

"How did you get into the country undetected?"

"Afraid we'll have to save that story for another venue. And while we're under orders from the White House, we were advised to insert and assess the situation before deciding what action to take. If any. I guess Marine command got concerned when they lost communication with your unit more than two days ago, and they weren't able to send an air patrol to find out what had happened to you."

Pringle snapped his fingers. "Of course, the no-fly zone."

"Now it would seem you have your hands full with a group of terrorists," James said.

"Out there?" Brock asked, doing nothing to hide his surprise.

Encizo nodded. "Seems you're dealing with the AQI. They've been planning this operation for months, apparently, and they're dug in well on that high ground according to our intelligence."

"They also have mortars and ordnance," Brock added.

"And they captured a squad from one of our platoons we sent up there on recon," Pringle added.

"How long ago?" McCarter inquired.

It was Brock who answered. "Two hours, give or take."

Manning leaned forward and said for McCarter's ears only, "We can't leave them up there, David. They'll be good as dead by morning."

McCarter nodded. There was no way they were going to leave even one American Marine to suffer at the hands of fanatics. The U.S. Army Rangers had a policy of "leave no man behind," and Phoenix Force honored it to the letter. They wouldn't have left a member of Stony Man behind if there were even the remotest chance of pulling that man out alive, and they weren't about to sacrifice Marines without a fight.

"What were they doing up there?" Encizo asked.

"Disobeying orders, I shouldn't think," Pringle said. "They were supposed to do a soft recon and only a soft recon. I don't think they were discovered. If I know the guy leading them as well as I think I do, Gunnery Sergeant Covey, there's a pretty good chance he tried to abscond with some communications equipment. Or at least to try to get a message out."

"What's wrong with your communications?" Hawkins asked.

"That's something you'll have to ask Sudafi," Brock said, his voice dripping with sarcasm as he added, "He's the, um, expert."

"We were assisted into Iraq with the help of members from the Jordanian Intelligence Service and army," McCarter said. "They have a mission of their own, to locate an agent they had inserted into this area who goes by the code name of Jeddah. Have you seen or heard of him?"

Pringle nodded. "He's here, as well. Apparently, Mr. Sudafi knew of his presence but we did not. It was only when this man encountered the AQI that he came to tell us what we were up against. We'd just been ready to recall Covey and his squad when the trouble started. We'd been engaged with the enemy maybe…" He looked at Brock for confirmation "What, Top? Twenty minutes before they arrived?"

Brock nodded.

McCarter said, "Well, the first thing we need to do is to come up with an evacuation plan."

"We've looked at every contingency," Pringle said. "We're short on supplies and completely out of water. We also have a lot of injured that could die if we move them. I'm not willing to risk those kinds of lives."

"If you try to hole up here until the cavalry comes, sir, you're going to have a very long wait," Encizo replied easily.

"Maybe so, but I don't see any other options. As I've already explained, we've looked at this from every angle and we don't have alternatives. We're best to hold out until our unit sends help. Now that we have you boys here, I'm hoping you can get communications out and get us some goddamned support."

"Such as?" McCarter asked.

"Well, we know for a fact that detachment 1-Two-7 of the 2nd Tank Battalion was on its way to Exit Point Tango, and they've easily arrived by now. Maybe we can't get air support but I know the Iraqis haven't objected to ground unit movements. After all, we can hardly be expected to bug out of this dung hole without being able to move men and equipment. I know Major Compton was actually going to leave a part of his unit behind to meet up with a squad of supply folks so we had an extra water buffalo, and if he learns that his people were killed by the same terrorists we're now up against, he'll pull out all the stops to send us armor."

"Captain's right," Brock agreed. "And terrorists or not, they sure won't last long against a dozen U.S. Marine tanks."

"There's only one problem with that solution," McCarter said. "We've gotten weather reports that say there are sandstorms brewing up both west and north of this position. There's no way they could get support here from either location for at least twenty-four to thirty-six hours."

"And we sure as hell won't last that long here, sir," Brock told Pringle.

"If there are storms expected, what chance do we have by evacuating now?" the captain asked.

"I said they were north and west," McCarter replied. "That still gives you two other directions to go."

"You want me to pack up my ill-supplied company of over a hundred men, with very little water reserve, and simply strike out for who-knows-what on a whim?" Pringle shook his head. "No way, Brown. No way in hell am I going to do that. You may be under orders from the White House but my orders are to keep these men alive. There's no way I'm going to risk this unit—"

"No disrespect intended, Captain Pringle," McCarter snapped. "But if you don't consider evacuating this unit from Camp Shannon immediately, chances are better than good you'll be wiped out in the next twelve hours. In which case you won't have another opportunity."

"What are you saying?"

"What he's saying is that the AQI terrorists out there have only been toying with you the past couple days," Encizo replied. "Chances are better than good they've only been stalling, waiting for just the right opportunity to execute their coup de grâce."

"Is that right?" Pringle's expression soured and he put his hands on his hips. "Listen to me and listen close, Brown. I don't give a damn who sent you. We've been fighting this enemy for nearly two days and holding our own. Now I would appreciate any assistance you wish to offer, but don't pretend for a second that you actually know this situation better than we do."

Manning stepped up and put on his best diplomatic face, trying to not let anybody see him glance at McCarter's reddening ears and face out of the corner of his eye. "Captain, if I could make a suggestion?"

Pringle didn't take his eyes from McCarter as he nodded.

"Maybe we could discuss the plan to retrieve your missing squad and leave these other details to later."

"Yes…yes, of course," Pringle replied. "Gunnery Sergeant Covey and his men *should* be our priority."

"Agreed," Brock said, and everyone let the uncomfortable moment pass. Brock looked at McCarter and asked, "What exactly do you have in mind?"

CHAPTER FOURTEEN

Muam Khoury studied the pair of resolute Americans with a burning hatred in his gut. He stood with one foot propped on a chair, arm slung over his thigh, an unfiltered cigarette dangling from his fingers.

The foolish bunch had attempted to breach the camp, for what purpose he had not yet extracted from them, but Khoury had been thinking ahead and considered they might try something like that. Four of the Marines had been lost in the battle that ensued but two had been taken as prisoners. One of the survivors, who bore the rank of a gunnery sergeant, had suffered a wound to his right leg—shrapnel from a grenade. Khoury's personal doctor had insisted on treating the wound in the hope of fostering good will.

Khoury knew it wouldn't work, but he'd approved the treatment, including a dose of antibiotics to prevent infection. After all, they had prisoners now and that meant leads to additional intelligence, not to mention the pair would last longer under interrogation if they were as fit as possible. Of course it wouldn't matter after Khoury had obtained whatever information he thought they might possess, because once he'd used them up he would have them summarily shot.

"You were caught attempting to subvert the security of my camp," Khoury announced through a cloud of smoke. "Several of my men have been murdered."

"A lot more Marines have been murdered, asshole," the gunnery sergeant replied.

"And who are you?"

The man gave his name as "Covey" along with his rank and unit.

This caused Khoury to smile. "You seem to be under the misguided idea that you are a prisoner of war. While true in the strictest sense, I should warn you that we do not accord enemies of Allah the same respect due those pure to the faith. But of course, you probably already know this."

Khoury dropped his foot off the chair and began to pace in front of them, hands behind his back. "I suppose it won't do any good to threaten you with death or torture. While I'm not aware that you routinely undergo techniques to resist interrogation, I do believe you will resist for as long as you think it possible."

"If you're saying we aren't going to tell you shit," the other Marine interjected, "you'd be right."

Khoury stopped and looked at the man, a private by his rank insignia, but he only smiled in response. "Your attempts at intimidation are wasted, American. We're not interested in torturing you, we're interested in *killing* you. Killing as many of you as possible, in fact. And if all goes as planned you will all cease to exist before the sun sets tomorrow."

"Is that right?" Covey asked.

"It is," Khoury replied with a curt nod. "We've known for months about your plans to evacuate that camp. It is this information that allowed us to plan how and when we would strike."

"And what are you waiting for? You've been hammering at us for two days with mortars and small-arms fire.

If you really had some big, bad weapon I would think you'd have used it by now."

"You're in no position to ask such questions of me, Sergeant, and I am not inclined to give you any answers. The only thing that will result of this conflict is that we shall send a message to your government, to the entire world in fact, that you cannot come here and destroy our homes and kill our children without repercussions. And what I have in mind to do will make that message clear, of this much I assure you."

"Yeah, blah, blah," the private said. "How's this for a message. Go fuck yourself!"

Khoury's face flushed as he stepped forward and crushed the cherry of the cigarette into the bastard's cheek. This brought a scream and flurry of curses from the American, a thing that only served to satisfy Khoury. He could not express in words how much he hated the Westerners and he had made his point abundantly clear in that act. While some might have deemed it more of a temper tantrum than much else, Khoury needed to get this pair under control quickly. If they thought he would respond to their resistance with swift and direct action it might be enough to break their respective wills.

Khoury stepped back and considered the two Marines with a thoughtful expression. "I think there will be plenty of time to apply more advanced methods of pain later. Perhaps you will feel more accommodating once I've decided exactly what those methods will be. For now, you are prisoners of Al Qaeda of Iraq, and you will be treated as such."

Khoury whirled and left the tent. He would've preferred to secure them in a different location—like the shithouse—but he didn't have such facilities at his disposal. Now he had more pressing matters to attend to, such as preparing their final assault against the camp. He'd considered everything his commanders had told him before making his decision. They would execute their operation in three parts. While they poured a barrage of mortar and small arms onto the camp, a special unit would already have set out down the back side of their hillside encampment and struck out for a flanking maneuver on the camp's relatively unprotected rear guard. Once they were close enough, that unit would give a signal and the remaining forces would evacuate.

Then would come the most devastating blow, a plan masterminded by their contacts in the United States. Hamza Asir and his men had devised a way to deploy a dirty bomb utilizing depleted uranium. Combined with chemical compounds designed to create maximum dispersal, the radiation would extend for at least a mile in every direction from the blast point. Even if the majority of the Marines survived the blast, they would suffer radiation poisoning without even knowing it. When reinforcements arrived, the exposure would set up a chain reaction and chances were good that at least two to three hundred Marines would suffer long-term exposure to the deadly gamma radiation from the nuclear waste material.

The team that had volunteered to undertake this terrible task knew the risks were high, that such an operation might be suicide. Khoury had managed to acquire radiation suits for them, however, so they might stand some chance of survival if they were able to get in, deploy the weapon and get out. A remote decontamination station had been set up at another point roughly twenty kilometers from their current position. Assuming the team members would not be killed during the operation, they had plans to drive a secret route to the decon area.

When Khoury had first presented the plan to his masters in Afghanistan, they had balked at the idea as too costly and not spectacular enough. Khoury had managed to convince the majority through either strong insistence, or just plain threats and intimidation. The council had finally acquiesced and the plan had been put into motion.

Khoury had to give some credit to Hamza Asir, his second cousin by marriage. Asir had been brilliant from the youngest age, demonstrating a natural talent for the sciences. Al Qaeda had spent a considerable amount of money and resources to get Asir and his colleagues into the United States, and even more time insinuating their spies into the military system in Iraq one agonizing step after another.

As Khoury headed toward his private quarters, just a short walk from the command tent, one of his lieutenants approached. "What is it?"

Bin-Jazeer replied, "We just confirmed that the Americans do have armor support now, Muam, although we're still not sure of numbers. We know at least one tank is present, although it would seem to bear markings of an Iraqi army tank."

"One tank? One tank has you concerned?"

"We're not concerned as much about the armor as that it seemed to have arrived out of nowhere, sir. Our analysts seem to think that this unit has somehow managed to get communications to others, and that reinforcements will arrive before we have implemented our mission."

"And what would you have me do?"

The commander seemed to hesitate at first, but when Khoury demanded an answer, bin-Jazeer said, "It has been suggested by some of the more experienced officers that you should accelerate the plans and make our attack now."

"Now?" Khoury raised an eyebrow.

"Or…at least, very soon."

Khoury contemplated this. So some of the underlings in his command had seen fit to send the weakest of their brood to deliver this news? What cowards! They had been forced upon him by the council and now he had to deal with their incessant whining and back-biting. Most of them cared little for the fatwas or jihad in truth—they were more interested in furthering their own ambitions. They were more like politicians than warriors and fighters in that regard, and Khoury found them contemptible for it.

"You can tell the other commanders I will consider it," Khoury said.

"Do you think they will mount an attempt to rescue the prisoners, sir?"

Khoury scoffed at that. "Hardly! They will most likely consider them dead. I have assurances from my spy that the Americans are short on supplies and will soon be forced to either attempt an assault against our emplacement or run. In either case, it will prove to be their undoing. We have the high ground and the advantage, as such. Go back and tell *that* to your comrades, bin-Jazeer."

"Yes, sir."

Khoury stomped the remainder of the way to his tent and considered bin-Jazeer's wild claims. The Americans attempt a rescue? They wouldn't dare. And one tank could hardly signal reinforcements. In fact, Khoury knew there weren't reinforcements because he'd seen such a tank as bin-Jazeer described it. It was a relic and had been seized from the Iraqi army by guerrillas in the Sunni Awakening. Most of the equipment on board was nonfunctional, and a working gun was hardly a threat. Ammunition would also be limited, as there was none within the Marine camp. No, there would be no rescue of the prisoners. The American officer in charge of the camp simply could not afford to lose any more men—any such attempt would exact a terrible price.

A terrible price indeed.

DAVID MCCARTER STUDIED the layout of the AQI camp. At least that's what Jeddah claimed to have provided in the crudely drawn plans he presented to the Phoenix Force leader, although McCarter still had serious doubts. There was a lot, in fact, that nagged at the Briton as he considered their situation. They couldn't even be sure any of the Marines in Covey's squad were still alive, not to mention Pringle's report of Paul Hobb's disappearance. That factor rankled McCarter more than anything.

McCarter wondered if it weren't Hobb who was responsible for everything that had transpired over the past few days, although Jeddah had vehemently protested the very idea. Yet nobody could explain what had happened to the CIA agent, and if he wasn't dead, he sure as bloody hell didn't just walk out of there without somebody knowing about it. And then there was Abu Sudafi to worry about—McCarter didn't trust that cock-knocker one iota. The entire situation stunk to high heaven and McCarter was about ready to wash his hands of it. Their mission was to find out what had happened to the Marines and they had done that. Now he had only one other objective and that was to kick the AQI full in the teeth.

"Okay. Gather 'round here, gents, and I'll show you what I've cooked up," McCarter told his teammates.

When they were gathered, McCarter directed their attention to a point on the other side of the hills. "This ridge here is where that Jeddah bloke claims we're most likely to breach the camp undetected. He said there are only a few large tents that make up the center, but the outer areas all use natural terrain. Lots of rocks and sand, slippery and treacherous."

"Not to mention we're going in at night," James said.

"What about numbers?" Encizo asked.

"Nothing definitive but Pringle's people estimated perhaps as many as fifty, and Jeddah thinks possibly even more."

"Can we get any support from the armor?" Hawkins asked.

McCarter shook his head. "No way, makes too bloody damned much noise and we have to get inside real quiet-like. I'm hoping if there are any Marines to rescue—and mind you I'm keeping my hopes up about it—that we'll be able to come away with the goods and they won't even know we've been there."

"Don't you suppose you should mention the second part?" Manning said.

McCarter frowned and scratched the stubble on his chin. He hadn't even had a chance to shave yet. In fact, they'd been going since their arrival and every one of them was looking a bit haggard. Well, the AQI didn't give a damn if they were unkempt or not. They would shoot at anything that moved, and that was not likely an exaggeration. Because Covey and his men hadn't followed orders—at least Pringle was assuming they hadn't, as there would otherwise have been no reason for a firefight—the terrorists would now be expecting anything at any time.

"Their people are going to be on high alert," McCarter said. "Despite that fact, we need to gather any intelligence we can about their plans. Maps, documents, anything that might give us an edge in planning our next move or figuring out what the AQI's up to."

James sighed. "That's just dandy. We're already up

against long odds and now we have to look for a needle in a haystack."

"It's a secondary objective," McCarter said. "It doesn't take precedence over rescuing any POWs and I sure don't want you to risk your necks over it. Just keep it in mind to snatch and grab if you find anything of interest. Questions?"

Encizo said, "Just one. Have we had any luck contacting the outside world? Maybe get this company's division to send reinforcements?"

"Unfortunately not. Sandstorms are moving across the northern peak of this operation grid, and our long-distance radios won't extend beyond that. We also think that's what might have brought down the landlines."

"And what about satellite phones?"

"Transmissions are being jammed and they don't have any of the repeater equipment necessary to get a signal out."

"So basically we're incommunicado until the storm passes," James said.

"It never rains but it pours," Hawkins added.

"We'll have to deal with things one at a time," McCarter said. "Let's see if we can save the lives of a few Marines and then we'll reassess."

"So while we're doing this, what do the Marines have planned?" Encizo asked.

"I've finally managed to convince Captain Pringle to get ready to move his teams out one unit at a time. He was resistant at first, but I told him there was little sense in them continuing to sit here and act as cannon fodder for the terrorists. Not to mention we know they have something planned against this base."

"That's what doesn't make any sense to me," Manning said. "There's no logic in anything the AQI has done up to this point. If they were going to attack Camp Shannon with some spectacular goal in mind, why not just do it? Why all the firing of mortars and conventional ground assault tactics?"

"I've been asking myself the same bloody question, but I'm not closer to any answers. I wondered if maybe they were simply trying to wear them down first, but that didn't sound like their cup of tea. I then wondered if they're looking to drive the Marines out of here sooner, but they had to know if that happened our boys wouldn't leave behind anything of use."

"Maybe they're worried about hitting a vital asset inside the camp," Hawkins ventured.

"I considered that, too."

James lowered his voice even though they were the only ones in the area. "Sudafi?"

"It's possible, but I can't see, outside of the PSIDS, how he'd be of any value to them. And while I don't trust the guy, I trust Jeddah even less. And this whole thing with Hobb just disappearing into thin air and nobody sees anything... Well, something's rotten in Denmark, mates, and that's all there is to it."

"So there's nothing we can do about it now," Manning said.

"Right." McCarter lit a cigarette and said, "Let's perform one more equipment check and get ready to go."

The men nodded in unison at him and then moved off to do it. McCarter took a long drag off his smoke and then wiped at the sweat of his forehead. They only had a couple of hours until dawn and were running short on time. The heat of the desert was already setting in, and just a few hours earlier it had been as cold as ice—cold enough to see their breath and the rise of smoke from the muzzles of the weapons they'd used to exchange fire with the AQI terrorists.

McCarter had to admit his friends were right. Not one single thing made sense about this, and it bothered him that he couldn't put his finger on it. He wished they could have connected with the Farm before having to step into the situation, but it was what it was and there wouldn't be any changing it. He knew Able Team was working as hard as possible to get answers.

Sooner or later the communications pipeline would open.

McCarter took his own advice and set about the task of checking his weapons and other equipment. They had to travel fast and light, and they had a couple of klicks to cover by taking the path Jeddah had recommended. When he'd finished the equipment check, McCarter slung his assault rifle across his shoulder and snatched a towel from his rucksack.

He then stepped out of the tent and looked at each of his comrades who were prepped and loaded for bear. "Ready, gents?"

CHAPTER FIFTEEN

Charging straight up to the ridge in vehicles was obviously out of the question; Phoenix Force had to make their approach with speed and stealth.

The increasing warmth had suddenly dissipated with a rise in wind, bringing a significant drop in temperature. The conditions were close to miserable. The five warriors practically froze their asses off as dust devils swirled around their boots. The cloud cover had dispersed and parted to a view of a crisp, clear sky filled with stars. The climb up the near vertical ridge didn't make the going any easier, and the many stumbles and scraped knees or hands brought forth grunts, grumbles and an occasional muttered curse.

McCarter wondered if Jeddah hadn't chosen the most difficult approach possible for this assault. Climbing treacherous, rock-strewed hills in the dead of early morning wasn't exactly the greatest plan they'd ever cooked up, and was proving more difficult than McCarter would've thought possible. The Briton reminded himself he shouldn't let the aggravating circumstance of the present situation get to him too much. The Marine prisoners somewhere inside the AQI camp, if there were any left alive, were more likely having a much harder go of it than Phoenix Force.

Snap out of it, McCarter, he told himself. Keep your head on mission.

It took them nearly ninety minutes to climb the ridge in the dark, but they were eventually rewarded with reaching the top of the crest. While the AQI leader would most likely have sentries posted, the bugger probably wouldn't be expecting an approach from the ridge side in the dark. In fact, he probably wasn't expecting any sort of rescue attempt. McCarter had thought the success of their mission would hinge on the surprise element and that was damned good because—

Movement to his left caught his attention.

Encizo and James, already in counterflanking positions, trained their assault rifles in the direction of the noise. They saw a triple flash from a small, blue light— the prearranged signal they had set up with Dakuwami and Nawaf if they got separated. The chance anyone else would know that signal was slim, and it confirmed itself with Nawaf's shadowy form as he emerged from some large brush.

"What the hell are you doing here?" McCarter whispered. "And where's Uthman?"

"On his way back to my country," Nawaf replied. "I sent him with Sergeant Dakuwami."

"I thought you didn't want to have any part of this?" Hawkins inquired.

Nawaf turned and looked Hawkins in the eye, something hard and cold set in his expression. "I have already told you that I have a stake in this, as well. I've made an oath to help you, and in Jordan that means something when a man gives his word."

"We don't need any more of your bloody help," McCarter said.

"What you need is inconsequential to me, American. But if I abandon you, then I abandon my mission and my goal of finding Jeddah. I will not go back to my country empty-handed, not for you or anyone. I will do it on my own if I must, but I would rather work with men of skill and integrity."

McCarter wasn't sure if he wanted to plant a sloppy kiss on the Jordanian or strangle him bare-handed right there. He'd always sensed something in Nawaf, a different something that was rare in the majority of men in today's world. Nawaf was still somewhat of an enigma. Maybe his reasons for summarily executing one of the Muslim Sunni prisoners had been justified. Whatever the case, McCarter hesitated on the point they couldn't afford any more "cowboys" in this already volatile situation. It was this thought that prompted the Phoenix Force leader to gain a better understanding of what had caused him to distrust Jeddah from the start. The two men were so much alike.

"All right, but I'm doing it against my better judgment." McCarter jabbed a finger at Nawaf. "But don't you bloody well step out of line once, mate, or I swear on my mother's eyes you'll wind up with holes I could drive that tank through. You get me?"

"What do you have in mind?" Nawaf said.

McCarter nodded at Manning to explain the deal to the Jordanian while he withdrew a night-vision device from a belt pouch and engaged the sensitive photoelectronics. The NVD doubled as a scope designed for spotting, so McCarter was able to get a pretty decent view of the terrain and camp layout. It was damned near identical to Jeddah's description and McCarter had to admit that impressed him.

When he'd finished checking it out, he handed the NVD to Encizo, who would take a look and then pass it along the remaining line of men. Each of them would have a very specific angle of approach to the camp, carefully designed so each could provide the man next to him with an interlocking field of fire if it became necessary. Certainly there would be sentries as they got closer to the camp, but again McCarter figured they wouldn't expect the enemy to approach from that direction.

That was fine—just fine.

After the last man had viewed the scene, McCarter retrieved the sensitive NVD and placed it back in its shock-resistant pouch. He then gestured for Encizo to take point. The Cuban immediately got to work negotiating the treacherous decline of the hillside. At least if they were detected before getting inside the camp, Phoenix Force would have the high ground to their advantage.

Hawkins came next, then McCarter in the middle with Nawaf, followed by Manning and James on rear guard. They kept a dozen yards apart, stopping whenever a misplaced foot would dislodge a cluster of stones or get a leg entangled in a bit of high brush. They were nearly at the bottom, or at least Encizo was, when the mortar fire started.

Every one of the men hit the dirt but they were quickly surprised when they weren't suddenly surrounded by exploding shells. It was in that moment Phoenix Force and Nawaf realized the mortars weren't firing at them—they were directing their fire against Camp Shannon. McCarter didn't know whether to count his lucky stars or be on double alert, since they hadn't expected to encounter such a situation. Well it sure as hell didn't matter either way, because the noise of the mortars and subsequent small-arms fire would certainly cover their approach.

McCarter whistled at Encizo and encouraged him to continue forward.

Encizo tossed a high sign and climbed to his feet, pushing toward the camp perimeter now as fast as his legs would carry him. He'd gotten a mere ten or fifteen yards from their intended breaching point when the first resistance appeared in the form of two sentries. The men were sauntering along, smoking, neither paying that much attention to Encizo, who now stood no more than half the distance to the perimeter, about eight yards. Encizo raised his assault rifle, readying the weapon by selecting the 3-round selector switch.

The sentries noticed him at that point, whether by his movement or silhouette would never be known, and clawed for their AKSUs slung casually over their shoulders. Encizo had chosen an MP-7 A-1 with suppressor for this mission, which fired the H&K 4.6 mm cartridge. The jacket of the cartridge was specially designed with a pointed steel core and brass jacket in a bottlenecked casing. The ammo had been designed to be lighter and to provide effective penetration of body armor.

The MP-7 was highly effective in the hands of Rafael Encizo.

The most noisy part of it was the ratcheting mechanism, which couldn't be heard above the machine-gun fire and mortar rounds. The first man took a short burst to the gut that doubled him over and exposed the second to a couple rounds in the chest. A third punched through his neck and tore out the better part of it. Encizo moved aside and reached the perimeter of the camp, and the rear of one of the smaller tents, before the sentries' bodies finished hitting the ground.

Hawkins followed behind his friend, sweeping the muzzle of his M-16A in every direction. It didn't take long for him to find his own trouble in an eagle-eyed sentry that had apparently spotted him. What the sentry didn't see was that McCarter not far behind Hawkins, or Encizo, who had blended into the shadows of the tent.

The two opened on the sentry simultaneously, dropping him in a crossfire before Hawkins had time to bring his own weapon to bear.

It was a good thing since a fourth sentry emerged from the shadows of another tent and practically walked right into Hawkins's field of fire. The former Texan and Delta Force veteran dropped to one knee as he brought stock to shoulder and sighted. The sentry tried to claw for his pistol, realizing he couldn't reach his assault rifle in time, but Hawkins had him dead to rights. The short burst Hawkins fired drove the sentry backward and through the tent opening.

"Aw, bloody hell!" McCarter groaned. "That did it."

"So much for quiet, eh, boss?" James quipped.

The remaining members of the rescue team charged down the hill, realizing they no longer had the advantage of surprise. They would now have to split up and search the three tents, hoping to find the prisoners in one of them. Encizo had already apparently considered that idea because, without prompting, he lifted the loosened canvas at the rear of the largest tent and rolled under it. McCarter shook his head, hoping even as a fresh cluster of terrorists seemed to come out of the woodwork that Encizo hadn't rolled right into bigger trouble.

RAFAEL ENCIZO HAD LEARNED a hard lesson long ago: inaction could kill a soldier much faster than action. It's the motto he'd lived by before Phoenix Force and it had served him equally well after joining their ranks. So it was pure reflex that drove him to lift the canvas and roll under it.

The warrior came through the other side and rolled to his feet, hoping he wouldn't be faced with a hoard of armed AQI fanatics. Instead of getting the expected, however, Encizo realized he'd stumbled onto a gold mine. Not only was there a large map on a table in the center of the room, two men were slumped in their chairs with hands tied behind them. Only one man stood guard over them, and he was facing the opposite direction, peering through the tent opening and oblivious to Encizo's entrance.

Encizo edged over to the two prisoners and slipped a Cold Steel Tanto fighting knife from his belt. He cut their bonds and when one of them looked in his direction with surprise, Encizo placed a finger to his lips. He then moved toward the diverted guard and with a quick yank pulled him into the tent. Encizo took his enemy with an almost surgical technique to the artery near the man's right kidney. The terrorist fell unconscious in ten seconds with a well-placed knee to the carotid artery. He'd be dead within two minutes.

Encizo returned to table and asked the Marines, "You guys can walk?"

"I'm okay," the private said. "The gunney, here, he's got a leg wound."

"You Covey?" Encizo asked, looking in the other man's direction. When Covey nodded, Encizo told the private, "You help him get up. I'll be with you in just a moment."

Encizo absconded with the map and all the papers he could, shoving them into the cargo pockets of his fatigues. What other choice did he have? He had no bags to carry them and it wasn't as if he had time to fold each and every one of them carefully. And if he got caught with them, the worst that could happen to him would happen anyway so it didn't much matter.

"Who are you?" Covey asked. "You're not from our unit."

"I'm just like you, Sarge," Encizo replied. "Same dental plan, just a different boss."

"He's Special Ops, gunney," the private said. He looked at Encizo with a glimmer of excitement. "You're Special Ops aren't you, sir?"

"Save it for later, Lewis, huh?" Covey said.

Rafael Encizo stepped forward and grabbed Covey's other arm. "Okay, let's get out of here."

MCCARTER AND JAMES hit the ground just at the edge of the camp as the fresh arrival of terrorist forces brought their weapons to bear. They still had surprise on their side but it wasn't much, and particularly not against a force of this size. McCarter could only remember the conflicting stories on the actual numbers of AQI terrorists amassed therein. Either way, Phoenix Force had faced such odds before and were accustomed to close-quarter battles of this kind. The terrorists, while probably having undergone training, were far from crack troops in the conventional sense. This played right into Phoenix Force's wheelhouse.

McCarter opened up with FN-FAL battle rifle, battering the terrorist force with 7.62 mm rounds. The terrorists had made the mistake of defending in clustered pockets, which only made McCarter's job easier. Two terrorists were recipients of his first volley, the slugs tearing holes in tender flesh. A second burst caught a third terrorist in the skull but McCarter missed a fourth, who narrowly escaped a similar fate by ducking for cover behind a large boulder at the camp's edge.

James followed suit by taking out another trio of terrorists with a sustained burst from his own M-16 A-3. The weapon chattered with familiar song as the muzzle swept in a corkscrew pattern. The 5.56 mm NATO rounds pummeled the terrorists, producing shouts of shock and pain from their receivers. One terrorist collapsed with a shattered knee, taking two more slugs to the chest on the way down.

NAWAF AND MANNING SPLIT from McCarter and James, moving offline and attempting a flanking position on the terrorists their comrades had already engaged. Some of the terrorists were completely unaware of the force they were up against, a force that had proved it was to be reckoned with time and again.

Manning decided to explain this concept to the terrorists in a way he knew they understood by leveling his M-16 and sniping the targets with short, controlled bursts. Nawaf had brought his own weapon, a design of which Manning wasn't that familiar, but that looked like an Italian variant of the H&K MP-5. The weapon stuttered with a report similar to that of an AK-74S, and Nawaf proved quite adept with using it in that respect. Manning couldn't tell which terrorists had fallen under his own sights versus those of Nawaf's, not to mention the hell being delivered by McCarter and James.

Manning had knelt behind the cover of a boulder and realized from that position he had the high ground. He turned to advise Nawaf they should hold there, confident the remaining members of his team could pull off the search-and-rescue mission. Unfortunately, Nawaf had apparently figured they weren't positioned for optimal results and broke his own cover, a heavy shrub with thick branches. Manning started to shout at him but he was a moment too late. It almost looked as if he'd stepped directly into the fire of the enemies below until Manning saw the awkward turn the Jordanian made.

As pink flecks of blood sprayed from Nawaf's mouth,

a clear indicator of chest trauma, Manning turned to see a lone terrorist approaching their position from his right flank, the muzzle of his weapon winking with unceasing fury. Manning realized even as he whipped his own weapon into play that Nawaf had spotted the terrorist and had broken cover to give the terrorist another target of greater threat, thereby preventing Manning from being shot in the back. The Canadian delivered a sustained burst that diced a bloody pattern up the terrorist's belly into his chest, and the last two rounds blew the man's skull apart.

T. J. HAWKINS REALIZED that the mission parameters didn't call for them to neutralize the terrorist force in support of the Marines, but he'd be damned if he escaped the enemy camp without at least taking some of the fight out of the AQI terrorists. He also made as much of this clear when accidentally and literally bumping into Rafael Encizo and two Marine prisoners.

"We need to get this guy out of here and back to a medic," Encizo said.

"I understand your concern," Hawkins said. "And I know the head cheese isn't going to be too happy with me. But I can't in good conscience give up an opportunity to dish out to some of these terrorists what they've heaped on our brothers-in-arms."

Encizo sighed. "What did you have in mind?"

"Nothing too extravagant," Hawkins replied with a wide grin as he tapped the satchel at his side filled with 40 mm HE grenades. "I was thinking maybe we could heap some of these babies down on their heads."

"All right, but you can't go alone. You'll need someone to cover your ass while you're handing out presents." Encizo turned to the two Marines. "You guys go out right there where I came in. You'll find our friends on the other side. They'll get you to safety."

"Give 'em hell, men," Covey said. "And don't worry about us. We'll be fine."

Encizo handed Covey his pistol and Hawkins did the same for Lewis. Encizo then turned to Hawkins. "Okay, my friend. Let's go state our case."

The pair burst through the tent entrance and moved across the camp in crouched runs, watchful for any new resistance. The alarm that had been precipitated by Encizo's encounter with the sentries had not apparently caused a camp-wide alert. Most were focused on the assault against Camp Shannon, and those who weren't participating were apparently disposed otherwise. Whatever the case, the situation would most certainly take a turn for the worse once the offense realized they were now on defense.

It wasn't difficult for Encizo and Hawkins to locate the mortar crews. They were clustered in a string of large rocks and natural outcroppings on the leeward side of the camp, which provided a perfect line of sight on Camp Shannon below. They had most definitely planned ahead when considering how they would mount their offensive against the Marine unit there.

Hawkins found good cover of his own and loaded up his first grenade. He slammed it home in the M-203 launcher, flipped out the special rangefinder sight and estimated the distance to the farthest emplacement. The flash from the mortars made it easy to identify locales of all five mortar positions, and with good timing and skill Hawkins knew he could bring the fight to the terrorists.

The stock of the assault rifle kicked against his shoulder like a shotgun as the first 40 mm high-explosive grenade left the muzzle with a powdery flash. He couldn't see the trail of the grenade but the resulting explosion left no doubt to the effects. As a bonus, the grenade had obviously struck close enough to the mortar shell magazine because secondary explosions followed a heartbeat after the grenade landed.

Hawkins repeated the assault, firing on each mortar position in turn until he'd fired every shell available. As the explosions died out from the grenades and the small-arms firing from machine-gun emplacements ceased, a deathly silence fell across the battleground like the quiet of a cemetery. To Hawkins's and Encizo's surprise, no terrorists rushed to engage them and the pair grinned at each other, bumping fists before they turned to leave.

As if on cue, a burst of static resounded in their ears and then McCarter's voice came in strong. "Team leader to our wayward boys, and you know who you are—where away?"

Hawkins let out a mischievous chuckle even as Encizo keyed up his radio. "Just wrapping up some last-minute details."

"Get your bloody arses moving. We'll hook up at the alternate rendezvous point."

"Did our two packages find you, team leader?"

"They did and they're fine. Now get moving and no stopping at the pub on your way."

"Roger. Out here."

"How did he know we'd stop for some suds?" Hawkins asked.

Encizo only shook his head.

CHAPTER SIXTEEN

Stony Man Farm, Virginia

Brognola and Price sat with stony expressions in the Operations Center of the Annex as Carl Lyons gave his report through the overhead speakerphone. Able Team was on its way to deal with the remnants of the militia first, determined not to let any more former Marines get killed by either Asir's men or get caught trying to battle on two fronts. Able Team had made one thing clear—they weren't going to kill those American veterans unless absolutely no other choice was left them. To Lyons, Blancanales and Schwarz, it was no different than shooting at the cops. Whether the former Marines had a justifiable role as law enforcement or not wasn't the point given the circumstances.

"They've been doing what any of us would've done if the situations were reversed," Lyons said. "And I think they at least deserve some payback."

Brognola said, "I'm in complete agreement. So regarding Asir, you've definitely acquired the intelligence to prove he and some of his cronies were plotting to destroy Camp Shannon. That's no longer difficult for me to swallow. But using a dirty bomb to decimate an entire company of U.S. Marines is unthinkable!"

"Well, if you'd seen the way they left this Lieutenant Bobinawski when they burned their makeshift operations camp to the ground using incendiaries, you might not find it as difficult to believe," Lyons replied.

Brognola grunted before replying. "We can also assume they don't know that *we* know about their plans, which means they think we'll send reinforcements and that the radiation poisoning will spread to even more Marines and equipment."

"What troubles me most is, we didn't think Asir had the kind of ties and influence with al Qaeda it's now clear he does," Price said. She looked at Brognola with a pained expression and added, "Apparently we were wrong—a lot more lives may be lost because of that."

"Don't go there, Barb," Brognola said. "We're not going to do anybody much good if we beat ourselves up over something we can't control. We just can't get personal about it."

"Yeah…stop fretting and turn that frown upside down, young lady," Schwarz said. "I can promise you that we'll take it personally enough for everybody."

Blancanales added, "He's right, Barb. We're going to find Asir and shut him down permanently."

Price smiled thankfully even though the Able Team warriors couldn't see it.

"You have any ideas where to start looking for Asir and his people?" Brognola asked.

"We were hoping you could tell us," Lyons said. "We're open to any suggestions at this point."

"Well, given their location, it would make sense they'd try to escape over the border into Canada."

"Yeah, which is exactly why we think they won't go that route."

"You have other ideas?" Price asked.

"Well, we started by considering all major routes of transportation out of the area. It's not believable they'll try playing hide-and-seek, especially since Asir was savvy enough to realize we're on to his game. He'll assume there's a statewide manhunt for them."

"Which of course we can't do," Brognola said. Price looked at him in surprise and Brognola added, "Not yet. If we alert officials too soon before giving Able Team a chance to track down Asir, it will create a panic and the White House will have to field a barrage of questions they can't answer."

"I don't know how much longer we'll be able to keep it quiet, Hal," Price said. "There are already reports of the press sniffing around the rumors of a recent loss of contact with the Marines at Camp Shannon. Which is another subject we aren't going to be able to keep out of the headlines for long."

"I understand all that, but we have a mandate from the Oval Office to wrap this up and do it quickly. Otherwise we not only risk an international political nightmare with the newly elected leadership in Iraq, the chances are also good that innocent bystanders will start getting hurt or killed right here on our own turf."

While Barbara Price didn't necessarily agree with the position of not alerting law enforcement in Montana, she would never have confronted Brognola in front of the teams. Her job title was mission controller. That meant she had to worry about setting the parameters and objectives for the teams that would keep them alive, and simultaneously satisfy any and all political constraints Brognola faced from the White House.

"So what do you need from us that you think might help, Ironman?" she finally asked.

"We need Bear to start digging into any and all modes of public transportation out of the state. I'd focus on trains and flights at this point."

Price nodded. "Done. Anything else?"

"Gadgets here had a thought."

Schwarz's voice came on the overhead. "Greetings. I just wanted to point out that Ironman's correct in thinking Asir and his men will probably think we've got every cop in the state looking for them. That means they'll want to make a fast, clean break. It also means they probably had a contingency plan in place for getting out of here while covering their tracks. So when Bear's feeding all of his search parameters into Big Brother it will make sense to look for the convoluted."

"What do you mean by that?" Brognola asked.

"Well, I don't know exactly, but Asir doesn't strike me as an idiot by any stretch of the imagination. The technical institute he attended here doesn't let anybody but brainiacs into their ranks. Just tell Kurtzman to look for flights out of both Bozeman and Great Falls that involve multiple stops or plane changes, especially the latter."

"You think they might have a place in Great Falls?" Price asked.

"Makes sense," Schwarz said. "That's where the Regional Science Institute is that Asir attended, so I'm pretty certain he would've needed some sort of local pad. I don't believe he would have commuted every day—wouldn't make sense. These terrorists would have some sort of place to retreat to, or at least a place to hide until they could get out of Dodge."

"Okay, we'll look into that angle," Price said. "And I'll ask Bear to investigate the, um, convoluted, as you put it. What else?"

"That'll do for now," Lyons said. "We're about ready to make our assault on the militia."

"Be careful and good luck," Price said.

"Always."

PRICE YAWNED as she entered the Computer room. Her sleep cycles had been anything but fitful the past few days, and that thought only troubled her more. She wasn't usually quite as concerned for the majority of the missions. The field teams always came through so it had nothing to do with confidence. What had her worried this time was having to wage the political wars while simultaneously juggling two separate missions where a very goodly number of human lives hung in the balance.

Price poured a cup of coffee and dropped into an office chair on wheels. She rolled up alongside Kurtzman and gently laid a hand on his shoulder. They had a platonic relationship, but on some levels it was quite intimate. Long hours had forced them together and forged an unbreakable bond. In fact, Price realized that a man and a woman couldn't have probably shared a deeper friendship with one another than she did with Aaron Kurtzman— not without moving it into the romantic arena. That's not a place either of them desired to go, mostly because of that bond they shared and not in spite of it.

"You found something?" Price asked after taking a sip of coffee.

"I did," Kurtzman replied. "I started running some algorithms Akira and I developed on the fly. We programmed in the factors that you passed on from Able Team. Looks like our man Gadgets was pretty on the money."

"That's the first good news I've heard today," Price replied. "Lay it out for me."

"You don't want Hal to hear this, too?"

"I sent Hal up to bed at the farmhouse. He was dead on his feet. I tried to get him to actually go home but he didn't feel comfortable enough to leave with the situation as it currently stood."

"Well, at least you got him to take his rest," Kurtz-man said. "Nice job."

"Thanks. And speaking of which, what about you? I assume you're about due for a few winks."

"Actually, I slept a good eight hours after we finished completing all of that tactical data on potential AQI force capabilities in Iraq. I've only been up about two hours."

"Okay. So what did you learn about the traveling hab-its of one Hamza Asir?"

"Well, Bozeman is just about a bust, based on what Akira and I came up with."

"Why?"

Kurtzman shifted position in his wheelchair, raised his arms above his head and stretched before reply-ing. "There's no connection between Asir and any of his known associates with that area. While that might make it seem ideal on the surface, it's not practical for any number of good reasons. So Akira and I agreed to focus our efforts on Great Falls, not only because that's where the Regional Science Institute was but because of Asir's obvious ties."

"But surely you're not going off his attendance at the school alone," Price interjected.

"Not at all." Kurtzman leaned forward and tapped a key on the keyboard, which brought up a section of the Great Falls municipal map. "Great Falls has a population of approximately fifty-nine thousand residents, which makes it the third-largest city in Montana. Because of that fact, the flights in and out of Great Falls Interna-tional Airport are severely limited.

"We also know that Asir had associates already work-ing within the area before he ever arrived at the institute, so it wasn't a stretch to reach into the electronic files of the school to find those connections."

"I'm impressed," Price replied.

"Not as impressed as I was when I saw what thorough records are kept at the institute. Not only do they keep the educational and personal records, they also have special files they claim are designed only for providing better educational offerings to more closely align with student interests. Frankly, I don't think keeping records on the religious and political affiliations of students is exactly geared toward the provision of tailored academia."

"Not that you're complaining too hard about it, either, though. Huh?" Price winked at him.

Kurtzman shrugged. "I don't know if I agree with it completely, although I am happy it proved fortuitous for us. I'm just not sure why this school happens to be doing it, and I don't wonder if maybe this doesn't have something to do with the increased amount of monitoring that's being done in universities and other similar facilities across the country."

"You don't like the idea that the government seems to be spying on everybody these days."

"I don't suppose," Kurtzman said. "In fact, it might seem pretty hypocritical of me considering who I work for and what I do, and maybe it is. But I don't go out of my way to snoop into the personal lives of my fellow Americans. I only look for the bad guys and the patterns that allow us to pick up their trails."

"But sometimes it's difficult to do one without the other," Price said. "Aaron, if I've learned anything in all the years I spent in intelligence and counterintelligence with the SIGINT Group of the NSA, it's that using cover intelligence to prevent evil is much different than using it to perpetrate evil. That's where I draw the line."

"Well, far be it from me to get into any sort of insane philosophical discussions with you on the merits of electronic surveillance. And back to the main point, the results from our probe did indicate there's some reason for us to believe that Asir might not have had his own hidey-hole in Great Falls but one or more of his supposed associates would. In fact, there's a guy who went by the cover of Abd el Malek, a supposed refugee from Afghanistan sent here under a sanctuary program. Come to find out his real name is Abad ibn-Habad, and he's one mean SOB."

"Even I know that name," Price said. "He's wanted in at least three countries for acts of terrorism. How did he manage to slip into the United States?"

"That would be a question for Immigration and Customs Enforcement, I suppose. I pulled the cover file and apparently photos the CIA had of him were sketchy at best. Trying to map that up against a young guy who is clean-shaven and has slicked-back hair, well—" Kurtzman put the CIA photo up against the immigration and student ID photos as he spoke for Price's inspection "—it doesn't leave much room for comparison."

"Okay, so we have Hamza Asir and Abed ibn-Habad, both known terrorists with al Qaeda affiliations, and they're in the country to figure out how to build a dirty bomb. But what they don't expect is an eagle-eyed former Marine who…who…"

"Maybe recognized one of them?" Kurtzman offered.

Price nodded. "Exactly, that's good thinking! So Lieutenant Bobinawski recognizes one of them from when he served in Afghanistan. He then tries to report his findings but nobody will listen to him. And who would? There are so many veterans who have cracked up from long-term exposure to combat over there, they see a terrorist hiding behind every tree."

Kurtzman nodded. "It's pretty sad, but you're right. And nobody's especially going to believe a terrorist sect is operating right under the nose of authorities. Because that's Great Falls, Montana, and why would any terrorists be way out there in the middle of nowhere?"

"That's terrible," Price said, shaking her head. "We had a chance to nip this in the bud long ago and our own police ignored the warning from a decorated Marine officer."

"That's why they launched this whole militia deal," Kurtzman said. "Cops wouldn't listen to Bobinawski so he did the only other thing he knew he could. He turned to other Marines he'd served with, men he *knew* he could trust, and convinced them they had to do something because nobody else would."

"So we've hammered down a pretty good theory that happens to fit much of what Weissmuller, Kapczek and Shtick have already told Able Team. But how does that help us find where they might be hiding out?"

"Well, that's where ibn-Habad, aka Abd el Malek, comes in. He arrived in Great Falls exactly three months before Asir. According to the information he provided, ibn-Habad was living right in the heart of the city." Kurtzman's images of ibn-Habad were replaced by a satellite picture with defined markings.

"So if I zoom in to this spot, this shows the exact location of the address ibn-Habad gave. It's in the heart of the downtown area, a boarding house above a coffee shop. Nice and quiet neighborhood."

"And the last place in the world anyone might think to look for terrorists."

"Exactamundo, my dear."

"All right, let's get this information to Able Team."

CARL LYONS HAD FINISHED loading the special shells in the combat shotgun when Blancanales rolled up to the short, squat building on the fringes of Hancock city limits.

Dusk was about to surrender to the evening and already things appeared to be in full swing at the Viking Steakhouse. A blue neon sign that looked older than the long, low squat building beyond it boasted live entertainment and the best steaks in Bear County. None of the men of Able Team doubted it, either, when they noted the sheer number of cars in the parking lot. One couple in jeans and cowboy hats had even arrived twenty minutes earlier on horses, which they tied up in a special corral adjacent to the restaurant.

"Ah, to live that kind of life," Schwarz remarked.

This produced a chuckle from Blancanales. "I didn't know you had any secret aspirations to be a cowboy, amigo."

"Why not? Sleeping under the stars next to a campfire, with my trusty steed standing watch over me. Stomach filled with beans and fresh-killed antelope meat. And, ah yes, let's not forget maybe a pretty girl along for the ride."

"Yes, it does sound very nice."

"That's quite a fantasy, Gadgets," Lyons snapped. "But now you think maybe you want to get your mind back on the business at hand?"

"What's eating at you now, Ironman?"

"Maybe he didn't think of the pretty girl in his fantasy," Schwarz joked.

"Yes, you're probably correct. I figure Ironman's more of a damsel-in-distress kind of guy."

"Put a cork in it," Lyons snarled.

Neither Blancanales nor Schwarz believed their friend was really mad at them. They all got tired and punchy at times, to be sure, but this was just one of those dynamics in their relationship. Blancanales and Schwarz would start cutting up, Lyons would insinuate into the bantering as the stolid voice of reason, and his two compatriots would then team up on their leader to try to loosen him up. Carl Lyons didn't know how to relax during a mission, something that Blancanales had warned him time and again might have a negative impact on his longevity.

"What's the plan, boss?" Schwarz finally asked.

"There are too many people in there," Lyons said. "I'm not sure how we should approach this."

"According to Shtick," Blancanales replied, "their group leased out the basement portion of that restaurant."

Lyons nodded. "Yeah, the proprietors thought it was nothing more than unauthorized poker games among Marine buddies. Instead they turned the thing into a bunker of sorts where they could brief and strategize on how to take down Asir and his operations. Meanwhile, patrons upstairs come and go without anyone being the wiser."

"A pretty ingenious plan, really," Schwarz said, not without some admiration in his voice.

"Maybe so," Lyons said. "But we can't allow it to go on. For their sakes as well as the innocent bystanders who might get in the way if full-fledged war breaks out between them."

"Yeah, well, I for one wouldn't half mind stepping back and letting them do that."

"The local law enforcement already tried that," Blancanales said. "Remember?"

Schwarz nodded in agreement, although he hadn't really been serious in his remarks. He knew they couldn't allow the militia to continue to operate unsanctioned against Asir's group, like it or not.

"All right, so we just waltz right into the place and locate the entrance to the basement. Nobody's the wiser and we won't act on anything unless it becomes absolutely necessary. Agreed?"

The others nodded but then Blancanales gave a diabolical laugh. "Oh, boys. I just had a great idea."

CHAPTER SEVENTEEN

Eddie Ponzo had served as a lance corporal in Second Platoon, Rifle Company Charlie, USMC, doing most of his tour in Iraq. He'd served alongside many other great Marines as part of the forward observation detachment assigned to rid the Iraqi-Syrian border of arms smugglers. Many of the Marines who had served with Ponzo agreed on one thing: that detail had been their own private little hell. Nobody had really cared about what was going on there at the border, or so it seemed, and Ponzo only had respect for the Marines and officers who were actually sticking it out at Camp Shannon, doing the best they could with a very bad situation.

What most of the Marines assigned there would've told anyone who asked was that they didn't have much confidence in the Iraqi technical wizard or his magical Perimeter Scanning and Intrusion Detection System. In fact, more smuggling operations had been stopped by Marine tactics, foot and air patrols than the inventor of PSIDS could ever hope to achieve. While the technology was great for detecting and tracking the enemy—certainly an important facet of destroying one's enemies relied on their numbers and location—it didn't do squat helping them destroy the smugglers of weapons that killed American military and civilian personnel.

"What kills more Americans than anything else is the apathy of other Americans."

Those had been the last words Ponzo ever heard uttered by Lieutenant Joseph Bobinawski. Damn how he missed that guy—the best Marine officer it'd been his pleasure to serve under. Bobinawski had been one of those men who knew how to motivate Marines, not only due to his brilliance as a combatant and strategist but his strength and compassion. A soldier's soldier, a warrior's warrior. Yeah, a Marine officer of the highest caliber and deserving of an end other than the one he bore.

Bobinawski was dead along with Madera, and three more of their men had been arrested by law enforcement. The baton of command had been passed to Ponzo as the most experienced in the group. Most of the remaining Marines had done shortened tours in Afghanistan, and not one of them still active had served at Camp Shannon. How could Ponzo ask them to fight for something they couldn't understand?

But then that's where he recalled the LT's words and realized all of them understood. Every single one of these fucking fire-pissers understood exactly. They had kerosene for blood and they weren't about to take any shit off a few weak-minded terrorist wannabes. This Hamza Asir had another think coming if he thought he could go up against hardened combat Marine veterans and live to tell the story.

Nick Peña moved over to sit next to Ponzo. A private from a small, dusty town in New Mexico, Peña had served with a field artillery detachment on the Afghan-Pakistani border. While he'd never really engaged in front-line combat, he was still a tough and unusually mean son of a bitch, his body and mind steeled by years of working in the inhospitable climates of his father's desert ranch. As he sat, a little of the foam head of the beer he drank slopped over the rim of his glass.

Peña cursed, took a big gulp from the glass and then offered a drink to Ponzo. "Wet your whistle?"

Ponzo shook his head. "No—thanks, though. And how many does that make for you?"

"You my mother now?"

"No, I'm the head of this unit now," Ponzo snapped. "And after what we experienced today the last thing I need is a bunch of my Marines getting sloppy drunk on me."

Peña nodded slowly and then set the glass between his booted feet. They had transformed the basement into somewhat of a makeshift barracks. One end had a set of eight bunks, stacked in pairs along one wall, with a kitchenette at the other end. The fridge was well stocked with cold cuts, bread and other foodstuffs, and the pantry contained dried goods and hygiene sundries along with a number of shelves stacked with boxes of MREs.

They also had a stove, and they kept their beer refrigerated in coolers that they resupplied with ice and brews as needed.

"It's actually my first one," Peña said quietly. "And only one. My dad was a devoutly religious man. Catholic, actually. And one of the most temperate wetbacks I've ever known."

"How can you talk about your own father that way?"

Peña laughed. "What way? My father used to regularly refer to me and my brothers as his spics. I thought I was being nice."

"Real sensitive, man," Ponzo said. "I suppose that would be like my dad calling me a dago."

"I don't know about that," Peña said with a shrug as he lifted the glass of beer and took another long pull. "But then, my dad was never a very sensitive guy. Kind of strange living with a staunch, nondrinking Catholic with a strong vocabulary and a bigotry doughnut you could drive a five-ton through."

That made Ponzo erupt into laughter and he punched the man's shoulder. "Yeah. You're a real enigma."

"What the hell is an enigma?"

"Forget it."

Something turned serious in Peña's tone as he asked, "What are we going to do, Eddie? We damned near got our balls scorched off out there at that camp. Madera's dead and Shtick's probably on his way to Leavenworth by now. Or worse, Gitmo!"

"They don't put former Marines in Gitmo, Nick. That's for terrorists."

"Right about now I wouldn't be surprised if they weren't looking at us as terrorists."

"They know we're not terrorists."

"Eddie, you know we can't go around shooting at the cops or feds. I mean, it's one thing trying to kill this Asir cock. I'm just as ready and willing as the next Marine to take it to haji, but we can't be shooting at the cops. It'll turn into like some Ruby Ridge thing all over again, man."

"I have no intention of ordering you guys to shoot at cops." Ponzo's eyes roved over the rest of the Marines hiding away in their makeshift bunker. "In fact, I'll take the hide off any Marine that kills another American and especially the cops."

"So what happens if we get caught? We just surrender?"

"No. The idea is not to get caught."

But even as he heard the words come out of his own mouth, Eddie Ponzo knew there wasn't much conviction in them. Most of the remaining men in their group were either seated in pairs at the dining table or resting in their bunks. Seven men was all that remained of their team. They had lost nearly half their members to either Asir or law enforcement. Twelve Marines, veterans of countless hours of combat under some of the harshest conditions imaginable, and they couldn't even wage an effective war against terrorists on their own soil.

After the events that morning in the Montana wilderness, Ponzo had thought about potentially convincing the rest of the team they needed to either surrender or disband. He'd decided not to suggest it in the end, fearing he would look weak and pathetic. These weren't traits in a leader that inspired confidence and got Marines to act. Bravery and honor were the orders of the day—anything less would mean the sacrifice of their comrades had been in vain.

"So what are we going to do, Eddie?" Peña asked again.

"I have to think about it," Ponzo said. "Which I could do a lot better if you weren't flapping your gums. No offense."

"Fine, I can—"

They were interrupted by thudding on the stairs that led to the upstairs restaurant followed by the most raucous of sounds. It wasn't until the noises got closer that it was the sound of two men singing at the top of their lungs, and it was immediately evident from whatever else, the two men were extremely drunk. They appeared a moment later, one practically tumbling down the narrow steps and dragging the other along with him.

It had happened a couple of times before, although not for some time. After the first couple of incidents, Bobinawski had gone to talk with the restaurant owner and advised that they didn't need people coming downstairs and disturbing their "poker games." While some forms of gambling were legal in Montana, with low bets and mostly the video machines, there was nothing legal about holding private poker games within the basement of an establishment that served liquor, whether under the label of a private club or not. It was allowed in a private home but not a business property, so Bobinawski's insistence in privacy wouldn't have seemed strange, not to mention the proprietor had been paid a pretty penny for the monthly rent.

"What the hell—?" Peña began. "Aw, not again!"

"I'll handle this," Ponzo said. He climbed to his feet, dusted his khaki fatigue pants and then walked toward the two men who were just about at the landing. One was older than the other, obviously, with a slight paunch and gray-white hair. The other was somewhat smaller, muscular, with a mustache and dark brown hair. Neither of them appeared to be threatening—in fact they were giggling at Paunch Guy's near disastrous tumble down the rickety stairwell.

"Sorry, guys," Ponzo said. "But you're in the wrong place."

"Huh?" the shorter one said.

Ponzo's nose wrinkled at the smell of strong liquor on the guy, and a downward glance made it appear that the guy might have urinated in his jeans. The man was staggering under the less steady embrace of his partner, and Ponzo was having a difficult time telling which of the men was more bombed.

"Whad'ya say?" asked the older guy, slurring his words. He turned and looked at his friend. "Whu-whud he say?"

Short, Busy Mustache Guy disentangled his left arm he'd used to support his friend and stepped forward unsteadily, nearly falling into Ponzo. The Marine stepped back and grabbed the guy to steady him, at which point the man's eyes suddenly appeared to clear, and with a speed greater than Ponzo had ever seen executed by another human being, he suddenly had the hand he'd laid on the guy pinned to his side, elbow locked in a position that made it strangely impossible to move without getting his arm broken.

"Just take it easy," the man said into his ear, all hint of a slur gone. "We're not going to hurt you."

CARL LYONS WAITED impatiently for his friends to get into place.

He stood outside the back door, an overcoat concealing his automatic shotgun, and tried not to call attention to himself as he leaned against one of the posts that supported the overhang. In addition to the large dining area indoors, the Viking Steakhouse boasted a considerably large back patio with a stage where the live bands performed for those wishing to dine al fresco. It even had an area where patrons could grill their own steaks if they desired.

In other times or circumstances, Carl Lyons might have taken the time to enjoy eating in such a place but right now he had a job to do. The poor schmucks around him had no idea that they were probably seated directly over armed veterans who had just tried to go up against a band of murderous terrorists. That was the way he hoped to keep it. Blancanales's plan had sounded crazy when he'd first proposed it, but Lyons eventually acquiesced when his friends outvoted him two to one. He could've overridden them, true, but that's not really how Lyons operated. Only if he felt strongly enough did he not consider their suggestions. After all, they were Able Team—

team being the operative word—which meant that if they didn't operate as such they were much less ineffective.

"And besides," Blancanales had reasoned, "it's probably not the first time something like this would've happened to them. So they probably won't be on guard."

"Security by ignorance, huh?" Lyons had said. "Okay, won't hurt to try."

Now Lyons waited as his two friends executed their little ruse. It wouldn't take long for him to know if it was successful or not. They had no idea the numbers they were up against, not to mention how the other Marines would react when they perceived a potential threat on their home turf. All he could do at this point was to trust his friends to pull it off and await their signal. Only time would tell.

As soon as Schwarz had executed the hold on the first man they encountered, Blancanales broke into action and sent Lyons the signal. He then whirled and moved in the direction of a second guy, who struggled to rise, upsetting a beer glass that had been positioned between his booted feet. Blancanales was on him before the guy could raise a shout of warning, slapping a hand against the veteran Marine's mouth while simultaneously clamping a second one onto the back of his head.

Blancanales leveraged the younger man into a position where he could take him down quietly and quickly by using his hip as a pivot point. The guy hit the ground, not too hard but enough to knock the wind from him and exercise control. Blancanales planted a knee on the young man's chest, pinning him to the floor, and turned as he heard the shuffle on his six.

Two more men were rushing him and one was reaching for a pistol tucked into a military-style shoulder holster. Blancanales reached for his own pistol, a SIG P-236 chambered for .357 Magnum, and whipped it into play. The one Marine had barely cleared the weapon when Blancanales squeezed the trigger repeatedly, each round driving the young man back as the reports cracked in the eardrums of all—although they weren't as loud as they would normally have been if they were "live" rounds. Instead, the rubber bullets were propelled by powder-cap-style casings that delivered a punch with each shot, but a nonfatal one.

Lyons dropped onto the landing and rounded the corner in time to neutralize the second threat to Blancanales. He leveled his Mossberg and squeezed the trigger, delivering a wide beanbag round that smacked into the running man's shoulder. He followed with a second shot and then charged behind it and managed to land a Shotokan karate kick that deflected the younger man off course and directly into the wall just inches from where Blancanales had his quarry pinned.

The noise of the shooting had now awakened the three Marines bunked down toward the back of the massive basement. Before any of them could react, Lyons had them covered with the shotgun and advised them not to resist. He then turned to cast a quick glance at Blancanales, who tossed him a thumbs-up signal. Carl Lyons grinned, damned glad to have friends he could rely on when the stakes were high.

They were truly the best.

It DIDN'T TAKE LONG for Sheriff Boswich and his reserve deputies to arrive at the Viking Steakhouse and take the remaining militiamen into custody. As they were being filed into the vehicles for transport, one of the men—the first one they had encountered—stepped out of line and turned on Lyons. Just by the way he held his head, Lyons knew immediately he was dealing with the de facto leader of the group.

"You in charge of this thing?" he asked.

Lyons was a little surprised the young man had picked Lyons out so easily as the guy in charge. Well, maybe it was where one leader knew another. This guy was still pretty young but he had the glint of experienced hardships in his eyes—something Lyons knew well because he'd once had the same glint. But he was still a young man and while he deserved a measure of respect for serving his country, he wasn't a law unto himself and would have to answer for his part in the whole scheme.

Lyons had already proposed with the help of Stony Man that they would find a judicial venue that would go easy on all of the survivors in these series of events.

"I'm in charge," Lyons said. "At least of the operation to take down Hamza Asir."

"You are?" the young man retorted, visibly brightening upon hearing that bit of news. "Well, I'd shake your hand if mine weren't cuffed."

"Come on, buddy, let's go," one of the reserve state policemen said.

"Can you give us a minute?" Lyons asked the man. When the officer nodded and moved away, Lyons said to the Marine, "What do you want to tell me?"

"My name's Eddie Ponzo, Lance Corporal, USMC," he said. "I just wanted to say thank you for not killing me or my men."

"We're not in the business of killing our young men and women who served us honorably, Ponzo," Lyons said in a quiet voice. "Like you, I know exactly who the bad guys are."

Ponzo nodded. "I just wanted to say that we wouldn't

have shot you guys had we known you were cops. In fact…in fact, me and Peña were just talking about it before you showed up. I told him I'd hold any man who shot a cop responsible. I know it probably won't buy me much leniency, and that's not really what I'm looking for anyway. It would be nice if they could go easy on the other guys. In fact, they were just following orders and I take full responsibility for it."

Lyons laid a hand on the young man's shoulder. "You're right, it won't buy you any leniency, Ponzo. But I appreciate you telling me that. We're not cops but it's nice to know you'll operate with the honor of a U.S. Marine. But the fact is that it was your country that let all of you down. Doesn't make what you did right, but I understand it. And you guys have paid a terrible price—a couple of you paid the ultimate cost, in fact."

"Thanks, thanks for saying that."

"You're right. And one other thing. We're going to find Hamza Asir and every one of his men—I personally guarantee it."

"I'll hold you to that promise, sir," Ponzo said. "Even if I never see you again, I expect I'll hear about what happened."

"Probably not," Lyons said. "We don't exactly televise our kind of work."

"Oh." Ponzo chuckled. "Yeah, I guess you guys fly under the radar a lot."

Lyons winked. "That we do."

"Well, all the same, go find them and give them hell." As he turned to leave, he stopped and said, "And, sir?"

"Yeah."

"Semper fi."

Lyons nodded and couldn't help feeling a sense of pride. He'd never served in the armed forces and yet this

Marine had just spoken to him as only one Marine would speak to another. He'd tendered the Marine greeting normally reserved only for another who could understand the impact behind it: the shortened version of *semper fidelis:* always faithful. Then Ponzo turned and climbed into the back of the state police cruiser.

The phone on Lyons's belt signaled for attention. "Go."

"Ironman," Barbara Price said. "How did it go?"

"We're good and no losses or serious injuries. The plan worked."

"That's good news. I wish you could take a breather and celebrate, but we think we've located Hamza Asir in Great Falls. I'm afraid you're just about out of time."

Something hard hit Lyons's gut as he replied, "That's okay. So is Asir."

CHAPTER EIGHTEEN

Iraq

"You've failed miserably," Muam Khoury told the commanders ranged around the empty tabletop. "I don't know how you can possibly live with yourselves. In another time you would be required to take your own lives and I, as your leader, would have to take my own alongside of you."

"It...it was like fighting an invisible army, sir," bin-Jazeer protested.

"Silence!" Khoury's face reddened. "I don't want to hear excuses or reasons. And since when has six men—*six*—ever constituted an army? What I want is for you to get out there and lead what remains of our forces by example. Colonel Shabbat?"

The officer stepped forward. Most of his face was bandaged, dried blood appearing in splotches along the crude dressing. He'd received a blast of shrapnel and stone chips in the face while overseeing his mortar positions. The force had taken them utterly off guard, and while Khoury was angrier at himself for not giving a possible rescue attempt of the Marines more serious consideration, he despised himself even more for doubting Shabbat. The man was not a coward, after all, standing his post even in the face of death.

"Yes, Muam?" Shabbat said.

Khoury didn't bristle at the break in protocol—Shabbat deserved a wide margin of consideration after what he'd been through. "I can no longer trust anyone but you to carry out the thrust operation of our plan. Do you feel up to it?"

"It would be my pleasure," Shabbat said.

Khoury nodded with satisfaction—he hadn't expected any less. After what Shabbat had experienced at the hands of the Americans, it only stood to reason he'd be looking for some payback. He deserved to be the leader of the mission, in addition to the fact the remaining men around the table had proved they were ineffective leaders bordering on just plain incompetent. Khoury hadn't lied when he told Shabbat he couldn't trust any of them to complete their plans. The thrust of their offensive—the planting and detonation of the bomb and covering the remainder of their force—would be best left to Shabbat, anyway, since he had more experience than the others.

"Very good, then," Khoury replied. "Prepare your men to depart within the half hour."

Once Shabbat had left, Khoury delivered another tirade of ridicule and curses at his remaining commanders before dismissing the entourage and advising them to prepare for evacuation.

The Americans had infuriated Khoury to the point he wanted to *kill* something. He could practically taste the blood of the Western devils on his tongue, thirsted for it like some crazed animal on the red-hot blood scent of its prey. His reaction surprised him for he'd never considered himself a fanatic of any sort, religious zeal or otherwise. Khoury had always desired to achieve greatness through his military savvy, to demonstrate his cunning as a soldier for the al Qaeda cause and not as a Muslim extremist.

Of course, he realized, to measure his goals by the

standards of the conventional world wasn't a fair comparison. The council had trusted him with this operation and he'd not performed as well as he hoped. They could not fail—they would not fail. Khoury would not be diverted in his mission by incompetent officers any more than he would let any of the men take the blame for what he deemed his failing. That was what Khoury felt separated him from so many others of those in the jihad. They had lost their way, squabbling over the politics of the organization—an organization that had been left in some disarray after the death of Osama bin Laden—while there were still a devoted few on the front lines willing to fight to the death.

Khoury didn't seek glory. He sought respect and he'd learned the only way to command as much was to fight and, if necessary, die by example. But he wouldn't go down quietly and he wouldn't allow this ragtag band of U.S. Marines to outwit or outfight him. Not that he didn't know who it was that had really been responsible for raiding their encampment, for Khoury had been aware practically from the beginning the Americans would send the squad of special troubleshooters to find out what had happened.

Well, before their contacts in Baghdad decided to acquiesce to American demands to lift the no-fly zone over the area and give the cowardly dogs the advantage of blanket bombing them all into eternity, Khoury would accelerate the operation. They had to achieve their objectives because they were out of time. Even so, Khoury knew even as he looked absently at his watch that it wouldn't upset their timetable that much. The decontamination area and fortified bunker was ready and would provide a safe point of retreat until they could quietly slip out while all eyes were focused on the rescue efforts that would surely come to the Marine camp sooner or later. But until that time, Khoury was satisfied that they could still accomplish their primary objective.

Yes—destruction of the infidels was imminent.

"I WOULDN'T HAVE believed it if I didn't see it with my own eyes," Gary Manning told his teammates. "Nawaf comes across as a solid friend and ally, then as a murderous fanatic, and then turns around again and saves my life."

"Well, the bloke warned us he wasn't anything like us," McCarter replied. "After what we've witnessed, I'd have to agree with him. But time enough later to chat that up. Right now we have other things to consider."

Before McCarter could say more, Captain Pringle entered with First Sergeant Brock on his heels. The officer's attitude had change considerably toward Phoenix Force after they'd brought back two live Marines and all but decimated the terrorists' mortar capabilities. Pringle had gone about the task of evaluating the intelligence the strike team had retrieved and the look on his face now told the rest of them he was worried.

"We've evaluated the information you brought back," Pringle said. "There's no question the AQI is up to something, although we don't have much more than some maps of the area with a few drawings. They look like troop movement capabilities. All of the papers were written in Arabic, so we have Jeddah and Sudafi translating those now."

Brock looked at Pringle and said, "Sir, if you'll permit me to brief them on what we discussed?"

Pringle nodded and Brock said, "As near as we can tell, it looks like AQI is planning some kind of a strike against the southwest corner of the compound, which is relatively unprotected. I'm convinced, and the captain and other officers agree with me, that this strike force isn't designed to overrun our position."

"What do you think they're up to, First Sergeant?" Encizo inquired.

Brock scratched his chin "My guess is a force that small is intended to provide a diversionary action, perhaps a feint and perhaps something else. Either they'll use it to divert our attention and hit us with a larger force at some other point they think is weak, or they'll use it to cover a tactical retreat."

"Sounds like you're on to something," McCarter interjected. "But I'm not convinced they'd just retreat. And while they are terrorists, whoever's leading their operation doesn't strike me as an idiot. There's something very deliberate about everything they've done to this point. I have the sneaking suspicion they're up to more than just a diversionary tactic."

"But what?" Manning asked.

McCarter shook his head. "We can't know that until we flush them out by providing a diversion of our own. And I have an idea how to do that, now that we have some idea what we're up against. Captain Pringle, I would strongly suggest you reconsider a plan to evacuate your men."

Pringle sighed. "I think you're right. Even with the mortars out of commission, we don't stand a chance of defending this facility if an attack should come on multiple fronts. Your actions on that hill have convinced me of that much, Brown."

McCarter nodded, acknowledging the offhanded compliment. "It's the best decision available to you at this point. That's my professional opinion. But this is still your company and I won't try to undermine your authority."

"I appreciate that," Pringle said, "and what you did to save some of my men. But this isn't the time to be stubborn and that's what I've been up to this point. No more. Here forward we'll work together to help each other, and you can be assured we'll cooperate with your efforts. We're on your team, Brown, one hundred percent and without reservation. You have my word on that as a gentleman and Marine officer."

"And mine, too," Brock added with a curt nod.

McCarter grinned. "Fair enough. I assume you already had some sort of bug-out plan in the works, yes?"

"We do," Pringle said.

"Good enough," McCarter said. "If you want our help coordinating it, we can do that, but you'll need to be ready to leave on practically no notice."

Brock snorted. "We're Marines, Mr. Brown. We're quite used to that."

McCarter nodded and the two Marine leaders made their exit from the area of the makeshift operations center Brock had assigned to them.

"Okay, let's go over our game plan," McCarter told his team. "We have to assume that this could go either way. If the Marines are right about the small number of this strike force, the chances are good we can stop them before they ever reach our location. But we'll also need to be ready for a holding action in the event it's a feint. At this point, I'm open to suggestions."

"Well, with some odd eighty to ninety Marines, it's going to be quite a convoy rolling out of here," Hawkins said. "I'd suggest we let the tank provide an escort, at least. An Abrams is cut out for swift maneuvers among armored units—no point wasting it on this alleged strike force."

"All right, that's a good start," McCarter replied. He glanced at the other team members. "What else?"

James leaned over the map of the compound spread in front of them and said, "It concerns me that the AQI would bother to send a small strike team like this. If they planned a tactical retreat, which I highly doubt, they wouldn't bother to commit any resources. We know they were using personnel in Montana for *something*—that much we knew before we lost contact with the Farm and the storms set in."

"Which is another thing," Encizo said. "We got a mother of a storm that's going to hit this region within the next couple of hours. Personally, I don't want to be caught in it and I don't think the AQI does, either."

"Maybe they don't know about it," Hawkins suggested.

McCarter shook his head. "No. I can't buy that, mate. They know about it. You can be bloody well sure they know about it."

"I don't like this," James said. "There's something more to this attack. I think the best option is to meet them out there where we can control the situation. We let them get up on us it may be too late and the Marines won't be able to evacuate this place."

"Actually, I think we ought to let them get right up to the back door."

All eyes turned on Manning, accompanied by expressions of mild interest. It wasn't something they would've thought might come out of the big Canadian's mouth. Normally, Manning held a typically conservative view toward tactics, always anxious to keep one step ahead of the enemy by moving *out* of the line of the attack. Now it sounded as if he'd just delivered a contrary proposal.

"You're suggesting we wait until we see the whites of their eyes," Hawkins interjected.

"Why not?" Manning said. He splayed his hands and said, "Look, we know if this information is to be trusted that they're going to come. It's not so much a question of *if* as *when*. They probably think the Marines will stay and fight because they believe there's something here to fight for. This system that Sudafi built is apparently dead, so I doubt that's their objective."

"So what are you saying?" Encizo asked.

"I'm saying that if they want to come looking for a fight, we should give them one. Not only will it give Pringle and his men time to make distance from here, but it will give us the chance to take a few more of them with us."

"It does have style," James interjected with a big grin.

"All right," McCarter said. "You may have a point. But I'd suggest we set up a two-tiered defense. Part of the group goes out to meet the strike team, part holds back here in case there's another force out there waiting for us to abandon ship."

"Splitting up doesn't sound like a good idea," Encizo said.

"Under other circumstances I'd agree with you, mate. But in this case I don't see we have much choice."

"We could ask Pringle to leave some men behind," James ventured. "A small squad to help shore things up."

"I want the whole lot gone," McCarter said with a shake of his head. "We don't have time to be worried about stragglers if we have to beat a hasty retreat out of here."

McCarter put enough in his tone to intimate he'd made his decision and it didn't require any more discussion. His teammates broke up and headed for their assigned stations. Even as they left, McCarter heard the start of diesel engines just outside the building. Pringle and Brock weren't wasting any time, and McCarter could at least find a reason to be grateful for that much. He didn't like going into the situation without a plan but he also knew without hard intelligence or a way to contact Marine forces waiting at the rendezvous point—hell, they couldn't even contact the Farm at this point—Phoenix Force would have to adapt to the situation and improvise their response as it came. There simply wasn't any other option left to them.

One thing McCarter was sure of: they weren't bloody well going to let the AQI escape if he had anything to say about it. Their fight with the terrorists had become a matter of honor and there would be a reckoning on that account. The odds were against them, sure, but Phoenix Force had been in worse situations. McCarter wasn't about to let the enemy escape, to go on wreaking havoc on American servicemen as they tried to make their way out of this shithole. This time they'd take the fight to the terrorists, a decisive battle with only one possible outcome.

Victory.

JEDDAH'S FACE FLUSHED with anger when he heard of the murder of his friend Nawaf. He didn't blame the Americans—they hadn't known Nawaf or been able to predict he would strike out on his own. Jeddah hadn't suspected it, even, and he knew the man pretty well. They'd grown up together in the same neighborhood. They'd served together in the Jordanian army and eventually were selected to undergo training with the JIS.

Now Nawaf was dead and Jeddah intended to make sure the AQI paid for it.

"Mr. Brown, I wish to speak with you."

"What is it?" the fox-faced commando asked.

"It is about Nawaf," Jeddah replied. "I wish to join you in fighting his murderers."

Brown cocked his head and squinted with a skeptical expression.

"I sensed immediately upon meeting you that you don't trust me, Brown. But I decided not to hold this against you or the other men of your team. Our countries had mostly shared a mutual alliance based on trust, even if it has not always materialized in the way either party might have expected. But I hope that Nawaf's sacrifice is enough to convince you of our resolve—and our faithfulness."

"I understand, mate," Brown replied. "But you also have to understand that I simply can't risk putting you on the team with my guys. We know each other well enough to be effective. We can predict each other's strengths and weaknesses. We're comfortable with our protocols and methods of operating and fighting. You, on the other hand, don't know anything about that, and all the trust in the world won't change that fact."

"Then I will do what I must on my own," Jeddah said, turning from the man with a new determination.

"Wait...please."

Jeddah stopped and turned to face Brown. "You Americans change your mind quickly."

"Look, I can understand you're looking for revenge."

"Not revenge, Brown. Justice."

"Fine, then you're looking for justice. But I just can't have another loose maverick. If I let you go off by yourself, that's even more dangerous than letting you join us." Brown smiled. "Beside the fact, you seem to have a bloody good inkling of these terrorists and how they operate. That could be a big advantage to us in the end. And it wouldn't make sense for me to not consider using that as additional leverage."

"It is agreed, then," Jeddah said.

"But know this. You'll take your orders from me and only me—don't try to get cute and do your own thing."

Jeddah inclined his head without taking his eyes off the American. "Consider me your servant."

"Okay. So any theories on what the AQI might have planned by sending a strike team to hit the rear end of this camp?"

Jeddah considered the question for a time, stroking his beard—he'd let it grow out in addition to dressing in the traditional garb of one of Iraq's rare nomadic citizens. While there weren't many left in the country, the Bedouin lifestyle still had some presence in the country, mostly the nomads keeping to the desert as their homes and surviving through either trading or horse and camel herding. Jeddah had managed to fit right in with these tribes by living with one for a couple of months, learning their ways and dialect to make his cover more convincing. At the end he wondered if his own mother would've recognized him, so well had he fit into the role of a desert wanderer.

"It is possible they are coming to steal the special equipment that is here."

"That's what we thought, but none of it works," Brown replied. "In fact, we think they may have been the ones to destroy it when they destroyed the other communications equipment."

"This is possible," Jeddah said. "It's also possible they have other plans, perhaps plans to destroy this camp and all of your Marines in it."

"How? From what we saw of their positions on that hill, these two forces are pretty evenly matched."

"There is something else, but I wonder if it is wise to make it known to you at this time."

"Now isn't the time to hold out on me, bloke. You got something you think is important, you best speak up."

Jeddah thought about it a moment and then tendered a curt nod. "They are only rumors I heard while I was moving about the region. There are rumors of a stronghold built close to here."

"How close?"

"Perhaps thirty kilometers in that direction," Jeddah replied as he pointed south.

Brown appeared to consider this new information as he dabbed his face. "Maybe they do plan to retreat. Maybe we hurt them enough they don't think they can carry through with their plans to overrun this camp. So instead they send a small team to keep the Marines busy while the bulk of their force makes its escape."

"This would be a suicide mission for the group they send here," Jeddah reminded him. "I would not call that typical for terrorists of this kind. In addition, the rumors of this stronghold are that it contains much unusual equipment."

"Such as?"

"Portable tents equipped with plastic piping, probably designed for the transportation of some kind of water system. Body suits that are not camouflaged but white, and trucks moving into and out of the area that are painted with strange symbols but look as if they are only carrying water."

"That sounds an awful lot like a bloody decontamination unit," Brown said.

"But if it is, what would they need this for unless

they were planning to use some sort of biological agent against the Marines?"

"That's a damned good question. I think maybe there *is* something more to this strike force than we originally thought."

"Perhaps you should reconsider your plans," Jeddah said.

"Yeah. I think you're right."

CHAPTER NINETEEN

Colonel Shabbat sat proudly within the personal vehicle that Muam Khoury had given to him. He knew this could be his last mission for the cause of Islam, but that didn't bother him. He wasn't the weakling as he knew so many whispered among the highest seats within the council. He'd fought for the fatwas since Osama bin Laden had first delivered them, handwritten edicts that would win a place for every fighter in the paradise of Allah.

Not everyone had been as dedicated to the jihad as his family, but that didn't trouble Shabbat. This was his opportunity to make history and strike a crippling blow against his enemies. The Americans had not only killed many of his men but they had also attempted to shame him, and Shabbat knew this was his chance to redeem his name and the name of his family. He did not want to have to stand before Allah and account for why he'd failed because of his cowardice, condemned to a life of agony and misery among his enemies.

Aboard his command vehicle they had placed the Radiological Dispersion Device. While Shabbat didn't understand the entire workings, he was educated enough to know that the chief contaminant within the bomb was Cesium-137, a radioactive isotope formed from the fission of nuclear material. The information on how to construct the RDD to provide the maximum amount of exposure effect had come from their contacts in America, particularly

Hamza Asir. Shabbat had never met Asir, although he'd heard of the young man's exploits. Asir was reputed to possess a substantially high IQ—some had even labeled him a prodigy although Shabbat had his own doubts—with a natural aptitude for the hard sciences.

In fact, it had been some of al Qaeda's other scientists that had first come up with the idea for constructing multiple devices of this type but using Cesium-134. Asir had disagreed with all of them, insisting that the 137 variant of the isotope had much greater potential for widespread damage and environmental contamination. Additionally, Casium-137 had a half life of more than two decades, making it ideal for the long-term penetration of food and equipment, as well as humans. The explosives packed into this particular RDD were also lined with radiated salt crystals to enable faster absorption into the bloodstream. While only those in the immediate vicinity of the explosion would suffer the most toxic exposures, the longer-term exposure would create a nightmare for rescue and military personnel.

Shabbat could remember his gut wincing internally as the effects of the bomb were described to him. Many within the core blast zone would be killed instantly, while those on the periphery would be exposed to the crystalline salt compounds. Still more, those inside the camp who were not injured, would of course begin operations to extract the wounded and make an accounting for the dead, as well as search for survivors. All the time they would not realize they were being exposed to the natural decaying process of the Casium-137 since the explosion had been designed to look like a conventional heavy explosive.

Shabbat glanced backward at the delivery device, a modified portable rocket launcher encased in lead aprons.

The actual shell was the size of a standard 158 mm tank round, but contained enough ammonium nitrate and PETN—Pentaerythritol Tetranitrate—mixture to create a blast zone more than twice that of a conventional HE shell. The Western dogs would not only be surprised by the terrible destruction, but they also wouldn't know they were being exposed to deadly radiation in the aftermath.

Of course, Shabbat knew they would have to arrive within firing range of their target first, and time their attack so that the remainder of their forces could escape. Because of the additional capabilities in the modified bomb, the engineers had been forced to remove a large amount of the propellant normally available to deliver the shell a great distance. This reduced the effective range considerably from which Shabbat's team would be able to fire the device, creating a natural hazard and potential for exposure.

Shabbat knew this posed a risk to the mission but he also realized there wasn't much they could do about it. For their plan to have the devastating effects they hoped, sacrifices had to be made on all fronts. Of course, once they had successfully delivered the weapon they could make good time to the retreat stronghold and undergo decontamination. Asir had been confident in his assessment that the chances of long-term ill effects from their exposure to the radiation were minimal and the probability of long-term survival high.

This had been good news to Shabbat—not because he cared for his own life but because it would allow him to continue fighting the jihad.

"We are approaching the American camp," Shabbat's driver announced.

"Very good," he replied. "We will hold position at this point and let our probe proceed on foot."

Once they had verified the target was still viable, the reconnaissance team would send back a signal to advise Shabbat they could proceed on mission. It was estimated the entire operation—including proceeding to the firing coordinates, preparation and launch, and retrieval of their team—would take no more than ten minutes. The odds were in their favor, not only because the Marines wouldn't be expecting the attack but also simply because Allah would show favor on his warriors. Yes, this would be a day the Americans would not soon forget. A day when Islam would emerge triumphant against its enemies!

DAVID MCCARTER HAD TO rethink his plan at the urging of Jeddah, and he damned well knew it depended largely on ensuring the terrorists didn't come even remotely close to the perimeter of Camp Shannon.

Pringle's men were in convoy and ready to proceed, the captain having already sent Brock out ahead with first platoon to ensure they didn't run into any nasty surprises. They had managed to supply themselves for two full days, after which they could implement survival rations for another two. By that time the storm would've passed and they would be well clear of any more encounters with the AQI.

While McCarter had argued the Marines should move away from the storm—which would take them farther from their rendezvous point—Pringle had wisely countered by pointing out they couldn't outrun the goddamned thing so why would they risk it. In his opinion, it was better to move directly toward the storm, something he'd called "the lesser of two evils" because the enemy damned sure wouldn't think to rush after them. Brock and the other officers had agreed with Pringle's assessment, proving once more just how bright and innovative Rifle Company Bravo's CO really was.

With the logistics hammered out, McCarter knew the time had come for them to move out. The desert winds were cold despite the fact dawn was less than an hour away. The first shimmer of another sunrise in Iraq peeked over the distant hills and the new cloud cover that had moved in—another sign of the imminent storm that would probably hit them by midday—proved to be a blessing by obscuring the formerly clear and star-dotted sky. McCarter hoped they could locate their quarry before they no longer had the night to work in their favor.

Small gusts of wind swirled at their feet, kicking up more of the dust devils they'd first encountered when setting out against the AQI hillside encampment. Once more the AQI had it in mind they were the aggressors, but it was Phoenix Force who had truly taken the offensive. They were hunting their enemies and ready to face them without fear. They would pin them down, corner them like trapped rats and they would strike like a cat pouncing on the mouse.

Once they had realized the terrorists might use NBC— Nuclear Biological Chemical—weapons, they knew keeping part of the team back in a holding action wouldn't be possible. They would have to come at their enemy with the swift and merciless resolve of fighters on a berserker mission to destroy every shred of the AQI threat in their path. No corner would be given to the murderous terrorists who had rained misery and destruction on American Marines for two days straight. Phoenix Force planned to dish out more than enough of what Rifle Company Bravo had taken.

While on the surface it might have seemed like the Marines were simply running scared, McCarter didn't see it that way. Those brave souls had held off their enemies for nearly seventy-two hours with minimal supplies and ammunition. It had been a stroke of luck that Phoenix Force arrived when they had to carry out the special operations none of the Marines at Camp Shannon were really trained for. They were a fighting force that knew how to wage war on a grander scale, maybe, but the men of Phoenix Force were specialized in surgical strikes designed to effect the maximum amount of damage and send the enemy reeling.

Each unit was capable in its own right but content to leave others to their own expertise.

"They're as fine a bunch of Marines as I've ever commanded," Pringle told McCarter before Phoenix Force set out. "I'm proud of them. And I'm grateful to you and your men, Brown. You'll always be a part of Rifle Company Bravo. I'll make sure everybody damned knows it in Washington when we get back."

"Probably not something you'd want to call the press about, governor," McCarter had said with a smart salute.

They were traveling along a natural patch of flat terrain running parallel to an arroyo cut by the flash floods of the previous monsoon season. The arroyo, according to the Marines' topographical maps, would eventually bifurcate with one leading into another channel of arroyos and the other terminating at a wash. This seemed like the perfect route for the AQI to attempt to use, so Phoenix Force had opted to string their patrol along that narrow path in the hope of intercepting the enemy far out.

The sound of movement—a crunch of boots on gravelly sand and clink of sloppily secured rifles slings—reached the acute hearing of Rafael Encizo first. The Cuban commando's senses went on high alert and he immediately signaled his teammates that the enemy was on the fast approach. By pointing at his eyes and then splaying his palm with four fingers held up, he signaled McCarter he believed at least four men on foot could be expected. A shake of his fist clinched that number as an estimate.

Phoenix Force moved into position.

Manning and James went prone where they were while McCarter and Hawkins circled out to the left to provide a flanking position. Jeddah moved to the right and took up a crossfire position angled forty-five degrees from where Manning and James had dropped, the Jordanian agent concealed by the slope of the arroyo. Encizo managed to find cover behind a boulder, a fortuitous find since he'd been on point and would be the first the enemy would have spotted had he not been able to secure concealment before the enemy patrol made contact.

Encizo got his weapon in position and held his breath as the shadowy forms became discernible. Phoenix Force wouldn't get a second chance, and it occurred to Encizo in that moment this was a scouting party with the main force behind it. Probably they were sitting in the wash, waiting for some kind of signal. Encizo reached back to his memory of the map and estimated the wash at better than a mile away, well within hearing range of any weapons reports. That simply wouldn't do. They had to be able to take these guys quickly and quietly. They were too close now for Encizo to risk using the throat transmitter of their radios, and since McCarter may not have realized this wasn't the entire enemy strike team, it would be up to Encizo to take the scouting party out before his teammates opened fire.

Encizo moved the selector switch on his MP-5 SD-6 to single shot, aimed at the first of the four targets and squeezed the trigger. The ratchet of the slide made more

noise than the actual report. The first 9 mm round left
the barrel at a velocity of just under 300 meters per second. It struck the target dead-on and drove him into the
man behind him. Encizo grinned at the lucky encounter,
fortunate the enemy squad had made a tactical blunder.

It would cost them, Encizo thought as he aimed and
fired at man number two. This one's head cracked open
as the hardball ammo did its grisly work. The other two
still hadn't realized they were under attack, bent over the
first one Encizo had dropped. They realized a moment
too late they were under fire but by this time Encizo had
broken cover and charged their position with his weapon
now on 3 round-burst mode.

Encizo cut the remaining pair to ribbons with several
sweeps of the muzzle. The flurry of bullets drilled holes
through them and in some cases left chunky exit wounds.
Encizo continued to advance until on top of them and
delivered a few more rounds into each of them to ensure
they were dead. It wouldn't do much good to assume he'd
killed them all only to have a survivor pop up and put a
few rounds through his back. Encizo's entire assault had
taken less than ten seconds.

"What the bloody hell is going on?" McCarter demanded over the radio.

"Scratch four terrorists," Encizo replied. "I'll explain
when we've rallied."

"Roger." McCarter didn't sound happy.

When they'd formed up on him and taken cover near
the boulder Encizo had used for cover, the Cuban said,
"Sorry, I didn't have any choice but to bring them down
on my own."

McCarter looked confused. "What happened?"

"It was only a four-man squad," Encizo replied. "If
I had let you guys just blast away at them like a turkey

shoot we would've alerted the rest of the team, which I'm guessing is probably hiding out in that wash."

"They sent those jive-asses ahead as a scouting party," James concluded.

"Bingo."

"All right, you did a good thing," McCarter said. "Probably saved the mission, too. But next time at least try to let us know what's going on before you just charge into the fray, mate. We didn't know what was going on and had about given up on you."

"I know," Encizo said. "But they were too close and I couldn't risk it."

Manning shook his head. "Do or die, brother."

"Don't you know it," the Cuban firebrand replied.

"Well, considering his quick thinking," McCarter told his teammates, "I'm of the mind we might still pull this off. But we're going to have to move fast because that wash is still some distance from here."

"It is at least another two kilometers," Jeddah offered. "We can make it within the next twenty minutes if we leave now."

"A mile or better in full gear and over terrain like this?" Hawkins said. "You don't ask for much."

McCarter grinned. "Who's up for a little Sunday stroll, mates?"

FOR A LESSER GROUP of men, the near 1.5 mile run through the dark, unforgiving Iraqi countryside would have been tough going. And while it wasn't easy, the observer would've sworn that Phoenix Force made it look that way. Even Jeddah had trouble keeping up with the five battle-hardened warriors as they negotiated the run with what seemed like a practiced ease—although they paid a small price. Sweat soaked the creases of their fatigues and their feet inside the combat boots felt like they were on fire. All of the men were gulping for air.

They wanted to take a rest, but McCarter reminded them that there wasn't time for such luxuries. "Somewhere ahead the enemy lies in wait for us. I didn't run my arse off just so I could let them win."

They did manage to get some rest as McCarter and Jeddah moved ahead to the rim of the wash and began to search the dry basin with their NVDs. McCarter had the one that he'd used when they'd assaulted the AQI camp and Jeddah had managed to abscond with a pair from a supply sergeant at Camp Shannon whom he had befriended. If nothing else, the Jordanian wasn't anything like Nawaf—all business, sure, but a lot different in a good many other respects. Somewhere along the way, Jeddah had taken time to familiarize himself with some of the social graces necessary for working with foreigners.

"You see anything?" McCarter asked after several minutes of a fruitless search.

"No, I— Wait!" Jeddah had swept past some area but then stopped and come back. "It is strange."

"What? What's strange?"

"I thought I saw a flash of light but then there is nothing there. Or is there, yes...I see it now. It is a smoke. One of the terrorist sentries is smoking."

"Can you be sure it's actually the terrorists?" McCarter asked. "I need to be sure of the target, chum. We're only going to get one shot at this."

Jeddah lowered the NVD and looked McCarter in the eye. "Believe me when I say it is them. No experienced man who has spent any time fighting in this country would openly smoke like that. It is too easy to be spotted just as I have spotted them now. These terrorists have shown us time and again that they are not experienced desert fighters. Their actions betray them as our enemies—of this I'm certain."

"Good enough for me," McCarter said, visibly impressed. "Let's go round up the rest of the team."

They returned to find the others double-checking their weapons or straightening up equipment that had shifted during their little jaunt. McCarter's chest swelled with pride—bloody pros to the very end, this lot. He briefed them on what they'd seen and then hunkered down to discuss strategy.

"We could go in close, try to take them out surgically," McCarter said. "The biggest problem I see with that is if they are packing some sort of NBC materials, we risk becoming exposed to it."

"And we're not packing anything that could protect us," Manning pointed out.

"Yeah, I don't think I'm real keen on the idea of coming out of this deal with glowing skin and gills, or whatever crazy thing might happen to us. We get a whiff of whatever nasty they're toting along and it's curtains for not only us but the rest of our mission."

"And let's not forget that even if we pull this off, we're still not out of the woods. We have to get back to Camp Shannon and retrieve our transportation so we can chase down the rest of the terrorist force."

"Doesn't look like we have much of a choice, then," McCarter said. "We'll have to take them from a safe distance and hope we can get the whole bunch in a single blow. How much ordnance are we packing?"

James and Hawkins held up the M-16 A-4s they'd brought, both equipped with detachable M-203 grenade launchers. Manning had also managed to acquire some antipersonnel explosives from the Marines, basically modern versions of the Claymore mine, in addition to a couple of antitank mines in the event the terrorists had managed to acquire an armored capability.

"All of that should do the trick," Encizo remarked.

"Would you allow me to make a suggestion?" Jeddah interjected.

"Absolutely," McCarter said. "Far as I'm concerned, you're a part of this team."

"It seems you could be more effective if you were to draw the enemy away from the staging area. They obviously have sentries and, as I said before, they are relatively inexperienced. A ruse could draw them out from the perimeter, leaving much of it unguarded."

"What kind of ruse did you have in mind?"

"It is an old trick that some friends in the Jordanian army have used before, and has proven very effective." He gestured at Manning. "If you would permit me to accompany your man here, the two of us could set up a trap and draw them into it. Then, while we provide the cover and diversion you need, the remainder of your men could move within striking distance and destroy the main force."

"And in so doing, destroy whatever weapons they might have without exposing ourselves to any potential NBC hazards," James said. "Nice thinking, bro."

McCarter looked at Encizo, upon whose expertise he often relied when it came to close-quarter battle tactics. "I think it'll work," the Cuban replied.

"Well what are we waiting for?" McCarter finally said. "Let's get this done."

CHAPTER TWENTY

Manning and Jeddah low-crawled along the brutal floor of the wash, the sharp stones gouging their chests and bellies. Hand after agonizing hand, right thigh and then left, they made their way to the area designated for the diversion. It wouldn't be easy, but at least they would be able to put a convincing spin on their plan. Prior to leaving the area where they'd encountered the AQI scouting party, Jeddah had lifted radios from two of the terrorists—this would work to their advantage, an integral part of Jeddah's contribution to Phoenix Force's plan.

As Jeddah had pointed out, the terrorists waiting in the wash would be getting concerned when they didn't hear from their men. They would have to develop a plausible explanation for the delay and then somehow communicate that to the main strike force. Jeddah had come up with the idea that once they were in position, he could call in posing as one of the scouting team.

It was purely good fortune McCarter had allied with the Jordanian, a man who not only knew the AQI methods well but spoke fluent Arabic. Good fortune, indeed, not to mention Jeddah had further come up with the idea of how they would make the ploy all the more convincing by making the strike team believe their men needed assistance.

"If we make our enemies believe failure to act puts their operation at greater risk, they will send as many men and resources as possible. And then they will be at our mercy."

It was a good plan, a solid plan, and Manning had every confidence it would work.

The Canadian explosives expert considered these things as he planted the first of the ten antipersonnel mines. From the armory at Camp Shannon, Manning had acquired six M-18 A1 Claymores—basically all the stock they had—along with four TS-50s the Marines had confiscated from a Sunni Awakening group they'd encountered on patrol. The latter was made for the desert terrain like this, an Italian-made job that was rugged, waterproof and versatile. It would do the job for which it had been constructed.

Manning continued forward on his belly, each movement seeming like thunder in his ears even though he knew the enemy would never hear him over the increasing winds. The cloud cover had now dissipated and dawn had broken. In the next fifteen minutes he would need to get the mines placed and they would have to execute their plan. They were simply out of time and every minute it took to end this here was another minute the other AQI terrorists were getting farther from their grasp. And they still had the three- or four-mile trek back to Camp Shannon to retrieve their transportation.

As if he'd been reading Manning's mind, McCarter's voice crackled through the static on his radio headset. "Firefox One to Firefox Three. Sit rep, over?"

"I'm working on it, Firefox One," Manning snapped. Then, quieter, he added, "Give me five mikes, top."

"Roger, Firefox Three. Out."

All fell silent in Manning's ears except the pervasive wind. The storm was another thing to consider but Manning put it out of his thoughts, forcing himself to keep focused on what he was doing. When one messed with explosives it was important to concentrate so as not to transform one's hide into bits of smelly flesh, fair game for the Iraqi carrions. In a short time there would be food enough for them all, Manning knew, and he had no intention of accelerating the process by any measure.

The other most telling part of this game was the careful placement of the mines. The Claymores could be remotely detonated but the TS-50s were timer activated, with a twenty-second safety buffer. That meant they would have to drive their enemy, assuming they fell for Jeddah's ruse, into the range of the Claymores and trigger them first. Then they would use assault rifle fire from a fair distance to corral them into the area where the TS-50s lay and then wait for whatever would happen to happen. To put the TS-50 mines close to each other in the hope one would set another off wasn't a good plan, since their tough exterior provided a significant safety buffer. After all, these mines were capable of being deployed from trucks and low-flying aircraft or choppers—they would need to be more strategically placed.

After Manning had set the last Claymore in position he looked at his watch and realized it wouldn't do any more good trying to keep low. He scrambled to his feet, gestured for Jeddah to head to the point from which they'd launch their ambush, and then headed to the most logical place for the enemy to hole up. Those who survived the initial blast would run for cover, and that meant the best place to put the mines would be near boulders and natural defilades.

Manning laid the TS-50 body-wreckers in haste, each covered with enough sand and gravel to obscure it, and then headed for the ambush point. Jeddah had chosen the area and it was a good one. The site was protected by both a large rock formation and a dried, gulch-like area immediately behind that. If the enemy had any kind of launch ordnance, such as rocket-propelled grenades or mortars, this point would afford them moderate protection. Manning and Jeddah didn't plan to give the enemy that kind of time, of course.

When Manning reached the cover he found Jeddah already prepared, the removable bipod he'd attached to his British-made LA-8 5 A-2 extended and weapon positioned for firing. Manning grinned with appreciation before he retrieved the FN-FAL Battle Rifle he'd pilfered from McCarter. Between the two weapons and the mines, the terrorists wouldn't know what hit them and even once they realized it, it would be far too late to respond. At least Manning was hoping the cards would fall that way.

He keyed up the radio and gave the signal to McCarter before he turned and nodded at Jeddah. Then he began to fire a steady barrage from the FN-FAL as Jeddah triggered some rounds from the AK-47 he'd lifted off one of the terrorist scouts. Jeddah then began to scream into his confiscated radio in a furious stream of Arabic, most of it unintelligible to Manning, although he did catch the occasional profanity. Jeddah was definitely selling the goods, and he sounded so convincing that even Manning found himself beginning to believe it.

Jeddah paused a moment and quit firing, gestured for Manning to cease firing, and then he started up again and shouted some more into the radio. He stopped in what sounded like midsentence and quite unexpectedly smashed the sensitive device into the rock, effectively preventing its further use. At first, Manning panicked. What the hell was he doing? Had McCarter been right all along to mistrust Jeddah? Manning got his answer a moment later when Jeddah turned and grinned, close enough that Manning noticed the slight gap between two of his lower teeth he hadn't noticed before.

"They are coming most assuredly," he said. "Be ready."

Manning tried to quiet the rapid thudding in his chest and scolded himself for being so paranoid. Jeddah had done it purposely, intent on convincing the enemy their position was about to be overrun by a whole platoon of very angry Marines. If that didn't draw them out then nothing would—assuming the strike force leader simply didn't tell them to turn the hell around and get out of there before they got their collective asses kicked. No, Jeddah had performed admirably and done just what he'd promised to do. Manning had just found a reason to trust the Jordanian, not willing to make the same mistake of not giving the guy a fair shake, something he'd failed to give Nawaf.

"Here they come," Jeddah said, pointing down the line and to the right.

Sure enough, a group composed of somewhere between ten and twelve emerged from a rock formation similar to the one behind which Manning and Jeddah waited. Manning withdrew the remote detonator from his pocket, flipped the arming switch and counted off the seconds in his mind. The terrorists slowed as they came into range of the Claymores.

"Just a little more, boys…" Manning whispered.

Then he depressed the firing button. For just a heartbeat there was nothing except the barely audible slap of terrorist boots on the gravel and sand of the wash floor—then the world went to hell for the AQI terror group. The M-18 A1 Claymores blew in near synchronized succession as the signal reached the detonator for each. Hundreds of steel fragments blew out, expanding in a sixty-degree arc at an effective range of 50 meters.

Backed by 680 grams of C-4 filler, each Claymore expended 700 1/8-inch steel balls. The effects were devastating as thousands of superheated metal fragments ripped flesh from bone or lodged deep in vital tissues.

Those fortunate enough to escape the effects of the shrapnel were either subjected to instant concussions or ruptured eardrums. Still more were knocked to the ground by the blasts. All were shaken by the sudden and swift consequences of rushing unprepared into the hands of their enemies, and the shame of such sloppiness carried over as Manning and Jeddah implemented phase two.

In sudden terror the terrorists realized they were under fire. Even though there were only two weapons directed at them, both from the same area, they probably felt they were surrounded on every side. Manning and Jeddah weren't selective, more intent on laying down a firestorm of lead in the hope of driving the survivors into the secondary trap. True to Manning's predictions, the terrorists that could still get to their feet did so in a hurry and dashed for the cover of the rocks nearby.

Even as they ducked out of the line of sight, Manning started the countdown in his head.

As SOON AS THEY HEARD the first shots, McCarter raised the binoculars to his eyes and watched with anticipation. He tried not to let his excitement show as he spied the apparent commander of the strike team step from his utility truck, a truck covered by heavy tarp, and begin to shout orders at his men.

They seemed to come out of the cover of the rocks and big, natural divots in the wash floor like locusts. At least a dozen had seemed to appear out of nowhere in just seconds. McCarter waited while their leader delivered another barrage of Arabic before the men turned and beat feet out of the area.

McCarter lowered the binoculars and said in an almost singsong voice, "They're playing our song, mates. Move out!"

The four men rose with James and Encizo paired as one team, McCarter and Hawkins as the other running a parallel course to them. They still planned to hit from a fair distance but they knew to launch an assault from that far away wouldn't be effective. Short of a fully fledged nuclear bomb, however, or blowing up a device that would disperse a toxic cloud of gas across the entire wash valley, McCarter figured they could get closer than this.

The terrorists remaining with the truck along with their commander were few and scattered, more focused on what was transpiring at the unseen point beyond their staging area than having any inkling trouble was coming up behind them. It surprised every one of the Phoenix Force warriors that they were able to get nearer. Each step, each foot, each ten feet they descended the slippery wall of the wash basin, the enemy remained oblivious to their approach.

As soon as they'd progressed to within what McCarter deemed a safe striking range, the Briton gave a hand signal and the others immediately took up covered positions behind the largest rock protrusions they could find. All but one—Calvin James—managed to find decent protection. James ended up having to take up a prone position behind a piece of dead wood lodged in the basin wall. Probably it had been forced there by the rush of heavy water.

Well, baking in the hot, merciless sun month after month it would be dry and cracked and fragile, at best.

McCarter saw his friend's dilemma but knew there wasn't a bloody thing he could do about it. They would just have to wrap this up quick, thereby reducing the chances they would get caught up in a battle with odds they hadn't expected. The echoes from the Claymores going up in the distance were almost equivalent to the trumpet blast of a cavalry charge.

McCarter opened the festivities with a well-placed shot from his scope-mounted FN-FNC that took out the driver of the utility truck. The bullet shattered the window the driver had raised to protect him from the steadily increasing wind and sand blowing down against the backs of the Phoenix Force warriors. It smashed into the side of his head and split his skull wide open before exiting out his neck. Gore showered the inside of the cab and some of it splashed into the eyes of the leader who had just been climbing into the cab.

With a concerted nod at each other, James and Hawkins sighted their M-203s on the base of the truck and triggered the 40 mm grenades. Even if some of their enemy managed to escape, they knew the first objective would be to attempt to immobilize the vehicle without utterly destroying everything that might be aboard. The grenades arced gracefully and touched down just forward of the driver's-side tires, which consisted of duals at the front and rear. The heat from the blasts instantly melted the tires and cracked part of the frame, ensuring that the vehicle wouldn't be traveling anytime soon.

Two terrorists attempting to flee the area by skirting the flaming destruction caught Encizo's eye. The Cuban raised his MP-5 SD-6, sighted down the slide and squeezed the trigger. The first and second 3-round volleys nipped at the terrorists' heels but none of the rounds managed to find flesh. His bearings now set, Encizo compensated for windage and the movement, gave the muzzle of the weapon a good lead and then opened up again. Encizo hit pay dirt, taking both opponents down. The rounds cut the legs out from one and sent him tumbling, a limp ball of blood and sand. The second terrorist died instantly when one 9 mm round clipped his thigh and spun him so a second shattered his spine. The man crumpled like a doll in a cloud of dust.

With the terrorists' means of transporting mobile weapons now effectively out of commission, Phoenix Force could turn its full attention to any remaining boots on the ground. And one thing was certain—there would be no terrorist attack against Camp Shannon today, be it biological, chemical or otherwise.

THE WASH OF BLOOD and flesh that slapped Colonel Shabbat full in the face stung his eyes. It caused him to misstep as he was climbing into the cab of the truck and he fell off the truck and onto his back. Shabbat sucked air, lungs burning as the wind was knocked out of him. He recovered quickly enough and moved to clear the gore of the driver with one hand while reaching for his canteen with the other.

Shabbat managed to get the canteen clear and the lid open. He tilted it to flush his eyes just at the moment that twin blasts caused his eardrums to vibrate and rattled his teeth. Hot gas licked at his boots and he could smell the rubber-lug soles as they half melted in an instant. Shabbat doused his eyes and face once more, snatched a small rag from the breast pocket of his desert fatigues and cleared his vision with an aggressive scrub.

Shabbat rolled from the truck and scrambled to his feet. He dashed in the direction of the rocky outcropping that concealed the personal vehicle Khoury had bestowed

on him as a reward for his faithful command under fire.
Even as he skittered toward it, he could feel the pain in
his left knee. He looked down without stopping his jaunt
and spotted the rapidly spreading patch of blood along
his left thigh—he'd obviously taken some shrapnel when
the grenades exploded.

Damn the American swine! They'd duped him with
that ridiculous call for help and he'd fallen right into their
hands, committed many of his best men to their deaths.
Shabbat reached his command vehicle without incident
and found his driver missing. Had the coward run away
or something? Shabbat couldn't believe that. Maybe he'd
abandoned his post to assist the others—perhaps he'd
even gone in search of Shabbat to ensure his leader's
safety. Whatever the case, Shabbat could only wait a few
minutes before he would have to leave the area.

No, he told himself. You will not abandon your men
to fight alone.

Shabbat couldn't believe he'd considered such a thing.
He was no coward! He was a valued warrior of the jihad,
and would sacrifice his life for Allah if that's what it came
to. Shabbat knew the ramifications of his decision but
he didn't care. Their position would be overrun within
minutes and he planned to make sure the Americans re-
gretted opposing him. He found the medical pouch in
the back of his vehicle, applied a hasty dressing to the
wound on his leg. The tight binding would staunch the
flow of blood and prevent his leg from buckling on him
as he returned to the truck.

Shabbat smiled as he thought about setting the self-
destruct mechanism. Their scientists, at Khoury's insistence, had equipped the weapon with a fail-safe so
that in the event they could not complete their mission
the bomb wouldn't fall into the hands of their enemies.

Shabbat had studied those instructions for arming the self-destruct very carefully, although admittedly he'd considered it a very remote chance he would have to use it. Now their plans to rain death and hell on the Americans were spoiled. At least Shabbat could have one remaining small victory. Once he took this step, however, he held no illusions about survival—at least he would take his enemies with him.

Shabbat double-checked his patch job and then grabbed an AKSU from the back of the truck. He turned and headed for the truck, summoning all of his will and courage. As he drew nearer to it the heat from the grenades the enemy launched had dissipated some, so it wasn't so intense he couldn't get close enough to complete his mission. Shabbat hurried to the truck bed and used his knife to cut a hole in the tarp—he couldn't risk being observed. He slung his weapon and then pulled himself up with a grunt, his arms straining as he hefted his body weight into position and scrambled through the tattered opening.

Sweat immediately beaded on his forehead, the interior of the truck bed already stifling hot. Shabbat withdrew a flashlight from his pocket and stepped over the heavy bolts attached to the launcher. He entertained the notion of attempting to reprogram the weapon so that it might still launch and strike the Marine camp but he dismissed it in the same moment. There wasn't time to reprogram it and he didn't possess the expertise to change the coordinates to a new valid setting. They had planned to launch the bomb from much closer to the enemy camp than their present location—at least this plan had the least margin of error and could still do vast amounts of damage to the enemy force.

At least Khoury and the remainder of the men would

have enough time to retreat to the stronghold. The Marines wouldn't recover so quickly from the device once it blew, and even if only a small force had been sent to conduct the ambush against Shabbat's team, it would take many more to rescue and evacuate the injured. In either case, they had won this round and Shabbat felt completely satisfied in his decision to self-destruct the weapon. In just a short while the Westerners would understand the might and resolve of al Qaeda like they had never understood it before.

And Shabbat would go down as one of the greatest heroes of the jihad, a champion over this day of blood and death.

CHAPTER TWENTY-ONE

Manning and Jeddah had implemented a firestorm with marked results; that much was obvious to David McCarter. He almost felt cheated in some strange way, since he and the other Phoenix Force warriors with him had encountered almost no resistance. Their ruse had worked better than even he could've hoped. Their fight with the terrorists had ended practically before it began. Dawn had broken sometime earlier in the hour and the sun was now full above the eastern horizon. The pink, purple and blood-red tendrils that had stretched across the dawn sky had burned into oblivion with the sunlight, the promise of another scorching day for the Iraqi desert.

As they proceeded in a fire-and-maneuver down the embankment, McCarter and the rest dispatched what few terrorists remained. Smoke and heat still poured from where James and Hawkins had targeted their grenades to take the truck and its enigmatic contents out of commission. McCarter couldn't be sure yet what the terrorists had concealed inside but he was about to find out. He signaled for the others to fan out while he inspected the contents.

McCarter eased up to the rear of the truck and checked the passenger side—nothing there but a depression and a little blood, probably where the terrorist commander had fallen. He would be long gone by now. The tarp along the side was partially torn, but McCarter didn't see or hear anything, and there weren't any places close enough that a terrorist could hide and wait to ambush him when his back was turned. McCarter slung his FN-FNC before grabbing the handholds on the truck and bracing his foot on the towing pintle assembly, which was currently locked in place by its pin.

The Briton eased into the truck bed, scurrying between the top edge of the tailgate and the tarp. He was nearly inside when he felt an arm encircle his neck. The move instantly choked off his air supply, the muscles of the attacker constricting around the carotid arteries. Pain lanced through his neck even though his neck muscles were much stronger than the average man because he worked them during physical training to prevent severe damage in an instance just like this one. McCarter couldn't move his head to either side, despite his strength. He quickly realized he had maybe ten seconds before going unconscious.

McCarter reached for the knife sheathed against his left thigh, yanked it free and drove it into the leg of his opponent. The ambusher let out a shout but was obviously a trained killer because he didn't release that much pressure. It was enough for McCarter to get some spare wind. McCarter levered the knife to drive the enemy off his back as he rolled by kicking off with one foot on the tailgate. The enemy was now pinned beneath McCarter like a turtle on its back. McCarter seized the moment by inserting a wedged hand between his neck where the two hands gripped each other, the weakest point at this moment, and then smashed his skull into the man's nose.

The grip broken, McCarter was able to draw his knife and scramble out of reach before his opponent could stop him. The Briton sucked for precious air as he stumbled over what he assumed to be equipment, the metal edges hard and unyielding against his shins. He finally managed to get clear enough that he could turn and face his enemy head-on, cursing himself for being so sloppy. McCarter couldn't see the terrorist's face well in the dark, the only light spilling through the tear in the tarp, but he could make out his figure well enough.

McCarter figured it was the strike force leader he'd seen earlier. The guy had probably torn the hole in the side of the tarp and climbed inside. But why? It didn't matter right then, however, since keeping the guy from killing him was the priority of the moment. He'd bloody near let the enemy get the best of him, and he wouldn't let his guard down again. Phoenix Force still had a mission to complete and they needed their leader.

And I'm not ready to go so easily, McCarter thought.

The terrorist rushed him, shouting like a banshee and seemingly unthinking of his wounds. His leg was already bandaged, McCarter oddly noticed just before he sidestepped the attack and delivered a slash to the side of the guy's face. The terrorist ducked aside in time to avoid having his cheek laid wide open and suffered a minor cut. McCarter danced back as the man, while a bit older, seemed quite small and agile. Whatever wounds he'd suffered didn't appear to be slowing him down.

In the flicker of sunlight McCarter briefly caught the wild glint in the terrorist's eyes, realizing that the guy had transformed from a human being into a raging animal. He would have to end this now. McCarter spotted the frame of the assembly bolted to the truck bed, realizing now that this was some kind of portable launching pad, got a handhold on it and dropped back as the terrorist adjusted and charged for a third time. The sole of his boot swung upward and caught the terrorist full in the crotch.

The guy howled and then hesitated, and in so doing he made the fatal mistake McCarter had been waiting for.

The Briton brought the point of the combat knife upward in a full thrust and caught the terrorist under the chin. The blade entered the soft, fleshy portion behind the jawbone, continued through soft, crunchy cartilage. The force was enough to sever the tongue, and the blade lodged fully in the roof of the mouth, effectively pinning the man's jaw shut. As the terrorist's eyes bulged in shock and terror, McCarter drew his pistol, aimed point blank and shot the enemy in the face. The bullet exited the back of the skull, taking brain matter with it, and the force of the close-contact wound flipped the terrorist onto his back.

McCarter breathed heavily and large globules of sweat soaked his face. The tarp at the rear whipped aside. Encizo appeared with his MP-5 held at the ready, and McCarter aimed offline as soon as he saw it was a teammate and not another terrorist coming to investigate.

"You all right?" the Cuban asked.

McCarter nodded as he holstered his pistol with some degree of disgust in the motion. "Got caught with my bloody pants down. Guy nearly killed me."

"Uh, what was he doing hiding in here?"

"Don't know," McCarter replied. "I think he may have been leading this operation."

Encizo appeared to notice the launcher for the first time. "Guess you were right about the strike force having some sort of weapon. They were probably planning to launch it at Camp Shannon."

"Wouldn't have been anybody there to kill with it, though."

"Maybe not," Encizo said. "But they didn't know that. He was probably trying to launch it…"

McCarter looked puzzled when his friend's voice trailed off. "What is it, Rafe?"

Encizo frowned. "That thing doesn't much look like it has the range to make it to Camp Shannon. It's not a particularly huge device."

McCarter glanced at the bomb now, realizing it was the first time he'd bothered to make a close inspection. Well, then again, his mind *had* been on other things up to that point. "You think so?"

"Yeah, I do. In fact, that looks just like a 158 mm. A tank-buster round. I can't see that thing doing much damage, and I surely don't think it's packing enough fuel to get it the four or five miles to Camp Shannon."

"Yeah, I think maybe you're right," McCarter said with another glance.

All was quiet between them a moment and then Encizo snapped his fingers. "That's why the scout party! They wanted to make sure there wasn't anybody within launching distance. They never intended to launch it from here."

"Then why would the departed here actually bother to hide inside?" McCarter asked. He pointed to the hole in the side of the tarp and said, "The crazy bloke even took the time to cut his way in along the side instead of just going through the back."

"He didn't want to be observed."

McCarter shook his head. "That sounds a bit daffy, Rafe. Surely he realized we'd search this thing eventually."

Both men's eyes met and then shifted simultaneously toward the bomb, coming to the same realization. The terrorist hadn't planned on launching the weapon; he'd planned on *destroying* it, and his enemies right along with it! It only made sense—the terrorists had gone into somewhat of a defensive mode with their recent thrust-and-parry tactics. It's the only thing that made sense.

McCarter and Encizo immediately got to work and searched the frame of the truck until they found what they were searching for. A panel covered an electronics board and Encizo opened it to reveal a set of red numbers actively ticking down. The timer read 7:36 and counting. Encizo and McCarter looked at one another and then McCarter reached to the radio on his belt.

Encizo stopped him and shook his head. "I don't know anything about anything when it comes to stuff like this, but I wouldn't necessarily key up the radio in here."

McCarter nodded. "Go find Gary. Fast."

MAJOR DOUGLAS COMPTON, commanding the 127th Armored, U.S. Army, knew something was terribly wrong. He'd brought his concerns directly to the colonel in charge of Exit Point Tango who, in turn, funneled Compton's concerns up to Brigadier General Maxwell. Maxwell had been the commander of the entire evacuation force in this area, which comprised both Marine and Army units in addition to a detachment of Delta Force operators and an entire unit of Army Rangers.

Yes, it was true that they'd had no word from Rifle Company Bravo at Camp Shannon, and yes it was true that they couldn't get any status because of a combination of bad weather and the no-fly zone restrictions put in place by the Iraqi leadership. No, they couldn't be sure when either of those situations might change because General Maxwell, after all, wasn't the hand of God and there were more politics to the evacuation than there were actually military decisions to be made. So what was the general to do?

"So that's the scoop," Lieutenant Colonel Jeff Karta

had said. "There's nothing more we can do until either we get communications restored or approval to send a spotter into the area."

"What about a satellite probe, sir?" Compton asked.

"Won't do any good," Karta replied. "Can't see anything with all the crazy weather right now."

"Not the best time to schedule an evacuation of this magnitude."

"Look, Major, I can understand your concerns but the facts are what they are," Karta said in a huff. "I won't pretend to understand why the Army does the things it does, nor will I pretend to understand why Washington, D.C., keeps putting its proverbial tail between the cheeks every time Baghdad whines. What I do know is that if we're to keep discipline among the ranks then we start by following orders. Those are our orders and I intend to follow them."

Compton smiled and delivered a salute. He started to turn but stopped when he noticed Karta deliver an almost disappointed expression. What the hell was that about? Had the old man actually expected Compton to push the issue here? Had he hoped Compton would resist the urge to acquiesce to avoid doing the easy thing—he'd leave it being the right thing to the armchair quarterbacks and the press—by taking the initiative to strike out on his own?

Seeing he may have nearly let an opportunity slip through his fingers, Compton said, "Sir, if I could have another moment of your time?"

"What is it, Major?"

"Sir, I suppose you've already thought of this but in the event you hadn't or someone else hadn't approached you, I have some concerns about perimeter security."

Karta tried to look annoyed but Compton could tell

right away the guy's face beamed with almost uncharacteristic delight. "Perimeter security?"

"Well...yes, sir. I mean, I know we have the fences and roving MP patrols and the dogs—that's all well and good. But I'm more concerned with what's happening farther out. You know, the far perimeter."

"Like what?"

"Well, for all we know there could be insurgents or terrorists or whatever just setting up a full-on assault right under our noses, and without some long-range perimeter patrols this could end up becoming a very dangerous position for us to hold in."

"I see." Karta leaned back and folded his arms. "And what exactly did you have in mind?"

"Well, sir, you must admit that armored parties on long-range patrol isn't necessarily unheard of. In fact, it's right out of Stormin' Norman's playbook, sir."

"Yes, I'm aware of that," Karta interjected with an enthusiastic nod. "Go on."

"Well, perhaps you could detail my unit to split into several long-range patrols. We could send the first squad north, three more squads in southerly directions."

"Only one squad north and three south? Sounds a little uneven."

Compton grinned like a proud cat. "It's all about where the most activity would be probable, sir. And an attack from the south is three times more likely than one from the north, not only where our northern flanks are already protected by naval patrols but also the sheer amount of artillery we have aligned there. An attack from the north would be sheer suicide for the enemy, whereas our southern flanks are still relatively unprotected."

Now Karta was grinning from ear to ear, clearly thankful—not only for his tank commander's diligence

but also Compton's understanding that Karta really didn't
want to just abandon Rifle Company Bravo. Compton
also knew, through the grapevine, that Karta had spoken
to Captain Pringle's CO and consoled the man. There
hadn't been much the Marines could do since they had
very limited numbers in this part of the region. Most of
their remaining forces were closer to Baghdad and the
other urban arenas, or tasked to provide facility security
for evacuation points such as this one.

"I think I agree with you, Major," Karta finally said
after a show of consideration. "And I don't have any orders contrary to the provision of providing, er, how did
you put it? Ah yes, long-range perimeter *security*. And
since the other units are tasked with important jobs and
the 1-Two-7 seems to be ready and able for an assignment, I think your idea has merit."

"Excellent news, sir. Then can I assume I have your
permission to depart immediately?"

Karta stood and extended his hand. "Permission
granted."

Compton shook the old man's hand, saluted and left
the S1 building. He would have a very short window in
which to get his tanks south and begin searching. Camp
Shannon, he knew, was too far for them to go. That would
be well outside the perimeter boundaries, about forty
klicks outside the perimeter boundaries actually, but it
might get him to the point where they could gather some
intelligence or at least get within radio contact. Of more
concern to him, however, was that they might be headed
right into the sandstorm the weather technicians had been
reporting was coming in.

Compton checked his watch and frowned as he headed
toward the billets of his men to give them the news.
Their time was short. Although not as short as those

of Rifle Company Bravo, potentially. Compton would shoot straight with his men, advise them they would be putting their lives at risk on a slim chance. But then he knew what their answer would be—they were U.S. Army tankers and a tough lot. It could've been a group of Iraqi refugees or a Marine unit in need and it wouldn't make a difference.

The message was and always would be the same: Leave No Man Behind.

AS HE WATCHED the dark clouds of the sandstorm approach, coming closer by the minute, Captain Colin Pringle found it odd that he thought of the special troubleshooters that had been sent to help them. Here they were, an entire company of Marines headed toward an evacuation point, and somewhere behind them were five men determined to ensure his safety and those of his men. Pringle shook his head at the very irony of the thought. In some ways he felt guilty, too, because it should have been Brown and his men who evacuated while the Marines destroyed the terrorist threat.

Pringle had twice considered turning back, finding the five mysterious warriors and offering his assistance. Brock had talked him out of it both times with one very strong argument. The five men, along with the assistance of the Jordanian they knew only as Jeddah, were much better trained for fighting a group of AQI terrorists. Additionally, if Rifle Company Bravo didn't do something to get out of Camp Shannon and at least attempt to reach the evacuation site at Exit Point Tango, the lives of many more men could be put at risk when they were sent to find out what happened.

Pringle couldn't have that on his conscience, especially not after wrestling with his decision to wait it out more than two days at Camp Shannon instead of evacuating immediately. Well, he had done the best he could and it wasn't likely the Marine Corps could fault him for that. And it made it damned frustrating that they were here fighting a political war with Baghdad. This was an occupied country, a country that had been at war for more than ten years. What right did they have to place restrictions on the country that put the lives of American servicemen at risk? Why was Washington kowtowing to these morons anyway?

Pringle knew he'd probably never find the answers to questions that soldiers had been asking the "statesmen" for thousands of years. It had been the same in the Roman army and probably the same among the knights of the Crusades and the same of the British Navy during their operations in the northern seas during World War II where dozens and dozens of ships had been lost along with thousands of lives as they attempted to deliver supplies to the Russian forces via the Siberian channel. That was the thing about fighting men and women, especially true among the American armed forces: they never questioned the insanity of it all, but merely asked their countrymen back home to protect the traditions so the sacrifices would not be in vain.

The radio squawked for attention, breaking Pringle from his reverie. He rode in the command Humvee with Brock at the wheel. His driver had been killed during one of the earlier assaults on Camp Shannon. The communications specialist, Margolis, answered immediately and then said, "Yes, he's right here. Stand by."

Margolis passed the phone to Pringle, who took it with a nod. "This is Bravo Leader. Go ahead. Over?"

"Sir, Lieutenant Dittmer here. I just spoke with our corpsman and he's advising one of my men has started bleeding internally. He's concerned about this with the coming storm. He's asking if we can hold back, find shelter and then when the storm has passed we'll catch up. Over."

"Request denied. Over."

"Sir?"

"Either we all stop and secure shelter or not. I won't split up the company for any reason short of we fall under attack. We'll move ahead and see if we can find shelter. Over."

"Understood, sir. Thank you. Dittmer out."

Pringle passed the radio back to Margolis and then turned to Brock. "First Sergeant, we need to find cover."

CHAPTER TWENTY-TWO

There were less than two minutes on the clock by the time Gary Manning arrived to inspect the terrorist launcher. The other men of Phoenix Force had stripped the tarp off the truck enough to admit adequate lighting so Manning could make an assessment of the timer. After careful inspection the Canadian stood and stretched, his back aching from being hunched over the console, and clucked his tongue.

"Well?" McCarter asked, probing. "Can you disable the thing or should we get the bloody hell away from here?"

"Don't think that's going to do much good," Manning replied. "In fact, we couldn't make enough distance that it would save us."

"What do you mean?"

Manning gestured at the launcher's electronics console. "I mean that this thing is wired directly to the explosives, which I'm guessing are probably radioactive."

"Dirty bomb?" Encizo said.

"Near as I can tell."

"So less than a minute now," McCarter said. "You want to save us the drama and disable this thing?"

Manning hunched over the console once more and inspected the wires that ran up the length of the launcher to the actual shell of the warhead. "I'm working on it, boss."

Finally, after another fifteen seconds of inspection,

Manning reached into his bag of tricks, which had held the TS-50 mines but was now equipped only with a few spare detonators and some tools. He withdrew a combination wire cutter and crimper and snipped all three of the wires running to the warhead, two black and one red, and then replaced the tool carefully in the pouch. None of the Phoenix Force warriors had bothered to attempt to escape, knowledgeable there wouldn't be time just as Manning had advised.

They stood frozen and watched the countdown, none realizing that all were possessed of bated breath. The timer hit 00:00 and...

Nothing!

Manning was the first to exhale, and none too quietly. He looked at McCarter with a grin. "See? Nothing to worry about."

"That's all you had to do?" T. J. Hawkins inquired. "Just cut the wires? We could've done that."

"Yep," Manning said. His brow furrowed. "Why? What else did you think there was to it?"

Hawkins shrugged, looking a little sheepish now. "I don't know. I guess I just thought it would be more complicated than that."

"That's only in the movies," Encizo told his friend.

"And nothing is too hard for he who remains calm in a crisis," Manning added.

"Listen to this jive turkey," James said. "Stops us from all getting blown to kingdom come and suddenly he thinks he's Carl Jung or something."

"Could think he was Jung," Encizo said, jerking a thumb at Manning. "Gary's a staunch Democrat, remember?"

"Well, whatever he is, he's all right with me," McCarter said. "Now you blokes do a full weapons and equipment check before we head out of here. And search every corpse that wasn't blown to ashes for intelligence. I don't want to leave anything to chance."

They did as ordered while McCarter conferred with Jeddah. "We'll have to get back to Camp Shannon as soon as possible, get those wheels under us. Are you in?"

Jeddah shook his head. "It is time for us to part ways, my American friend. I must go back to my country and report everything that I know. With the Marine camp abandoned and the PSIDS equipment no longer functional, I must move on to other places and assignments more important to my government."

McCarter nodded. While he'd hoped they could hold on to Jeddah a bit longer he understood the man's reasoning. The ways of the Jordanians were truly not like those of Americans. There would be other times and opportunities to work with Jeddah again, potentially, so while McCarter felt a strong urge to try to change Jeddah's mind he didn't want to alienate him. They had done that with Nawaf and all it had done was get the guy killed.

It was eerie to McCarter, almost as if Jeddah had seen his thoughts because the Jordanian clamped a hand on his shoulder. "You have been both an able and worthy ally, Brown."

"You, too."

"I do not blame you for what happened to Nawaf, and I will not attempt to do so when I return to Jordan. As far as my government is concerned, Nawaf was a hero of the people and he risked his life to enable your mission against the AQI. This is what my report will reflect, as well as your cooperation with me in accomplishing my own objectives."

McCarter nodded. "Much appreciated, mate. And since we're going on the record here, I don't want to break up this happy little band before I say it's been a pleasure and honor to fight beside you. You ever need us for anything, don't hesitate to reach out. And I mean *anything*."

Jeddah nodded. "It is the same here."

"Okay, so I suppose this truck isn't going anywhere. We'd better get moving 'cause we got a long walk back and it's getting hotter by the minute."

"You will not have to walk," Jeddah said with a smile. "There is another vehicle concealed behind that rock formation. Probably the command vehicle. It is more than adequate to transport all of you back to Camp Shannon."

McCarter could only smile at their good fortune. "Then what are we waiting for? Let's blow this soda stand!"

"What does this mean?" Jeddah asked with a queer expression.

McCarter smiled. "I'll explain on the way."

THEY HAD BARELY MANAGED to find shelter within the cleft of a small ridge when the sandstorm hit with all the force of the gale winds of a tornado. The troops had managed to split into two groups and find refuge in different caverns dug naturally into the rock from thousands of years of water and sand cutting paths through their cores while another thousand years of heat baked the saturated limestone and shale. The creation of these natural formations had ultimately saved the lives of every Marine in the company.

Just outside the cavern entrance they could hear the abrasive sand, powered by the winds of the storm, pelt the equipment with raspy noises they could hear even above the wind. Those sounds echoed through the caverns and reminded First Sergeant Brock just how precarious their situation. Pringle had been forced to allow the company's two medics to perform an emergency surgical field procedure on their comrade's leg to find and stop the bleed. Chances were good if they couldn't find the bleed and stop it the Marine would lose his leg, possibly even die. And Pringle's approving such a thing would most likely wind up before a board of review if not buy the man a straight-out court martial.

Well, Brock would stand by his CO and the decision, even if it cost him his stripes. He'd watched Pringle grow and mature as a Marine officer, and he was proud to serve under the guy. Pringle had led his men to hell and back, and they were still alive. That was pretty good for spending more than forty-eight hours under practically constant enemy barrage. Not to mention that it was Pringle who had opted to listen to Jeddah when Brock thought it was a bad idea, and it was Pringle who had agreed to evacuate Camp Shannon and trust the Special Operations team to handle the AQI terrorists.

"How you doing, Top?" Brock looked up from where he sat with his back against the cave wall and made out the outline of Pringle in the gloom. He started to rise but Pringle added, "As you were."

The captain had just come back from making his third trip around the Marines, chatting with them and making sure their needs were attended wherever and however he could. Now he took a moment to sit next to his senior noncommissioned officer. In a surprising twist, he not only told Brock "smoke-'em if you got-'em" but also offered a nip from a small flask. In all their time together, Brock had never seen Pringle take a drink. Well, that wasn't strictly true. The captain had drunk a beer in the enlisted men's mess once when the USO sponsored a tour for Miss September.

"Care for some?"

Brock took the flask with a nod and after a good pull

he passed it back. "What is that? It's almost like...I don't know, like I've tasted it before but it's been a really long time. I do remember I liked it!"

This produced a chuckle from Pringle. "It's a good chance, being all your years in the Corps. It's Asbach Uralt, a brandy from Germany."

"Yeah, that's it. Wow—didn't know you were into brandy, sir. Frankly, you always struck me as somewhat of a straight shooter, kind that never really enjoyed any sort of liquor, if you know what I mean."

"I know what you mean," Pringle said after another pull. "A prude."

He handed it to Brock, who took another drink, this one not quite as large. Brock laughed as he returned the flask with a wave to indicate he didn't want any more. "I guess that's what I was thinking, yeah. I meant no disrespect by it, sir."

"I understand, First Sergeant," Pringle said. "I'm not so much a wimp that I'd take offense to something like that. I've been around the block or two."

"That right?"

"The neighborhood in south Atlanta where I grew up was pretty rough. My family was poor, and we didn't have a whole lot besides each other. My brothers and I got into more scraps than you can believe, and my oldest brother was always getting into some kind of trouble. Practically killed by Dad by the time he was fifteen when he called at three o'clock in the morning to say he was sitting in jail for stealing a car."

"Sounds like a handful," Brock replied politely.

"He was a dumb son of a bitch, rest his soul."

"Sorry, sir."

"No need, Top," Pringle said. "Like I said, I've built a pretty thick skin."

"How are the men doing?" Brock asked in an attempt to change the subject.

"I think they'll be just fine once we get the hell out of here. You should go around to them, yourself, talk to them some. I'm sure it would lift their spirits a lot more to know they have you than me in their corner."

"Excuse me, sir, but that's hardly fair," Brock said, doing nothing to hide his disdain for the CO's assessment. "You're a first-class officer and every one of these Marines owes you their life, me included. Now I wouldn't let anybody in this outfit talk that way about you and that means you, as well. Do we understand each other, sir?"

Pringle nodded as he put the flask away and patted his cargo pocket with a grin. "Best to save the rest for later. We never know if we'll need it."

Brock nodded and then got to his feet. "With your permission, sir, I think I'll do as you've suggested and check on the men."

"Carry on, First Sergeant."

Brock saluted and walked away. He made a cursory glance of the situation, chatting it up with the men here and there, but mostly small talk as he did. Brock had always believed in a certain amount of professional distance with the Marines under his command, although he loved and respected every damn one of them. These were the best of the best, men who had decided to serve their country and go wherever they were told. They weren't here because they wanted to defend the people of a country who were less than grateful for their very presence; they were here because they were defending an ideal. That's what the bleeding-heart liberals back home didn't understand. The men and women of the American armed forces were doing what they'd been doing since the first organized army under George Washington marched out to meet the British in 1775. They were defending the ideas of liberty and freedom, of equality and justice for every man, woman and child. That was what it meant to be a Marine, to be a patriot. It wasn't just about honor; it was about duty. Brock wondered if there would ever come a day when Americans could unite on that fact alone and just accept it for what it was, denying the politics and the religious prejudice.

Aw, who the hell cares anyway, Brock thought.

It was their job as Marine leaders to keep these men alive and get them back safely to their loved ones. And that's exactly what Brock planned to do.

MAJOR COMPTON FINALLY removed his helmet for the fifth time in a half hour and mopped the pools of sweat off his brow. If there was something every tanker could agree on it was that even with the modern conveniences of air-conditioning, the inside of an Abrams was still damned hot in the middle of the desert. The hammer of sand against the exterior of the tank armor made the conditions even less bearable.

Compton had ordered the other three units running abreast of their position to halt when the storm finally hit. He couldn't risk continuing the search when visibility had dropped to nil. Too many tanks had been lost or ditched in similar conditions because some dumb-ass TC grew overly confident in his nearly impervious chariot and thought he could press on even when conditions were bad. And while it was true that sand couldn't "hurt" a tank in the conventional sense, driving blindly across a treacherous desert was another thing entirely. Nobody spit in the eye of God without repercussions, and failing to think was like spitting in the eye of God.

"What was that, sir?" Compton's driver asked.

"Huh? What did you say?"

"I was just asking you to repeat the order, sir."

"I didn't give you an order."

"Well, then what—?"

This time Compton heard it. At first he didn't think it was possible but after spending time listening he realized it was radio chatter. They had brought two spare radios for purposes other than their own communications. One they used to monitor the main command frequency back at Exit Point Tango and the other was to surf the private channels dedicated strictly to transmissions between Marine units. They were now hearing the buzz of repeated calls and responses between somebody, but it was still too faint to figure out whom.

"Sir, do you hear that?" the driver asked.

"I do, Sergeant," he replied. He turned to his communications specialist. "Beltzer, I want a Report Document Format on that traffic and I want it as soon as you can get it for me."

"I'm not sure the RDF will be accurate while the storm's passing, sir," Beltzer replied.

Compton shook his head. "Just do your best, Specialist."

"Yes, sir."

This was good news—very good news! Compton had thought finding anything would be a long shot, but to hear the faint hint of unit traffic in an area where there weren't supposed to be any units was a big comfort to Compton. It was George Patton who had once said, "A pint of sweat saves a gallon of blood." The thought of it brought the flicker of a smile to Compton's lips. He didn't want to get his hopes too high but it would be a beautiful thing if they not only found the members of Rifle Company Bravo alive but that it was also an Army tanker unit that actually rescued the group of Marines.

"Oh, the jarheads would never live it down," Compton muttered.

"What's that, sir?" the driver asked again, but Compton didn't answer this time.

I'm going to have to get that man's hearing checked when we get back, Compton thought.

IT DIDN'T TAKE ANY TIME for Phoenix Force and Jeddah to get back to Camp Shannon.

The trip in the late terrorist leader's utility vehicle had been nothing short of a luxury, and especially welcome news when McCarter broke it to the rest of his team they wouldn't have to jog the five-odd miles back to the deserted camp. Once they arrived, Encizo and Manning began to work on transferring all of their remaining equipment to the Humvee while Hawkins and James conducted perimeter security. Wouldn't do to attempt to chase down the remaining AQI terrorists if they never even got out of the compound before somebody blew them to smithereens.

"It's going to be a tight fit," Manning announced as McCarter and Jeddah watched them pack things in.

"You could bloody well walk instead, if you like," McCarter remarked.

Manning made a face. "Thanks, but no."

McCarter turned to Jeddah and extended his hand. "I guess this is where we part company, chum."

"A pleasure, Mr. Brown. I wish you speed and good fortune in your hunting."

"Likewise."

With that, Jeddah began to climb into the AQI utility when McCarter restrained his arm at the last moment. "Hold up a second, mate."

McCarter turned to Encizo and Manning. "Yo, mates,

I just had an idea." He looked back at Jeddah and said, "How would you feel about trading this old clunker for a brand-new Humvee?"

Jeddah looked puzzled at first but then a cool smile played across his lips. "Ah, I think I understand."

McCarter grinned back. "I thought you might. And besides, this Humvee belongs to your government anyway. I'm sure they'd like it back in one piece."

Jeddah nodded and helped Encizo and Manning get the gear stowed in the AQI utility vehicle. When they were finished, he waved goodbye one last time before piling into the Humvee. Shortly he was headed down the crude road that led to the entrance of the camp and, before long, was out of sight.

With the utility vehicle loaded, McCarter called the group together where they could plan their next move. He had a map spread open on the hood of the vehicle. "Now according to Jeddah, the AQI have some sort of base about forty klicks south of here. Assuming we don't run into a storm or a full-up ambush party, we should be able to make it to that region within an hour."

"Any chance we might catch up to the terrorists before they can make it to this mysterious base?" Encizo asked.

"Not likely. They had a good three- or four-hour head start on us while we were tangling with their little death squad. Even traveling in a convoy there's no way they'd still be out there, and even if the base is farther than we think, they had enough of a lead we wouldn't be able to spot any trail they left without air support."

"Which we know we aren't going to get," Hawkins interjected.

"Okay, so it's straight to this base," Manning said. On afterthought, he added, "Wherever the hell it is."

Hawkins scratched his neck where he'd wrapped a

camo scarf around it to keep from getting sunburned. "Seems like this is a real long shot. How are we supposed to find this thing?"

"I don't think we'll have to search very hard," McCarter said. "By the time we get that far south the storm will have passed and we should be able to make contact with the Farm."

"I'll bet they'll be chomping at the bit to find out what happened to us," James ventured. "We've been out of contact with them for almost thirty-six hours straight."

"I'm sure they'll understand the situation," McCarter said.

"You know, if we're able to contact them, then that means the satellite system should also be in position and they can do more advanced scans and pinpoint the exact location of the AQI stronghold," Encizo pointed out.

"That's exactly what I'm counting on, mate."

"I just hope that warning beacon we placed on that dirty bomb will remain active long enough to keep everybody away until our forces can dispatch a properly equipped EOD team to neutralize it," Manning said.

"I'm sure it'll be fine where it's at," McCarter replied. "It's not easily accessible and we did a pretty good job of camouflaging the thing so it can't be spotted by air."

Manning nodded. "I realize that. I just don't want to be responsible for killing some innocent bunch of nomads."

"Everything will work out. I'm sure the natives around here have learned to leave well enough alone when they come upon military equipment of any kind."

"And the storm is probably moving into that area as we speak," James added. "So nobody's going to be anywhere near there if they're smart."

"Speaking of which," McCarter said, "we would be

smart to get the bloody hell out of here if we want to beat the storm."

All mumbled in mutual agreement and they piled onto the utility vehicle. They had an appointment with the AQI death merchants—an appointment that was long overdue.

CHAPTER TWENTY THREE

Great Falls, Montana

Able Team had come to settle a score with Hamza Asir. The first thing they had to do, however, was to make sure they had a viable location on their target—the next step would be to verify no innocent bystanders were endangered once they decided to make their move. Able Team understood Brognola's decision not to involve law enforcement or to notify authorities in Great Falls about the presence of a terrorist threat hadn't been a terribly popular one. At least not popular with those at the Farm, particularly Barbara Price. Sure, it had bought him some good will from the Oval Office but that didn't do much in the way of saving lives. That's the business Able Team was in, and while the three warriors could appreciate Price's feelings they also mutually agreed with Brognola's decision.

"Last thing we need is the law getting in the line of fire," Lyons had reminded his friends. "When the shooting starts I don't want to have to be looking to make sure my target's not wearing a badge or uniform."

Now the trio sat in their SUV in one of the residential sections along the riverfront. Given the Missouri River provided much of the prosperity in the city because it provided a waterway that practically screamed for industry, there were more commercial holdings along the river than residential. To no great surprise, in fact, Great Falls boasted a healthy economy from both manufacturing and machining, a rarity considering modern social technologies ran rampant through most American cities. It also commanded a healthy tourist population, and even catered to a military installation. On the east side of Great Falls, just off Highway 87, was Malstrom Air Force Base. Home to the 341st Missile Wing, the base had served to provide national air defense with intercontinental ballistic missile capabilities. As part of the command, the base also housed the 819th Rapid Engineer Deployable, Heavy Operation Repair Squadron, Engineer, aka RED HORSE.

"It's strange that considering there's an Air Force base so close to this city that Bobinawski's reports weren't taken more seriously," Blancanales remarked.

"More than strange," Schwarz added.

"Well, it's kind of water under the bridge now," Lyons said. "And I'm thinking that after the death of a number of U.S. veterans, in the future they'll sit up and pay more attention."

Schwarz shook his head. "Let's hope so. The whole reason they ignored him was they thought he was suffering from PTSD. As long as we have the attitude every service member that comes home from the war is paranoid and socially maladjusted, we don't stand a chance against the enemy."

"And neither do they because the enemy they're fighting is in their heads, not in front of them," Lyons interjected. "It's often why they don't get the help they need and wind up going off the deep end."

"Modern psychiatry's never had a very good handle on post-combat illnesses," Blancanales said. "Makes me grateful the people the Farm provides us with are experienced combatants themselves. They understand what we face every day."

The conversation drifted to more superficial and mundane matters, including a brief quibble between Schwarz and Blancanales about whether rocky road or butter pecan was the better ice cream. Lyons tried to ignore their bleating and continued to observe the coffee shop. Above it was where the enemy had supposedly sequestered themselves, but Lyons hadn't seen any movement or lights in the place. Surely there would be more activity by the college kids that "rented" the space above the coffee shop from its proprietor on a Saturday night.

Lyons lowered the binoculars. "Something doesn't feel right."

"There he goes talking about his feelings again," Schwarz quipped, punching Blancanales's arm. "Maybe if we—?"

"Wait a minute," Blancanales said.

The warrior stared into the rearview mirror intently, the glint of moonlight reflected off the river casting a sheen to his eyes. "There's a sedan that pulled to the curb behind us about ten minutes ago."

"So?" Lyons said.

"Nobody got out of the car," Blancanales said, looking at Lyons with a wrinkled brow. "Don't you think that's a little strange?"

"Maybe it's two kids necking."

As if on cue, Blancanales watched as two men emerged from the sedan. They both exited from the passenger side and were carrying what looked like large tubes similar to the kind utilized by architects or used to package posters. That was until they started putting everything on computers. To Blancanales's trained eye, the canisters the two men carried were much more ominous than that. And a hell of a lot more deadly.

"And maybe it's terrorists with grenade launchers?" Blancanales countered.

"Bail!" Lyons said.

Able Team did that just as the pair of newcomers raised the tubular devices to their shoulders. The muzzles flashed a moment later as a twin pair of RPGs exploded on impact, turning the Able Team SUV into a fireball of superheated metal, fiberglass, plastic and glass. The gas tank, munitions and ordnance provided a secondary explosion and the shockwave knocked all three Able Team commandos to their bellies—not that it wasn't the safest place to be at the moment anyway.

Lyons was first to recover, rolling as he hit the pavement until he came to a stop behind a telephone pole. Braced on one knee, the Colt Anaconda .44 Magnum in his fist, Lyons sighted on target number one. He squeezed the trigger and blasted a hole through the windshield, continuing on to catch the driver full in the face. The skull-busting slug caved a major indentation in the driver's face, effectively neutralizing the vehicle.

Blancanales was next to take a fighting position. He climbed to his feet and burst toward a U.S. postal cluster box. The thick aluminum and metal boxes arrayed inside the steel frame would surely go a long way toward providing protection. It wouldn't stop another grenade launcher but it would be more than adequate in the case of small-arms fire. Fortunately for Blancanales the terrorists—and there was little doubt in his mind they were terrorists working for Hamza Asir—appeared to be fresh out of grenades. That was fine with the Politician.

Blancanales steadied his forearm against the frame of the cluster boxes, sighted down the slide of his SIG-Sauer

P-229 and squeezed off three shots in rapid succession. Two glanced off the hood, one apparently ricocheting, a fragment catching one of the terrorists in the forehead. The guy spun right into the third shot.

Blancanales and Lyons were simultaneously honing in on terrorist number three when they heard the unmistakable reports of autofire coming from near their wrecked SUV. The impact of bullets from that weapon drove the surviving terrorist against a fire hydrant with enough force his body flipped over it and landed on the pavement at a very awkward angle. The shots had come from Schwarz, who had found cover from behind a telephone pedestal. Blancanales tossed a thumbs up at his friend, realizing Schwarz had managed to grab at least one of their assault-class weapons from the SUV before the thing went sky high.

The warriors waited patiently for further trouble to appear but none did. Finally, Lyons gave the all clear and the three converged on the sedan. Sirens were already wailing in the distance so the men got to work frisking the deceased terrorists for any intelligence. As expected, they didn't find any.

"You want to check the driver?" Blancanales asked Lyons.

"If these two don't have anything on them, I doubt he does."

"What made you think to take him out first, Ironman?" Schwarz asked.

"I didn't want them to be able to run away if Fate showed favor upon us," Lyons said with a deadpan expression.

"That was good thinking." Schwarz looked at Blancanales. "I'm actually impressed. Normally we have to keep trying to talk him out of tempting Fate."

Blancanales nodded as if in enthusiastic agreement.

Lyons went to the driver's-side door and opened it. He yanked the terrorist's corpse from the car and poked his head inside. Keys were still in the ignition, which meant that at least they wouldn't have to head out of the area on foot, allowing them to make some distance from the approaching police. The timeline was too narrow for them to risk compromising the situation now. Lyons also noticed the majority of the gore had been confined to the man's head and shoulders so only a few small bits were visible on the headrest.

Lyons looked over the roof of the car and said, "Uh, I think one of you guys should drive this time."

THE INCIDENT at the riverfront had left the men of Able Team stymied. In addition to their befuddlement about the ambush, they were equally amazed that they hadn't been stopped by a passing squad car for the bullet hole in their windshield. Then again, the squad car had flashed by them so quickly with its lights and sirens—passing them on a divided road that was poorly lit—it wasn't any wonder the cop had failed to spot them. They kept to the primary roads until they were a fair distance from the area and then got onto the First Street Bridge, which took them over the Missouri River and into the west side of Great Falls.

"So now what?" Schwarz asked after they'd ridden some distance in silence while watching for cops—and more terrorists.

"That's a very good question," Lyons said. "Unfortunately, I don't have an answer for you."

"Should we call the Farm?" Blancanales suggested.

"I don't know what good it will do," Lyons said. He punched his palm and exclaimed, "Blast it! I thought for sure Bear would be right on about this. Now we're back to square one with no idea where Asir is or what he has planned."

"Well, we know they're going to try to get out of here," Schwarz said, "Maybe they headed out of the state by highway after all."

"Gadgets could be right," Blancanales said. "We might have to accept they managed to escape from us. But we'll get them eventually."

"I won't accept that," Lyons countered. "I *can't* accept it. I made those Marines a promise that we'd find Asir and stop him. I refuse to give up that easily just because we didn't hit pay dirt on the first try."

"Look, I don't want to be the naysayer here," Schwarz said. "But someone has to play devil's advocate."

"No! We're going to stay optimistic about this, Gadgets. You hear me?"

"I hear you, I hear you."

Blancanales stepped in at this point, always the calm and steady voice of reason. "If we're not going to give up yet, then it stands to reason we need to come up with some way of finding where Asir's hiding."

"Or…" Lyons said.

"Yes?"

"Let's consider where they might be running *from*."

"What are you talking about?" Schwarz said, his tone betraying he still didn't think the odds of finding Asir were in Able Team's favor.

"We've already assumed they won't attempt to leave by private vehicle, but it's too easy to be spotted. A bunch of Mideast types riding around with bulges in their jackets isn't exactly inconspicuous. That means they'll attempt some other form of public transportation. Until they make their move, they would have to find some place to wait."

"What's your point?"

"Where else, without drawing attention, could Asir and his men wait until it's time to go? Where have they been seen together over and over—someplace where they wouldn't get a second glance?" Silence weighed for a time and Lyons finally said, "Oh…come on, guys. Think!"

Then Lyons noticed something on the floor at his feet, something he hadn't noticed before. He bent over and scooped it up—unfolding the massive piece of paper. It was a map and there were points drawn all over it in felt-tipped marker. "What the hell is this?" he mumbled.

Then he saw the legend and the keys written at the bottom. Lyons held it up, waving the map victoriously at his friends. "I think I just found the answer to my question."

"The institute," Schwarz and Blancanales blurted simultaneously.

"Right!" Lyons flashed them a wicked grin. "It's the one place we didn't think to look and that's probably what they're counting on."

"That's a pretty big campus," Schwarz said. "How do you plan to get in?"

"Turn up here, Pol," Lyons said with a wicked glint in his eye, utterly ignoring Schwarz's question.

He already had considered the possibility Asir might hide out at the Regional Science Institute and he now had to find a way to flush the rats from their hole. The only way to do this would be put the focus on alleged trouble somewhere else. Such a move would make Asir and his terrorist friends nervous, and when terrorists got nervous they made mistakes and jumped the gun. That's when Able Team would pounce.

They entered a block that was jammed with cars, and

Lyons's grin began to widen. He thought he'd seen a lot of traffic down this way when they were on the bridge and his suspicions were confirmed. He ordered Blancanales to slow down, match the speed of the other cars that cruised up and down the street. A smaller town like this wouldn't have much for college students to do at this time on a Saturday night, and in one regard it was refreshing to Lyons to know that "cruising" of this kind still went on.

Of course, a few things had changed—the obvious prostitutes and occasional drug dealer were one of those things. The innocence of the 1950s had been lost, for sure, where burgers and shakes had been replaced by booze and drugs, internet porn had replaced the drive-in movie theater, and so forth.

Lyons whipped out a cell phone and gestured for one of the prostitutes as he indicated Blancanales should pull to the curb. The woman was black and big-busted, attired in a skimpy dress and bright blue lipstick. Lyons handed her the cell phone and flashed a hundred-dollar bill.

"Not out here, honey!" she snapped. "You want to get us busted? And what's with the phone? You want me to talk kinky to you over the phone or something?"

"No. I want you to make a call."

"For a hundred bucks?"

"Yeah, as long as you say exactly what I tell you to."

"Oh my…we're going to get thrown in the klink," Blancanales moaned, putting a hand over his face so passersby couldn't get a good look at him.

"Why?" Lyons said. "Nothing illegal about paying a prostitute to make a phone call for you."

"Call to where?" Schwarz asked.

Lyons produced another wicked smile. "Campus security. We're going to provide them with a wee little distraction."

IF ANYTHING COULD GET the attention of a bunch of campus security guards—mostly novices who were barely out of college themselves—it would be a report that students from a rival school were about to break into one of the labs and pull some sort of practical joke. Five minutes after the call came through, two campus SUVs with orange lights pulled up in front of the labs in Building B. The security teams exited with nightsticks at the ready. One guy even had a stun gun. They were also carrying mace.

Across the campus on the opposite side, the three men of Able Team were on their own search operation. The difference was that they were toting pistols and hunting for terrorists, not pranksters. Lyons had hoped that the activity would flush out the terrorists. He was gambling, yeah, but it was one his gut told him would pay off. If they didn't find Asir at the institute, then Lyons knew he might have to concede the point that they'd lost Asir. Maybe forever, maybe not—a lot would depend on how fast he could get out of the country.

The labs at this end of the institute were dark. During their trip, Lyons and the others had managed to get Kurtzman to send them a full breakdown of the campus—every room, every building delivered instantly to the secure portable device Schwarz carried everywhere with him. The detailed specifications would help them negotiate their way through the darkened labs.

They had left their vehicle parked a block from the scene and hoofed it onto the campus, climbing the tall fence and continuing toward their objective. They'd found it easy to stay out of the range of the cameras. Wasn't any point in distracting campus security only to get caught on camera and have them come running. If Lyons got his way, they'd be in and out before anyone even realized they'd been there.

Lyons wasn't particularly keen on the idea of going up against Asir's men, who were probably well armed, with only one M-16 A-3 and three pistols. Well, they didn't have any choice. If they played their cards right and managed to locate Asir and his men, Lyons was betting they could either take them down one and two at a time or box them in and cut them down like fish in a barrel. Either way, Lyons didn't give a damn—he just planned to make sure that whatever happened, Asir wouldn't be walking away from it. This guy had been responsible for murdering veteran Marines. He would have to answer for that.

They crossed the expansive lawns and eventually reached the first building. This one had been the favored choice because it's where Kurtzman indicated Asir had spent most of his lab time. The guy was smart but that didn't mean he wouldn't head for some place that wasn't the most comfortable to him—familiar surroundings would give him the false hope of security. He knew the area well, so he would figure it more difficult for somebody to get the upper hand on him.

Well, that was just fine with Lyons. Let Asir underestimate his enemy and put on an air of false bravado. There wouldn't be any corner the guy could escape into—no massive terrorist force to save him. His men hadn't even been able to conduct a successful ambush against Able Team. Twice they had eluded his best attempts to kill them, and now Lyons could almost *feel* Asir's presence. Yeah, this was where the ambush team had originated and any moment Asir was probably expecting his men to report the three Americans were dead.

Asir was going to get a message, all right—and Able Team was going to deliver it in person.

CHAPTER TWENTY-FOUR

The plate-glass entrance doors to the lab building were heavy but hardly impassable. Able Team had managed to make it across the campus lawn undetected and Schwarz now studied the heavy glass and steel lock with professional interest. Lyons and Blancanales kept checking their surroundings while Schwarz pondered how to make entry quietly. It wasn't something they had considered before.

"Well?" Lyons finally asked after more than a minute.

"Well what?" Schwarz asked.

"You know how to get in or what?"

"Just give me a minute. Rome wasn't built in a day, you know."

"Well I'd like to get the terrorists *before* they get on a plane out of the country."

"I think what he's trying to say, Ironman," interjected Blancanales the peacemaker, "is that pestering him about it won't help the situation to go faster."

"Well, if you can't defeat it, then just step out of the way and I'll shoot the damned thing off," Lyons said, Anaconda held in the ready position.

"Oh…like *that* won't bring a bunch of people running," Schwarz countered.

"Not to mention alert the terrorists to our presence," Blancanales reminded their impatient team leader.

"This is going to be next to impossible without any equipment," Schwarz said.

"You don't have your tools?"

He shook his head. "No. Just a pair of lock-picks and a butane torch in my belt pouch. Everything else went up in our SUV with the ammo and weapons."

"Could we—?"

"Wait!" Schwarz said. "I think those will do the trick."

Schwarz tapped his head and grinned before reaching to the belt and pulling the torch from the pouch along with the elongated pick portion of the lock-pick. He then pulled a Leatherman multitool from his belt, used the knife to cut off the cargo pocket of his khaki fatigue pants and then applied it as a bulky wrap to one end of the pick. He fired up the torch with the windproof lighter he always carried on him and jammed the pick into the key lock. Applying the torch, the metal began to melt and drip into the opening. Schwarz worked for about a minute until some metal actually began to extend out of the lock.

"This particular brand of pick is actually a composite alloy that includes, among other things, copper and zinc with a bit of silver," Schwarz explained. Neither Blancanales nor Lyons really cared all that much but they knew it helped Schwarz to concentrate if he was also permitted to teach as he went. "This mix is about fifty-fifty so that makes the metal harder to melt but also much stronger when cooled. For example, if I were using straight soft or lead solder this wouldn't be possible."

Schwarz killed the torch—apparently satisfied with the job to this point—then withdrew a can of breath spray from the breast pocket of his black T-shirt. He removed the cap, turned the can upside down and then sprayed the metal while his friends watched with interest.

"The propellant for breath spray is just like any other," he explained. "By inverting the can the propellant becomes a supercoolant. Metal alloys of the kind the pick is constructed from harden much better when cooled rapidly."

It didn't take long for him to expend the coolant. In fact, the whole process had taken less than two minutes. Schwarz clamped onto the stub of metal protruding from the lock with the pliers from the multitool. He crossed his fingers as he gently turned the makeshift key that had been formed by melting the metal into the lock and the expansion of the heated alloy pushing against the tumblers to create an in-lock master key.

Schwarz said, "Now we just turn gently…gently… and—"

Click.

The lock disengaged and the door popped inward under the weight of Schwarz's shoulder.

"Nice!" Lyons whispered. "Let's go."

The three warriors moved single-file through the vestibule. The inner doors were decorative—thank God they had no locks or that would've been end of the line for Able Team. The fearsome trio fanned out in the modern and broad foyer beyond the vestibule that included a reception desk. One small light on the desk shelf behind the vestibule illuminated a sign-in sheet along with a radio and recessed computer terminal. All of the devices were on and active. Lyons looked up and immediately spotted cameras in a number of corners. The red lights winked steadily as the cameras whirred silently on servos to get a panoramic scan of the entire entrance.

Lyons cleared his throat to get the attention of his teammates and then gestured at the cameras.

Blancanales mouthed an "uh-oh" but before they could decide what to do next, one of the doors of the nearby elevator bank dinged for attention and then slid aside. A campus security officer, obviously just returning from his rounds, emerged from the elevator. He'd been sitting at the desk and Able Team had just been lucky, or perhaps *un*-lucky, enough to come upon the building when the guard had been walking his beat. Lyons moved swiftly and grabbed the guard from behind, snaking a muscular forearm around his neck and dragging him back into the elevator. Blancanales and Schwarz joined him a moment later and Blancanales stabbed the all-stop button before the doors could close.

The four looked odd standing inside the elevator, but Lyons was betting the cameras couldn't pan this far inside the elevator car and with campus security tasked on the bogus call they'd made, he hoped this would buy them some time before reinforcements arrived. With luck, maybe the cameras were only recordings and not actually live feeds monitored by staff. Either way, they were rapidly running out of time.

"Listen good," Lyons growled into the guard's ear. "We're not here to hurt you, understand. We're federal undercover agents and we have reason to believe there are terrorists in the building. Now I'm going to let you go but if you try anything you'll be taking a very long nap. Understand?"

Lyons flexed his forearm for emphasis and the security officer nodded in short, rapid movements of his head. He released his hold and said, "Is there anybody else in the building? Faculty or students… I mean *anybody*."

The man nodded as he rubbed his sore neck. "Yeah… I mean, yes, sir."

"You don't have to call me 'sir,'" Lyons said. "Next question—who are they and how many?"

"There were nine of them, I think I counted. I remember they all had valid student IDs. I thought it was kind of funny that they'd come here on a Saturday night and all, but I've seen it before."

"You didn't think nine men were a bit much?"

The guard shrugged. "I've seen them work in large study groups before. It's not that unusual, especially since the new year just started up. This is a busy place. Lots of students."

"Did they have any equipment with them? Bags of any kind or suitcases?"

The guy nodded. "One of them was carrying a long bag. I looked inside and all. We're required to search every bag, you know. If we don't search them then we get in huge trouble, so I always make sure to search every bag that comes in or out."

"Stay on topic," Blancanales said. "What was in the bag?"

"Nothing," he replied. "Just some testing equipment and books. It was pretty heavy but I didn't find anything unusual."

"False bottom?" Blancanales asked his friends and they both tendered nods.

"So we're looking at nine, then," Lyons reiterated. "Which floor?"

"Fifth but no—there weren't nine of them," the guard said.

"What do you mean? You just said—"

"Three of them left just a short time later. Kind of in a big hurry so I figured they were probably done with their assignments and heading out to a party somewhere."

"They told you that?"

The guard looked sheepish. "No, but...you know, like I say—it makes sense being it's a Saturday night and all."

Blancanales grinned. "The three that left would probably be our friends down by the river."

The other pair nodded and Lyons said, "All right, here's what's going to happen. You're going to return to your station like nothing's wrong. We'll handle this. You don't call anybody and you don't let anyone else in. You have a supervisor that makes regular checks?"

The guard said, "Well, yeah, but…"

"But what? Lyons could understand this young kid was a bit inexperienced but he was fast losing patience. "Out with it, dude, we don't have all night!"

"He's supposed to actually come by but usually just calls in. I think he's got a girlfriend and she's a student. You see he's not—"

"We get it, son," Blancanales said easily. "He's fraternizing with a lady friend and you don't want to get him in any trouble. But don't worry about that."

"Yeah," Schwarz added with a wink. "We promise not to tell anybody."

"Just act normal," Lyons said. "If you sound the alarm and the terrorists have a bomb or heavy weapons, a lot of people could get hurt. We don't want that, understand? We just want to keep everyone away until we can neutralize the situation."

The young man nodded with enthusiasm. "I get it, I get it. I'll do whatever you want."

"You're a good citizen," Blancanales said.

"And a true patriot!" Schwarz added.

Lyons gave the pair a look that said they were laying it on a bit too thick and then gently shoved the guard into the corridor with a reminder he was to return to his post, sit and keep quiet. They had no way of knowing if the kid would actually comply but there wasn't time to find something to bind and gag him with, and they didn't want to hurt him by knocking him out cold. Besides, Lyons reasoned, if a supervisor did happen to even drive by he'd see the guard seated at his station and figure all was well.

Lyons stabbed the button for the fifth floor and then checked the loads in his Colt Anaconda. Blancanales and Schwarz followed suit, Blancanales ensuring he had a full load in the magazine as well as the two spare clips in kept in holders on the opposite side of his shoulder holster. Schwarz verified the action on the M-16 A-3 and he knew the clip had somewhere on the order of twenty-five rounds remaining. That, coupled with his Beretta 92SF, would surely do the trick.

"Okay, so we're okay on ammo," Lyons said. "Gadgets will take point since he's got the only AR. We're pretty evenly matched on bodies, basically two on one so at least we have that going for us."

"Yeah, really not bad odds at all," Blancanales agreed. "We've faced worse."

"I'm hungry," Schwarz said. "Can we get something to eat when we're through here?"

WAR HAD COME to the doorstep of Hamza Asir and his murderous associates, and it would be a war only the men of Able Team could wage.

Their appearance coming off the elevators took the six terrorists by utter surprise, and although they reacted with admirable swiftness it would prove too little too late. Asir's expression was visible through the vast expanse of windows that separated one part of the lab. The terrorists happened to be holed up in the technical section of the combined classroom and lab facilities on the fifth floor that were divided by folding walls. The entire floor was laid out in similar fashion, one side composed of alternating lab areas and classrooms while the other half was taken up by a massive classroom that featured stadium-style seating and room-wide blackboard, white board and projection screen.

The terrorists broke apart and brought their weapons to bear, intent on defeating their enemies before it got out of control. They didn't get their wish. Per Lyons's instructions, Schwarz took the lead and brought his M-16 A-3 to bear on the enemy, all too aware of his ammunition limitations. Every round that went down range was precious and, as such, Schwarz had the obligation to make each of them count.

Schwarz brought the stock to his shoulder, held tight and squeezed a 3-round burst that shattered the terminals of two computers. The plastic and LCD monitors burst under the impact and showered sparks onto the terrorists who had taken cover behind a long counter composed of a half dozen workstations. The terrorists popped their heads over the counter and returned a few sporadic shots of their own, but oddly none of the reports sounded like those of automatic weapons.

Lyons and Blancanales had hit the polished linoleum in the hallway just outside the lab where Asir and his friends were making a stand. Blancanales looked at Lyons and grinned. "They only have semiautomatic assault rifles."

"Or they're conserving ammunition," Lyons observed.

"Either way, our chances just got better."

"Agreed."

Lyons counted to three on his fingers and then the pair jumped to their feet and charged the terrorist position, each firing a round alternate to the other so at least they could maintain a somewhat steady barrage of lead to keep the heads of their enemies down. They reached the doorway that opened onto the lab and took refuge behind the metal frames opposite one another. Schwarz had retreated down the hallway with the plan to circle around and attempt to come up on their flank. The terrorists had to know at this point they were trapped and their only alternative would be to fight back if they had even a glimmer of a chance to escape.

That was fine with the men of Able Team because it's exactly what they had been prepared for from the start. Whatever they did, they couldn't allow a single terrorist to escape this building. The line had to be drawn here and now, without holding back or hesitating for all their lives. The terrorists delivered a new volley of rounds, still firing one at a time to no effect. Lyons just wasn't buying it. They had been using automatic weapons at the mock camp and he had no reason to believe they weren't fully equipped with those same weapons now.

Judas priest—they just sent some of their goons after us with rocket launchers! Lyons reminded himself.

Lyons made a signal at Blancanales, who nodded, then dropped to his belly and began to crawl across the floor. Blancanales fired a few rounds from his pistol to cover the noise of Lyons's approach. It was a pretty ancient tactic but they had used it before in a similar manner with a modicum of success so there wasn't any reason for them to believe it wouldn't work again. The counter was high and the terrorists wouldn't necessarily be able to see him if Lyons could get close enough to end up in their blind spot. The plan worked and Lyons reached the perimeter of the workstation counter unscathed, now completely concealed from view. He wished for a grenade right at that moment, thinking how easy it would be just pull the pin, let it cook off, and then toss it over the counter right into the terrorists' laps.

The sudden arrival of Schwarz to their left was just as good, though. Schwarz had the M-16 A-3 held at the hip and was sweeping the terrorists' position, completely exposed from his angle of attack, with a steady series of 3-round bursts. The terrorists were so completely surprised and distracted by the abrupt appearance of their enemy that three of them broke cover in a panic and tried to find a way to escape the onslaught. They dashed from the counter and rushed toward an adjoining lab, unaware that they'd made a mistake and exposed themselves to Lyons and Blancanales.

Lyons got the first of the three with a clean shot from his Anaconda. The .44 Magnum roared in the confines of the lab, ringing the ears of everyone within proximity as the 230-grain bullet accomplished its deadly work. Lyons found his mark and a terrorist caught the round in the upper rib area just behind and below his right shoulder. The bullet continued through a lung and blew out a tennis-ball-size hole in the chest. The terrorist kept going, unable to stop his forward motion since he was for all practical purposes already dead. His head crunched against a hard counter before he hit the floor, never to rise again.

Blancanales fired two rounds, both of which narrowly missed the moving terrorist's skull. The third hit home, the .357 SIG round tearing through the man's neck. The impact spun him off course and he crashed against a tray upon which sat a collection of beakers filled with multicolored liquids. The terrorist upset the tray and both tumbled to the ground.

Even as Lyons was aligning his pistol sights on the remaining terrorist, something very hot and oppressive suddenly passed through the room. It felt to all the occupants as if someone had thrown an enormous hot, wet towel over them and it suddenly got very difficult to breathe. Something had gone terribly wrong in the mixing of those chemicals and the only one who managed to escape the majority of the effect was Schwarz, just given his distance.

An acrid cloud of smoke whooshed through the lab and, in a flash of insight, Schwarz saw what was about to happen. The electronics wizard hopped to his feet and rushed toward Lyons, holding his breath and blinking rapidly to keep his eyes clear of the fumes. He got to his leader just in time, grabbed his arm and practically dragged him from the lab and down the hallway. He got Lyons a decent distance before turning and heading back to the hot zone. He found Blancanales facedown near the door, nearly unconscious, choking and gagging with copious fluids running out of his mouth.

Schwarz tossed the rifle aside so he could get both hands on his friend. He heaved the massive frame up over his shoulder and beat feet down the hallway until he reached Lyons, who was now recovering, gulping for air while his back was pressed against the wall. Another moment passed and the air seemed to come alive in the lab, as if charged with electricity. Seconds followed before a flame whooshed across the ceiling.

The explosion wasn't massive. In fact, it was more like a set of miniexplosions inside the lab. Once Schwarz had verified his two friends would be all right without him, he rushed back to the lab and slapped a red switch mounted to one of the walls. A thick glass door framed by steel began to lower from the ceiling just behind him and Schwarz had to duck to avoid being trapped inside the lab. Plaster and dust rained from the ceiling as the whole hallway seemed to quake with each miniexplosion from inside the lab.

Sucking the clean air, or at least air that wasn't filled with toxic fumes, Schwarz didn't even notice that the room beyond the door suddenly filled with chemical extinguishing agents that were designed to protect the sensitive electronics inside the lab. It didn't really matter since it would take many days to clean up the mess beyond the hermetically sealed door, the only thing really protecting the Able Team warriors from near instant death.

Blancanales was still coughing but his color had returned. There was some drool at the corner of his mouth and a bit of reddening of the mucosal tissues, but Schwarz knew his friend would be okay. He'd need a full checkup by a physician, but Schwarz doubted there were any chemical burns to the lungs, given Schwarz had pulled his friend out of that toxic environment before things really went south.

"What the hell happened?" Lyons said, still coughing intermittently.

"Whatever was in those beakers mixed to produce ammonia hypochlorite. As soon as I smelled it I knew the terrorists who were shooting at us would set off an explosive reaction we couldn't have stopped if we wanted to. That's why I risked pulling you two the hell out of there instead of trying to kill the bad guys."

Lyons shook his head incredulously. "So Asir and his men killed themselves."

"Basically, yeah."

"Amazing," Blancanales managed to rasp.

"What's that, *compadre*?" Schwarz inquired.

"All that training—" he experienced another coughing fit before continuing "—all that training in chemicals and those dudes didn't even know enough to get the hell out of there. Yet you did."

"It's ironic, I'll grant you that."

"Ironic?" Lyons gibed. "You think it's ironic?"

"Well, what else would you call it?"

"I don't know, just doesn't seem like that's the right word."

"Well, what word would you have used?"

"I wouldn't have called it ironic, that's for sure."

As the quibbling went on, Blancanales coughed and mumbled, "Saints preserve us..."

CHAPTER TWENTY-FIVE

"Damned glad to hear your voice, David," Brognola said. "I know I speak for all of us on that note."

"Thanks, governor," McCarter said, fighting to be heard over the hot winds passing outside the open door of their confiscated AQI utility vehicle. "We're blowing hugs and kisses."

Brognola cleared his throat. "I doubt that, but we appreciate the sentiment."

"Able Team pull through okay?"

"A few bumps and bruises, but they're fine," Brognola said. "And the AQI's contacts here were obviously masterminding a dirty bomb. But then, you probably already know that."

"Indeed we do," McCarter confirmed, then launched into a full report of the past two days.

When he'd finished, Brognola grunted and said, "You've definitely had your hands full. First order of business will be to get word to our forces at the rally point and advise them of Rifle Company Bravo's situation. Barb's already gone to find Aaron and get him working on pinpointing the location of the stronghold even as we speak. Looks like the storms have passed so it shouldn't take long.

"We've also positively identified the leader of that local AQI group. His name is Muam Khoury. He's an experienced fighter with the AQI. Khoury's much more like a military commander than a terrorist, per se, with the training to match. So don't think you'll be going up against a novice on this one."

"Roger that," McCarter replied.

For a moment the signal faded but then it came back immediately. McCarter looked at the phone when it had sounded like the transmission cut out but then shook his head in amazement. This particular device had the ability to hold the signal in a buffer for up to minutes in a computer aboard Stony Man's dedicated satellite. That meant even though there might be a delay or interruption in the signal, there was still an actual connection maintained that would automatically switch the encoded transmission to another frequency once the linkup had been reestablished. It was all kind of like something out of a science-fiction movie, and McCarter had to admit the latest gadgets to come out of the Farm—originating in the minds of Kurtzman and his team—never ceased to amaze and confound the Phoenix Force leader.

"Lost you for a moment," McCarter said. "What was that last?"

"I said that Khoury has been around the block a few times. He's reputed to be not only a skilled technician but a fierce leader of the al Qaeda cause. Some rumors in the intelligence community are that he may even have studied the fatwas from bin Laden himself."

"Well, isn't that bloody lovely," McCarter muttered.

"Hold on a second, we have something coming through from Aaron now. Okay…yes, that's got it. He found what he believes to be the hard site and he's sending the exact coordinates through to you now. According to what we see at this end, you're less than a kilometer from the location."

"That's what I wanted to hear," McCarter said.

McCarter put Brognola on standby long enough to
check the coordinates against the map references Jeddah had provided him. Once more, Jeddah's information
pretty much checked out and his guess at the location of
the stronghold wasn't actually that far off. This revelation
didn't really come as any surprise to McCarter, who then
got back to Brognola with the news they were on track.

"David, don't take any chances, and I mean it,"
Brognola said. "You hit that place with everything you
got and don't leave anything to chance. You're autho-
rized for total destruction on this one. If they have other
dirty bombs we can't risk them getting out. Understood?"

"Perfectly," McCarter said with a cocksure grin.
"That's just the way we like it."

"Good hunting, then."

McCARTER LAY ON a promontory overlooking the floor of
a shallow valley. Through his binoculars he spotted the
natural archway entrance in the side of a rocky hill that,
according to Stony Man Farm, provided the only way
into the base. McCarter had to wonder why they hadn't
known about the base before now. After all, it hadn't
been that long since the Iraqi government had put the no-
fly zone into place for this half of the country, and Mc-
Carter doubted Khoury would've had the manpower and
resources to mount a major operation like this in such a
short period of time.

Then again, McCarter remembered what Nawaf and
Jeddah had told him about the AQI. They had originally
flourished by working with remnants of the former Iraqi
regime to put down radicals inside the Sunni Awakening. It wasn't until they'd sought support from outside
parties in places like Iran and Syria that the influence

of al Qaeda eventually permeated their infrastructure to such a degree that they took on their very namesake.

Yeah, the AQI hadn't always been the AQI, McCarter reminded himself.

The Phoenix Force commander took one last look at the layout below and then withdrew on his belly until he could safely make his way back to his waiting men without risking the enemy spotting him.

"Well?" Encizo asked.

"Whole lot of quiet," McCarter said. "That entrance is supposedly the only way in or out of that place. It looks dark and narrow, and I would be surprised if it was booby trapped."

"If it's the only way in, I don't see that we have any alternatives."

"Agreed."

"Seems to me like if we have to play with only the hand we're dealt, our best option will be to go in hard and fast," James said. "I say we just drive up to the door and knock really, really loud. We have this old clunker here, so I'm sure when they spot it they won't be inclined to blow us up on spec."

"That might work for the first minute or so," McCarter said, "but Hal said to be careful with Khoury. Apparently the guy's no fool and he'll have anticipated an attack of that kind. They probably have some prearranged signal and if we come driving up without giving it, Khoury might just order his men to open fire. And even if he buys it, he may have something in place to stop us once we're in that narrow entry corridor."

"What about a two-pronged attack?" Hawkins ventured.

All eyes turned on him and McCarter said, "Explain."

Hawkins shrugged. "Well, they say there's only one entrance, but do we know that for a fact?"

"I see," Encizo said with renewed excitement. "You're thinking there might be another way in we don't know a thing about. And neither, then, would our terrorist friends."

"Exactly. I think it's at least worth a couple of us taking a look-see into the ridgeline directly above their AO. The rock formations out here are filled with tunnels that act as natural air shafts that could take us straight into the heart of the camp. And even if the AQI's had time to build up resources inside, they've been using it awhile as a point from which to strike out against UN forces. They have to be running low on supplies and ammunition. We still got some explosives left, Gary?"

Manning nodded.

McCarter rubbed his eyes and considered Hawkins's proposal, admittedly intrigued by the idea. "We take out their munitions and ordnance, we take away their teeth."

"That's a good point, David," James said. "And didn't Jeddah say he thought the primary purpose of that place would be as a decon point? I would hardly call that a veritable fortress."

Manning nodded in agreement. "Cal's right, David. There's not much chance Khoury's planning for anyone to be crazy enough to risk a ground assault against him. He's probably as much in the dark as we are right now about whether his strike force succeeded or failed."

McCarter's brow furrowed. "You think he'll be chomping at the bit for news, good or bad."

"Yes, I do."

"All right." McCarter nodded. "We'll play it your way this time, since you're already two-and-oh this trip. You take whatever's left of your little bag of tricks, and you and Hawkins will get up that ridge and see what you can find. Meanwhile, the rest of us will plan our assault through the front door. Hopefully, we'll meet up in the middle."

"And what if things go the wrong way?" James asked.

"Then those who survive should try to find each other and do what they can to make it back to Exit Point Tango. Understood?" When they all nodded with murmurs of assent, McCarter added, "Tallyho."

THE HOT WINDS and blistering sun made Hawkins's and Manning's ascent seem like a stroll through hell—definitely not a walk in the park, and Manning wanted to kick his friend's butt for having even suggested it. If he'd had his way, they would all have been in the utility vehicle and crashing through the enemy's proverbial front gates with guns blazing. Oh, who was he kidding anyway? If he really had his way he'd be enjoying a camping and hunting expedition in the mountains of his native Canada during the day, and soaking up suds by a campfire in the evening.

"Have I mentioned lately how much I hate this place?" Hawkins asked in his Texas drawl as if he'd been reading Manning's mind.

"You're the one that suggested it, Mr. Two-Pronged Attack."

Hawkins shrugged and chuckled at his friend's good-natured ribbing. "Seemed like a good idea at the time."

Hawkins hit a slippery patch of loose rock and gravel and his foot gave.

More loose ground shifted under his weight, the impact of his leg against a loose boulder opening to reveal a 150-foot drop into a gaping yaw of sharp rocks.

A viselike hand wrapped around his forearm just as Hawkins's heart leaped into his throat.

His pulse thudded in his ears as Hawkins sought purchase with his free hand behind him. Eventually he found it and with Manning's assistance he managed to gain solid footing again. The two lay next to one another and panted with the exertion for several minutes. Hawkins could only curse himself for volunteering to undertake such a treacherous assignment, but at the same time he thrived on the excitement. In any case, he realized Manning's quick reflexes and rugged strength had saved his life. He shook his friend's hand in a firm, blood-brother-style grip before they rose and continued their journey.

McCarter had agreed to give them a full sixty minutes before he, James and Encizo commenced their approach to the camp. There was a bit of absurdity to this plan, almost a craziness that seemed so bold it might actually work. Khoury wouldn't assume there was any trouble if he saw one of his own vehicles approaching, especially in light of the fact he was probably under the illusion that his enemies didn't even know the location of this base.

Still, they were proceeding under the assumption Khoury was smart enough to have an alternate plan if things didn't go exactly right, a plan that might involve rigging this little base of operations with enough explosives to leave nothing to chance if it was breached. It wasn't the first time the AQI had demonstrated its willingness to revert to a scorched-earth policy and it certainly had the Phoenix Force warriors mindful of that being an all too real possibility.

The two men continued for another fifteen minutes when Hawkins stopped without warning and Manning nearly walked into him. He opened his mouth to deliver a rebuke when he looked to the right and realized why

Hawkins had come up short. A deep, dark circle—too dark to be a shadow or water vapor—seemed to grow out from a natural divot in the ridge wall.

"Well, what do you know," Hawkins said, turning to Manning with a grin. "I do believe we've struck oil, partner."

Manning wasn't totally ready to get his hopes up but he nodded all the same. "Let's see where it leads."

WHEN THE WORD CAME IN from headquarters about the plight of Rifle Company Bravo, Compton ordered his tanks to prepare to depart. The storm still blew outside but the most powerful section had passed and within fifteen minutes the weather technicians at Exit Point Tango were reporting the skies would be clear. That was one nice thing about sandstorms—they were largely unpredictable in their genesis but once they started up they were easy to track, especially the bigger ones like this because they left such a massive trail in their wake.

Compton's unit was ready to move out and at five minutes before the storm was scheduled to abate the four armored vehicles struck off and rolled toward the coordinates HQ had transmitted to them. As the storm became less severe the traffic on the dedicated Marine channel became clearer and clearer. With each transmission the grin on Compton's face grew—there was little doubt they had found America's wayward sons.

It took another twenty minutes for the tanks to arrive, but when Compton ordered them to halt and emerged from the turret, he immediately spotted the convoy of Marine trucks, trailers and Humvees covered by tarps. They were aligned in perfect bumper-to-bumper configuration in a line just in front of a formation of dense, rocky protrusions. Compton had seen these before scattered throughout the Iraqi desert—many of them had caverns cut into the rock and served as perfect shelters from the sandstorms that pelted the region.

Compton climbed down the tank and dropped to the sand from a forward compartment overhanging the tank's track. He could see his breath in the midday air even though the storm had passed, a natural phenomenon that occurred in the tail of a sandstorm—a swirling vortex of entropy that sucked the heat off the ground and left a dense cloud above to trap the cold air.

The major didn't let it concern him much since he knew that within the hour this area would heat up quickly as the sun penetrated the vapor cloud and dispersed it to dump copious heat on them all. Compton stood utterly still, remnants of sand swirling around his boots, and then he saw it. Movement—faint at first through the mist, but then more pronounced as the fog started to clear and the first shafts of sunlight peaked through.

It was a glorious sight, to be sure, and the Marines began to shout at Compton—shouts that he didn't realize until he got closer were actually cheers and calls of adoration. Compton's spirits lifted immediately and a glow formed in his chest, beating away the icy chill of the air against his exposed skin. He pulled the goggles from his eyes as he approached the growing crowd of Marines and by the time he reached them a number were slapping his back before realizing they had forgotten themselves and immediately rendered more formal salutes.

Compton's arm shot up and down like a piston again and again as he returned each one. Eventually he came on a black Marine officer wearing the rank of a captain and accompanied by his first sergeant along with a lieutenant.

"Captain Pringle, I presume?" Compton inquired as he returned the other officer's salute.

Pringle nodded. "I am. And I hope you don't mind saying we sure as hell are glad to see you, sir!"

"I've been searching all over this region for you, Captain. I believe we've already spoken." Compton grinned and extended his hand. "I'm Major Compton of the 1-Two-7. When your men never rendezvoused with us and you didn't show up at Exit Point Tango, I knew something bad had happened. I just couldn't get those turkeys up at HQ to believe me."

"Well, obviously somebody believed you," Pringle said, "because you're here."

Compton nodded. "You can thank Lieutenant Colonel Karta for that. He's the one who approved my request to perform perimeter security operations."

Pringle looked puzzled. "Perimeter security?"

"It's a long story," Compton said. "I'll fill you in later."

"Long stories we understand, sir," First Sergeant Brock said. He shook his head and with a chuckle added, "We've got one of our own to tell."

Compton laughed. "I'm sure you do, Top. I'm sure you do."

"SIR, THERE IS A VEHICLE approaching the entrance," the head of the guard unit announced to Muam Khoury.

The al Qaeda leader looked up from the small field table where he'd been studying potential routes of escape into Syria. "One of ours?"

The man nodded with excitement. "It would appear, sir, that it's your personal vehicle. The one you gave to Colonel Shabbat."

Khoury looked at his watch and frowned. He hadn't been expecting Shabbat after this amount of time. When the strike force commander hadn't reported in at either of the designated times, Khoury had assumed he'd either been unsuccessful or killed in the explosion. Communications had been practically impossible, however, given the storm, and it was possible there had been survivors in the mission but they hadn't been able to communicate for some other reason. And besides that fact, Shabbat would be the only one outside of their group to know the exact location of this retreat point. It hadn't been marked on any of the intelligence material retrieved by the American strike force sent to rescue the Marine prisoners.

"Send a squad of men out to meet them," Khoury finally said, rising from his chair, the map totally forgotten now. "We've received no communication from Colonel Shabbat, but there is a chance their equipment was damaged in the strike. Still, I don't want to take foolish and unnecessary chances. You *will* verify that it is Colonel Shabbat or his men before you permit them to enter, and once you have done that you will direct them straight to the decontamination area. Are those orders clear?"

"Yes, sir." The captain of the security team turned and left to carry out his orders, completely forgetting to salute.

Khoury let the moment pass, realizing that the man was so pleased to see that Shabbat and his team had survived he'd neglected protocol. Indeed, if they had managed to launch the bomb against the American Marines it would be a cause for significant celebration. The Americans had done much to undermine the success of past al Qaeda missions and the aftermath of their device would result in ramifications that would have the press and military communities talking for many months.

Khoury could not think of a more glorious time in their jihad since the attack on the World Trade Center. Now, just like then, the citizens of Islam would dance in the streets and the whole of the United States and its allies would come to understand the fierceness and determination of al Qaeda. The mere execution of Osama bin Laden, the trials and imprisonment of other al Qaeda leaders, wouldn't stop Khoury. This most recent success would prove it. He would continue to fight them and their attempts to resist would be the very path leading them to destruction.

The sound of an explosion echoing through the cavern caused Khoury's eyes to widen in shock. He turned toward one of his officers and said, "What the hell was that?"

"It…it sounded like an explosion, Muam."

"I know it was an explosion, you idiot! Go find out what's happening. We may be under attack!"

"Yes, sir."

The officer sprinted for the exit from the sheltered area Khoury had chosen for his operational headquarters. It was really just a narrow alcove with a piece of canvas over the entrance. He'd selected it because of the natural stream of water that trickled from an overhead opening into a pool in one corner, a source of fresh water and a place to clean up when he felt the need. It was the one luxury he'd afforded himself with the provision officers could use the natural spring to replenish the water supply for their men.

Khoury turned to the only other officer remaining in the room, the young bin-Jazeer, who Khoury had appointed as his personal adjutant. He'd decided to take the young man under his wing and teach him everything he knew. Since he had no children, he secretly aspired for bin-Jazeer to grow into the kind of man Khoury would have hoped for in a son from his own loins. Since bin-Jazeer was an orphan, Khoury had come to feel it was an omen.

"It would seem perhaps we've allowed the Americans to outwit us once more."

"Perhaps," bin-Jazeer replied. "But it is not by any fault of yours, sir."

"Nonsense!" Khoury spit on the ground. "It is always my responsibility as your leader. I will not put the blame on someone else. Never forget this!"

"I shall not."

Khoury turned to look toward the entrance to his quarters and whispered, "Not this time, infidels. This time we shall be the victors. Even unto death."

CHAPTER TWENTY-SIX

The terrorist looked mightily surprised when Calvin James refused to stop or even slow the utility vehicle. By the time the AQI guard realized the approaching men weren't allies, his attempts to bring his sub-gun to bear didn't do him any more good than waving down the vehicle. That mistake was the last one he ever made as James clipped him with the bumper while the terrorist was still trying to open fire. The hit drove the terrorist into the rock wall and snapped his back on impact.

At the exact same moment of that impact, McCarter was leaning out the passenger side and triggering his FN-FNC. A torrent of 5.56 mm NATO slugs cut a bloody spiral pattern up the man's body while making him dance like a puppet. The terrorist's corpse eventually had no place to go, stopped by the rocky protrusion of the entrance, and he crumpled to the dust in heap.

McCarter grabbed the roll bar above his head, stood in the seat and then threw back the tarp to expose Encizo. The Cuban had the HK-23E machine gun they'd pilfered from the Humvee loaned to them by the Jordanians primed and ready for action. He held on to the roll bars on either side as James negotiated the narrow entrance while still under full speed. Encizo felt like a milkshake as the utility vehicle fishtailed and nearly wrecked. Its metal frame scraped against the unyielding rock and sent up a shower of sparks as the metal squealed in outrage before part of a rear panel was torn completely off the vehicle.

They rolled into the darkened entrance in time to see a squad of six terrorists approach them, muzzles winking as they tried to lay down suppressing fire. James and Mc-Carter rolled clear and rushed for the back of the vehicle as cover while Encizo covered the retreat with some suppression fire of his own. The HK-23E erupted into a sustained rhythm as Encizo swept the area where a gaggle of screaming terrorists approached. The air came alive with 7.62 mm lead, and that seemed to bring a change of heart to the terrorists.

These definitely weren't typical terrorists the Phoenix Force warriors were matched against—that much seemed immediately evident. Whatever else the terrorists might have felt about Allah and the Islamic jihad, these men operated like trained soldiers and not fanatics with the scream of "allahu akbar" frozen on their lips. These men were concerned with both how to fight and how to survive against their enemies. Only half were taken down under Encizo's initial defensive fire zone while the remainder sought cover behind rocks, vehicles and—in one case—a fellow terrorist.

James decided to even those odds some more by wrapping his hand around an M-67 fragmentation grenade and detaching it from his LBE harness. He yanked the pin, let two seconds go by and then tossed it high and deep to ensure he cleared any obstructions immediately in front of them. Wouldn't do to have the damned thing bounce back and straight into his lap. There was just a moment, a weird heartbeat where things went silent before the frag went live. Then all hell broke loose as the seven ounces of explosive filler blew and sent fragments slicing in every direction. Only two terrorists actually fell under the deadly effects of the M-67 but a few more got their teeth rattled in their head from the shock of the explosion.

One man staggered from cover for a better position while still disoriented and Encizo cut him down with a short burst from the HK-23E. Another terrorist jumped from cover and tried to kill Encizo while his attention was fixed on another, but McCarter had been waiting for something like this. The Briton swung his FN-FNC into acquisition and delivered a short burst that blew off the top of the terrorist's head. As he fell, the terrorist's finger jerked at the trigger and spit a cluster of rounds that buzzed uncomfortably close to Encizo.

Time to abandon that position and move deeper into the battleground.

McCarter broke cover first and headed for where he'd cut down the terrorist trying to take down Encizo while James angled in the opposite direction to take down two terrorists that had exposed their position when they saw McCarter. They had thought the Briton would be easy game but James was happy to show them the error of their hasty assumptions. He leveled the muzzle of his M-16 A-3 and delivered a sweeping firestorm of 5.56 mm hardball at his enemies. The terrorists realized in a moment and one shouted in horror just before a bullet entered his windpipe and cut the scream to a grisly gurgle. The second terrorist was struck in the hip and side. The impact slammed him into the unforgiving rock wall and James finished him with a shot that connected with his skull. The man's headless body froze there a moment and then he slid to the ground, leaving a trail of blood to mark his passing.

Encizo abandoned the HK-23E and jumped to the ground, MP-5 SD-6 held at the ready. Three terrorists emerged from a recessed opening not immediately visible to Encizo. They were like termites or something coming right out of the walls. It reminded Encizo of a vermin-infested slum and he was reminded of just what kind of murdering *cucarachas* they were. These men had attacked and slaughtered United States Marines without any provocation, and Encizo was more than satisfied to explain the price of American blood to them.

The Cuban steadied the H&K against his muscular forearm and triggered one short burst after another, each one intended for a specific target. Encizo was renowned for his skills with a knife, but he was equally reputed to be a steady marksman in close-quarters battle situations. The MP-5 SD-6 made no audible reports, drowned by the unsuppressed reports from other weapons, as the first terrorist got his legs cut from under him and tumbled to the dust with a shout of anguish. Encizo took the second man down with a burst in a pattern so close that blew apart the terrorist's heart and upper left lung simultaneously. The third terrorist caught two slugs in the chest, one that cut out a chunk of his windpipe while the other splintered his sternum and drove jagged shards of bone into his vital organs.

HAWKINS AND MANNING were halfway down the narrow shaft, dangling on a rope fifty feet above terra firma, when the echo of an explosion boomed and rolled in their ears.

"Sounds like the party's started," Hawkins said.

"You think? Let's get the lead out."

"Your wish is my command."

The pair continued their hand-over-hand descent, their only purchase the knots spaced at regular intervals along the special climbing rope. The walls of the shaft had been narrow enough at some points that the men could barely squeeze through them. Still, they could feel the cool blasts of air that occasionally swept through the shaft and that left no doubt that there was an opening at the bottom. It was only a few minutes later that they hit that opening—an opening about as wide in diameter as a man's waist.

"Ain't no way we're going to fit through that," Hawkins said.

Manning hung above him and said, "Well, going back up is out of the question."

"What? We don't have any other choice, Gary."

"We have one other choice."

At first Hawkins didn't know what his friend meant, but then when he thought about it he realized just what the Canadian explosives expert was proposing. "Oh, no... uh-uh, pal. You ain't going to blow no holes in this."

"Give me one good reason."

"I'll give you two good reasons—me and you." Hawkins looked around in the gloomy, narrow shaft and added, "Not to mention there's an awful lot of moisture in here."

"Exactly right," Manning said. "I noticed that, as well. Which means that the walls here are going to be much more pliable. Can't you smell that? That's shale, brother, and it's lightweight and very responsive to explosive materials. It wouldn't take much and we can get high enough in the shaft to protect us."

"Correct me if I'm wrong, but aren't shale deposits extremely notorious for experiencing regular cave-ins?"

Manning ignored the question and instead withdrew a dinner-plate-size charge from his ordnance satchel. It was pure misery having to work with this stuff in such confined space but he didn't have any choice. There hadn't been time in their sixty-minute window to stop to prime a few explosives before descending into the shaft. They were already behind the eight ball and if they didn't accomplish their mission of sabotage it would go a long way toward hurting the outcome for their friends who were ducking it out with the terrorists to buy Hawkins and Manning the time they needed.

Finally, Manning crimped the blasting cap in place and passed the circular object to his friend below. "Here. Feel that and tell me if you can feel a difference."

Hawkins complied and finally said, "Yeah, I think so. One side's real smooth and the other's kind of rough."

"Exactly, that's exactly right! Now take the rough end and place it facing toward the outermost wall."

"How am I supposed to know what that is?"

"Feel around you and you'll eventually detect the running water."

"Okay, I got it."

"Good. Now just put the rough edge of the plate against that wall but just above the entrance. You want to stand the plate on its side, and make sure it doesn't fall over."

Another minute elapsed and a fresh echo of autofire echoed through the shaft. Their friends were getting closer and the fighting was growing more intense by the minute. If they didn't get this done quickly it would be curtains for the entire team. When Hawkins confirmed the charge was in place, Manning began to climb as fast as his muscles would allow. He could hear Hawkins grunting, but the guy was holding his own. He was as strong as an ox and Manning knew his comrade's years in Delta Force had taught him how to survive for very long periods at a time with very little food or sleep.

Manning had undergone the same training but in different arenas, such as his training in the rugged mountains with the RCMP and then again under special loan to the infamous GSG-9. Finally, Manning had been forged through the fire-and-steel initiation with Phoenix Force, a participant in hundreds of successful missions against the very nastiest of foes on a truly global scale. The two men were in their element, despite the risks and the grueling physical demands of their present predicament.

Manning stopped when they'd reached a safe distance and withdrew the detonator. He extended the antenna, flipped the actuator and switch and was about to depress the fire control button when Hawkins called to him.

"Ho! Wait up a second."

"What now?"

"How do you know that we aren't going to get our asses blown off?"

"I don't," Manning said as he depressed the button.

The only real tense moment wasn't when the charge exploded but when the shaft suddenly filled with enough smoke and dust that neither of the men could breathe. Through fits of coughing and wheezing, Manning began to coax Hawkins to descend the rope as fast as possible. They reached the bottom and true to the Canadian's prediction they emerged in some sort of antechamber and slid down the slippery rocks into a pool of water.

The cool, refreshing water that splashed onto their pants was enough incentive for Hawkins to grab his partner around the neck and deliver a quick head rub. "Gosh darn it but you're the best, Gary."

"Aw, stop it," Manning said, trying to sound annoyed but gloating all the same. "People will talk."

"Killjoy," Hawkins muttered as he retrieved his slung MP-5. "Now let's go get us some terrorists."

IN A STROKE OF BAD fortune, McCarter and his teammates had somehow managed to get pinned down by a group of about twenty terrorists. Khoury had obviously had time to regroup and was now defending their position in a vast chamber where the ceiling rose several stories above them. They had definitely chosen their location well, nestled into the massive desert caves they'd all heard plenty of stories about but couldn't imagine existed until they actually found themselves inside one.

Deafening reports of autofire echoed off the walls of the chamber, creating more confusion and noise as the acrid clouds of spent gunpowder hung low in the air. These were the only telltale clues of the enemy positions, the same clues they knew would give them away in conjunction with the muzzle-flashes. At one point, the terrorists had rained a firestorm of hot lead on their position. One of the rounds ricocheted and buried itself in the side of McCarter's foot.

"Bloody hell!" the Briton shouted.

While Calvin James assessed and treated the wound, Encizo took whatever opportunities he could to reduce the odds. A couple of terrorists had been stupid enough to expose themselves while trying to find a better vantage point. Even as Encizo took them out he could hear someone shouting at them, probably ordering the idiots to get out of the line of fire before they got themselves killed. He wondered if it was Muam Khoury.

Encizo dropped behind the shelter of the enemy truck and checked the clip to his MP-5 SD6. He reinserted it and then turned to assess his friends. James was already securing the supplies in his medical pouch and McCarter was lacing his boot.

"The ammo situation is grim. How about you guys?"

McCarter gestured to his FN-FNC, which he'd already chucked aside with its chamber in an open and locked position.

"Everything okay with you, O fearless leader?" Encizo asked.

James nodded. "Just a bite. He'll have a trophy scar."

Encizo rolled his eyes at McCarter. "Oh, as if you need another scar to brag about."

"You're just jealous," McCarter said with a cheesy grin and waggle of his eyebrows.

The radio squelch sounded in their ears and then Hawkins's voice cut through the interference. "Firefox Four to Firefox One. Over?"

McCarter keyed up his microphone. "Go ahead, Four."

"We found the mother lode. You guys clear?"

"We could be if you'd get a fire under your arse."

"Well, get ready for the new Big Bang."

"Roger that. When you're clear, fall down on this position and we'll try to cover your retreat."

"Negative, Firefox One," came Gary Manning's voice. "When this goes, it'll go big. You need to get out of there as soon as you hear the first charge. After that, it'll be too late."

"What about you?" McCarter asked.

There was a long silence and when Manning's voice came back McCarter thought he heard just a minor crack in it. "Mission first. You guys…well, stay frosty. Firefox Three, out."

The radio squelched again. They'd gone dark. Damn it all to hell! He didn't like it but he knew Manning and Hawkins were doing whatever they had to to accomplish the mission. If that meant they went down with the terrorists, then that's what it meant. The boys were pros and would do whatever they had to do. It was what it was and McCarter couldn't do a damned thing about it. Even Mc-

Carter's desire to see all of his team come out of it alive couldn't take precedence over the mission objectives.

That thought didn't ring more true for all three of them when they heard the first boom. The sporadic fire from the terrorists fell silent and then the cavern seemed to take on a life of its own. McCarter shouted at his friends and the three scrambled from cover and dashed across the open cavern toward the exit. They made it more than two-thirds of the distance before the terrorists began to open fire, and McCarter risked a glance to his right to see one of the terrorists emerge from cover and raise a pistol in his direction.

McCarter never broke stride as he whipped out his Browning Hi-Power, sighted down the slide and triggered three rounds. A champion pistol marksman, McCarter rarely missed what he aimed at and this was no exception. The terrorist took all three rounds in the chest, each one driving him back until he tumbled over a large equipment box, a puddle of blood spreading across his chest. It wouldn't be until some days later that McCarter would recall the exchange and upon seeing Khoury's face would be able to confirm the death of the revered AQI leader.

The Phoenix Force warriors barely made it through the narrow egress before tons of rocks poured into the cavern, covering the entrance and effectively sealing the terrorists inside. The place the AQI had used for the last few months as shelter while they conducted their brutal and vicious attacks against hapless natives, the impregnable rock that had protected them as they schemed and planned the destruction of American serviceman, had abruptly and necessarily become their grave. It was a fitting end, to be sure.

And yet David McCarter couldn't help but think only of Gary Manning and T. J. Hawkins. They had suffered a fate alongside the terrorists they didn't deserve. Mc-Carter had to wonder if they would at least get permission to perform a search and rescue, maybe if not now they could get it down somewhere down the line. He didn't want to think about their bodies having to share a resting place with the enemies of freedom and liberty. That wasn't a thought he was sure he could live with—at least he couldn't think about it and still desire to remain the leader of Phoenix Force. But then again, that's not what Manning and Hawkins would've wanted. They had sacrificed themselves for the good of all and to save their friends. They had died with honor and dignity.

And for that reason and that reason alone, David Mc-Carter would carry on the fight.

EPILOGUE

Exit Point Tango, Iraq

"We appreciate all of your assistance," David McCarter said. "But I can't ask you to risk your men or your career."

Captain Colin Pringle shook his head and frowned. "Brown, you guys saved a whole bunch of Marines. Many of those men owe you everything. You've also been through hell these past few days. I can't imagine what it would feel like to be in your position. You can't possibly believe I'd leave you just hanging. My men are going to help find your guys if it takes us the rest of our natural lives, and I don't give a rat's ass what Maxwell has to say about that."

Pringle had been put in charge of all the remaining companies present while the division commander was absent and tasked to assist in evacuation logistics for other units that were still either missing or requiring additional support. Pringle, by virtue of his elevated, if albeit temporary, position hadn't been lying when he promised to use every resource at his disposal—a force that comprised more than one thousand Marines and a couple of wheeled and armored units.

Even Major Compton had offered the use of his tanks if it came to it.

McCarter, Encizo and James were about to argue with Pringle when a private stepped into the tent, his eyes wide. "Uh, sir...um, excuse me, sir."

Pringle turned. "Not now, Private."

"But, sir, I really think you need to come outside and see this." He looked at McCarter, Encizo and James and said, "All of you."

Pringle let out a sigh and then gestured for the Phoenix Force trio to follow. They stepped into the hot sun and at first they weren't sure they could trust their eyes. Through the shimmering heat of the tarmac they saw two figures approaching, the swirl of chopper blades churning dust and sand around them, distorting their faces. Like ghosts, they eventually materialized into view—and a jaw-dropping view it was.

Hawkins and Manning looked tired and dirty, but other than that they were unmarked.

Their teammates could hardly believe what they were seeing. When the five men connected there were a lot of shouts and fist bumps and back slaps. There were even a few hugs—not the full embrace but the kind men did where they sort of grabbed hands and wedged them between their chests, and maybe delivered a slap on the arm.

The team was reunited, the latest threat neutralized. Shortly they would be on their way back to Stony Man Farm for some much needed R and R—until the next crisis erupted.

* * * * *